CHANCE

CHANCE

STEEL BROTHERS SAGA
BOOK TWENTY-FIVE

HELEN HARDT

WATERHOUSE PRESS

ISBN: 978-1-64263-361-0

For everyone who dares to take a chance.

PROLOGUE

Ava

My mother and father got married on Thanksgiving twenty-five years ago.

Twenty-five years with the same person.

It's unimaginable to me.

I'm a Steel by birth, but I've never felt like a Steel.

I don't want my family's money. I like being on my own. I opened my bakery and sandwich shop with my own money—money that I earned, not money from my gigantic trust fund, which, even though I gained control of it when I turned twenty-one three years ago, I've never touched.

I'll never touch it if I can avoid it.

Don't get me wrong.

I love my family. All of them, without condition.

I just don't want their money.

I'm kind of the black sheep of the Steel family. Or rather, the pink sheep, if my hair color makes me who I am. So I like pink hair. Sue me. I can pull it off.

My little sister, Gina, thinks I'm crazy. She's gorgeous, of course. Looks just like our father, Ryan Steel, who's the pretty boy of the Steel family. Gina has his dark hair and light-brown eyes that are fringed with those ridiculously long lashes.

I look more like our mother, Ruby Lee Steel. I have her

brown hair, lighter than Dad's, but of course I color it. I also have her blue eyes. That's where our similarities end, though. I'm not nearly as pretty as Mom is.

I'm just me.

Ava.

Simply Ava, who loves to bake, and who's damned good at it, if I do say so myself.

I learned at an early age from my aunt Marjorie, who's a trained chef. I'm supposed to be meeting with her now, as we're planning Mom and Dad's twenty-fifth anniversary party.

It will be huge and lavish and at the main house, where Uncle Talon and Aunt Jade live.

Just like all the Steel parties.

And man, we Steels *love* to give parties.

I'm running late, of course, because I got sucked into a tarot reading with some of my online pals.

Gina rolls her eyes at me whenever I pull out the tarot deck, but that's fine. I don't think of it as fortune-telling or witchcraft or anything. I simply use it to tap into my own intuition. Plus, I enjoy it.

I'm about ready to log off when my phone dings with a text.

Darth Morgen is alive.

Huh?

I wrinkle my forehead and check the number. I don't recognize it.

Darth Morgen? Is this some kind of *Star Wars* reference?

Who is this?

No reply, until—

Darth Morgen is alive.

O...kay. Whoever sent this message probably mistyped a number. It's not meant for me. Still, I'm curious, and I want some guidance.

I shuffle my deck and pull a single card.

The hierophant.

I jerk slightly.

Not because the hierophant represents anything that concerns me, but because in the ten years I've experimented with the tarot, I've never drawn this card in a reading for myself. Others, of course, but not myself, which always made sense. The hierophant can represent conformity and group identification.

That's not me. Not Ava Steel.

I'm the Steel who didn't use her sizable trust fund to open my bakery in town. I'm the Steel who colors her hair and wears a lip ring.

Definitely not a conformist.

But...a hierophant is also someone who interprets secret knowledge and seeks a deeper meaning.

Darth Morgen is alive.

Secret knowledge? A deeper meaning?

Was this message meant for me after all?

CHAPTER ONE

Ava

I'm still staring at the strange text when a new one comes in from Aunt Marjorie.

Where are you? Everything okay?

Right. Mom and Dad's twenty-fifth anniversary party. A Steel grand occasion can be put on hold for nothing or no one—especially not some bizarre message that may not have been meant for me anyway.

I text back quickly.

On my way.

A half hour later, I arrive at Aunt Marj's home.

Her husband, Uncle Bryce, is the chief financial officer for the family company. I don't concern myself much with what goes on with our finances. It's not that I don't care, because I love my family. It's just that it doesn't really affect my life. I live by my own means, and I'm proud of it.

I give the door a quick knock, and I walk in, giving some head scratches to their black labs, Thad and Gary.

"Ava, is that you?" Aunt Marj calls from the kitchen.

"Yeah, it's me."

"Great. Come on back."

I'm on my way through the foyer when Uncle Bryce, Uncle Joe, and my cousin Brock walk toward me, clearly having come from Uncle Bryce's office. Brock is Uncle Joe in miniature—except Brock is hardly miniature. But for Uncle Joe's graying temples, they could be twins with their strong builds, dark hair, and dark eyes. Uncle Bryce is silver-haired with bright-blue eyes and also nearly as tall as Brock and Uncle Joe.

"Hey, Ava," Brock says. "What are you doing over here?"

"I'm helping Aunt Marj plan the big shindig for my mom and dad."

"Right, the anniversary." Brock nods. "Have fun."

"What are you guys all doing here?"

"Just some business," Uncle Bryce says. "Nothing to concern your pretty head about." He smiles, and for a moment I think he's going to tousle my hair.

Brock, Uncle Bryce's son David, and I are all about the same age. Uncle Bryce used to tousle heads all the time, and he still does it on occasion, though he does it less often now that my hair is pink. He also still resorts to infantilizing and chauvinistic remarks—like my *pretty head*. I've learned to ignore it—it's part of Uncle Bryce's charm.

Uncle Bryce and Uncle Joe walk toward the front door and talk in low tones, leaving Brock and me standing in the foyer.

"By the way," I say to Brock, "congratulations on your engagement to Rory."

Brock smiles. "Thanks."

"So when's the wedding?"

"We're not sure yet. Have you heard the news, though? Rory and Jesse and the band are going on tour. A huge international tour beginning in January."

I raise my eyebrows. "Seriously?"

"Yeah. Two guys from Emerald Phoenix—"

I drop my jaw. "What? *Emerald Phoenix?* Jett Draconis?"

"Yeah. You heard it right. It's incredible. Jett and the keyboardist, Zane Michaels, were at one of the band's gigs last weekend, and they asked Dragonlock to open for them on their tour."

Happiness for Rory and the band flows through me. I've been a huge fan of Jesse Pike and his band for as long as I can remember.

"That's unbelievable. And great! So no wedding yet, I suppose."

"Probably not until after the tour. Besides . . . there's so much else going on . . ."

"Yeah."

I've heard the talk about some things coming to light regarding our family, but honestly, I don't know a lot about it. I try to stay in my own space. I'll be there for my family if they need me, but unless they require baked goods, I'm not sure what I can do for them.

But I *am* curious.

"You okay, Brock?" I touch his hard shoulder. "For someone who just got engaged to the most beautiful woman in Snow Creek, you don't look all that . . . happy." I can't help a chuckle. "I never saw you settling down. Not anytime soon, anyway."

Brock sighs. "I'm ecstatic about Rory and me, cuz, but . . . there's just some shit going down that's . . . well . . . *bothersome.*"

Bothersome? Interesting word.

"Anything you want to talk about?"

"Ava?" Aunt Marj's voice nags me from the kitchen.

"Maybe some other time." I roll my eyes. "I've got a party to plan."

Brock nods. "Everything's okay. Or it will be, anyway."

Uncle Bryce and Uncle Joe are still standing by the door, engaged in low conversation. Are they waiting for Brock?

Must be, because when he joins them, they head outside. The Steel Boys Club. I hate to say it, but it's true. The Steel men are good men, manly men . . . but they can be a little hard to take sometimes. They're overprotective to a fault.

I walk into the kitchen where Aunt Marj is seated at her large oak table, notes and cookbooks strewn in front of her.

I gaze around her perfect creative space. She's a trained chef, and her kitchen shows it from her six-burner Viking gas stove to her marble countertops, which are perfect for kneading bread. I spent many days here when I was a kid, learning to bake. It became my passion, and I had marble counters installed in my kitchen at the bakery because I swear nothing works better for hand kneading. With the right amount of flour, your dough never sticks to the surface.

Aunt Marj's stainless-steel refrigerator looms tall in the corner, and her Italian espresso and cappuccino machine is the centerpiece on the opposite wall. She designed the kitchen herself, right down to the artwork—all vintage advertisements that she found in old cooking magazines.

"So what are you thinking?" I ask.

"Thanksgiving theme, of course," she says. "Since they were married on Thanksgiving."

"But this year their anniversary falls on a Saturday evening."

"Right, but that's only two days after Thanksgiving, so the theme is still relevant." She flips through a couple of pages of the cookbook in front of her. Another one is open to a full-color photo of a turkey next to a cornucopia of fall vegetables. "Plus, gratitude is always a good thing, don't you think?"

"Yeah, of course it is. But I was wondering…"

"What?"

"What about a wine theme? Dad is retiring as master winemaker, and Mom loves his wines."

"Wine isn't really a theme, Ava."

"Why can't it be?" I take a seat at the table and grab one of the cookbooks. "It's our party. We can make it however we want."

"I suppose so." She wrinkles her forehead. "Maybe a Greek theme. Celebrating Dionysus, the god of wine."

"Dionysus was also the god of fertility and ritual madness," I say dryly.

Aunt Marj laughs. "Sounds like a Steel party to me."

"I do like the idea of a Greek theme," I say. "My mom has always said she's half Greek, but she says nothing about her father other than that."

Aunt Marj drops her gaze.

Weird.

"Can you make Greek food?" I ask.

Aunt Marj makes a note on one of the recipes in front of her. "I can make any kind of food, Ava."

I laugh. "Sorry, I forgot who I was talking to."

"The real question is, can *you* make Greek food?"

"I can *bake* anything."

"Have you ever baked pita?"

"Of course I have. I just don't sell it in my bakery."

"We'll need lots of pita," Aunt Marj says. "Maybe some Greek olive bread as well."

"Easy enough. I make a really awesome kalamata olive loaf, as you know. I can just adjust a few things."

"There's also Greek Easter bread."

"Aunt Marj, how many kinds of bread do we need?"

"I'm just thinking out loud. I think pita and Greek olive bread will be fine."

"Good. So that'll be my contribution. What else do you need from me?"

"I need you to help me plan the menu."

"Of course."

Aunt Marj rises, picking up the cookbooks that are spread out in front of her. She takes them to a cupboard, inserts them, and pulls out another—this one with kabobs and eggplant on the cover.

"*Opa!*" She brings the book to the table and opens it. "I haven't used this Greek cookbook in a long time. It'll be great to delve into it."

"What about baklava for dessert?" I ask. "I'm experienced with that."

"That's a thought."

"Of course, it wouldn't be a Steel party without one of your cakes."

"True enough." Aunt Marjorie taps her cheek. "But I like the idea of baklava. Do your parents like it?"

"You know my parents. They'll eat anything."

"True. Let's do both," she says. "I'll make one of my cakes, and you make baklava."

"Good enough."

"Now, invitations."

"I'm no graphic designer," I say.

"No, and neither am I. Jade can handle those."

Aunt Jade is usually Aunt Marj's second-in-command when it comes to all the Steel parties. I just provide the baked goods, except for the cakes. I make a darn good cake, but Aunt Marj's cakes are legendary. I've tried to get her to work for me at the shop, to make some cakes, and I'd give her the profits. She always says no, that it would take the joy out of it for her. I don't understand that, since I get all kinds of joy out of baking, and I make a living from it.

Aunt Marjorie leafs through the book. "We can go traditional, or we can go a little more modern."

"Honestly? I like the idea of traditional. We don't get to eat much Greek food here on the western slope."

Aunt Marj laughs. "Somehow I don't see your cousins— the male ones—getting excited about stuffed grape leaves."

"So we'll make sure there are lots of gyros. Beef gyros. Plus, I think Mom and Dad would love it. Dad can do the wine pairing. You know, come out of retirement and all."

Aunt Marj taps her cheek again. "You know? You're right. This party is for them, after all. They may like this Greek thing. Especially if we tie it into Dionysus with the wine."

"Right," I say, "and we can forget about the fertility and sex fest."

"Well, we won't mention it anyway." Aunt Marj smiles.

I make a few notes on my phone. "How many pitas and olive loaves are you thinking?"

"Invitations haven't gone out yet, but Steel parties are always very well attended."

"True. Can we expect maybe a hundred guests?"

"I'm thinking close to two hundred. This is an anniversary party."

"Okay. I'll need to order my supplies and make sure I can get enough bread made in time along with all my Thanksgiving orders."

"I know. We probably should've started planning a little earlier."

"I shouldn't have any problem getting supplies," I say. "I get all my flour and other grains from a heritage supplier in Grand Junction. I'll give them a call first thing tomorrow."

"Okay. Let me know if you have any trouble. I have some contacts as well and can probably get you what you need."

I nod. "So what else?"

"If we're going to go traditional Greek, make a list of what you'd like to see."

"Moussaka," I say.

Aunt Marj closes her eyes. "Mmm. I love moussaka! It's easy to make, too. Bryce hates eggplant, but like you said, we'll have lots of gyros."

"Although…" I rub my chin. "Maybe kabobs would be better. Gyros are usually made with chicken or pork. Sometimes lamb. Or a lamb and beef combo. Rarely beef by itself."

Aunt Marj nods. "We do have beef in abundance here at Steel Acres."

"Kabobs would be easier, too," I say. "We'll marinate the meat and veggies, and they can be grilled ahead of time and kept warm. Gyros require a rotisserie, and though it would be amazing to watch, it's a lot of work."

"True." Aunt Marj smiles. "You've convinced me, Ava. Beef kabobs, moussaka, and then traditional Greek salads with pita and your olive bread. Baklava and cake for dessert."

"Sounds like a lot of work," I say.

"Are you kidding? Jade and I live for this stuff. You just let me know if you can't take care of the bread and baklava. Or if you need some extra hands, I can send some people."

My family always offers to help.

I never let them.

I can handle Thanksgiving and a Steel party. I've done it before—although I usually have to hire extra help as well. But the profits more than cover it.

"Okay, great." I rise. "If you need anything else from me, just let me know. If I can't get the supplies, I'll call you tomorrow."

"Sounds good." Aunt Marj smiles. "I just have to tell you, you look absolutely radiant tonight, Ava."

Radiant? Not usually a word that describes me.

"Well...thank you."

"Have you done something different?"

"Not really. I did get my hair touched up." I finger a pink wave hanging at my shoulder.

"That must be it. It's really pretty. Has a little more depth."

"I asked Willow to mix the color the way Raine did, but maybe she added something extra."

"Raine was a wonderful hairstylist," Aunt Marj says, "but I just went to Willow myself for the first time last week, and I have to say, she's more of an artist than Raine. Plus she gives these amazing scalp massages every time she does a shampoo."

I laugh. "Yeah, I really like that too. I wonder why Raine never did that?"

"I don't know. Probably because Raine did a little bit of everything. She did hair, nails, facials. She never had time to give a little extra."

"I know," I say. "Willow told me she doesn't do facials and

nails. Not that I ever had a facial, but I like a good manicure every now and then."

"I think Willow is looking for someone to come in part time to do nails and facials."

"That'll be kind of hard to find in Snow Creek. We were lucky that Raine did everything."

"I guess we'll just have to do our own facials," Marj says. "I read about this amazing honey and oatmeal facial you can give yourself. We should try it."

"Right now?"

She laughs. "Not right now, silly. But you and I are the cooks in the family. Let's give it a shot sometime."

"Sounds good."

I really do love Aunt Marj. She and I have a lot in common.

"I should get going," I say.

"Okay. I'll see you out."

I gesture with my hand. "No, don't get up. I know you're ready to immerse yourself in all things Greek."

She laughs. "You know me too well, Ava. Thanks for coming over."

"No problem."

I walk outside and raise my eyebrows at Brock.

"Hey," I say, "what are you still doing here? Don't you have a gorgeous fiancée to get home to?"

"She and Jesse and the band are working tonight. She has a concert to plan for mid-December, and they have to be ready for this tour in January."

"Does that mean you're not going to see much of her now?"

"She's moving into the guesthouse with me, so I'll at least be able to see her every night."

"That's great."

"But I'm alone tonight, and ..."

"Brock ... do you need someone to talk to?"

Brock's shoulders are visibly tense. "What I need, Ava, is a drink. Feel like going into town?"

My family likes to drink, but they know when to stop, thank goodness. I've never had much of a taste for the stuff, but Brock and I have been buddies since we were in diapers, and I get the sense he needs someone to listen tonight.

"You know what? A drink sounds great. Let's go."

CHAPTER TWO

Brendan

Finally.

Finally the investigation of my trashed living quarters above the bar is done, so I can move back in.

Except not yet. I have to get it fixed, and I was fortunate to get a massive insurance check to make that happen.

I'm so sick of bunking at my parents' house. I'm thirty-five years old, for God's sake.

At least I have work. A man has to make a living, of course. Except now, instead of walking up the stairs to go home at night, I walk a few blocks to my parents' place in a residential part of town.

I have to tiptoe through the house so I don't wake them, because it's very late after tending bar. I go into my old room, which looks exactly the same as it did when I was in high school over fifteen years ago, right down to the old movie posters on my walls and my hockey trophy from eighth grade.

I love my folks.

But I'm so ready to get back to my own place.

I wipe down the bar and make my way around the tables, checking if anyone needs a refill. Laney's here tonight, but that's it. Just her and me. It's a weeknight, so things aren't as rowdy as usual.

For a small town, Snow Creek has a fair amount of action on the weekends. The pool tables in the back of the bar are always crowded, and we usually have a full house.

I jerk as the bell on the door rings, signaling a new patron.

Then I nearly jump out of my skin when Ava Steel enters.

For the past year, I've been horny as hell for Ava. I'm trying to keep my dick in my pants, though, because she's so young. Twenty-four, I think. Plus? She's a Steel. With a big Steel father, big Steel uncles, and big Steel cousins. I can hold my own against any one Steel, but all of them? Not so much.

But damn...

First of all, she has a body that won't quit. She's not as tall as her sister, Gina, but she's built just like her mother, Ruby Steel. Perfect tits, a small waist, just the right amount of ass. Her legs are luscious too, when she lets anyone see them. Tonight she's wearing baggy boyfriend jeans.

Except I know she doesn't have a boyfriend.

Yeah, I keep tabs on her.

She walks in with her cousin, Brock Steel—one of the Steel cousins. They're the same age, and they've always been close.

I suck in a deep breath. I always do that when I see Ava Steel. I have to calm myself and make sure I act like a normal person around her. I'm thirty-five fucking years old, and she makes me feel like a high school kid.

It doesn't help that I've been sleeping in my high school room. In the bed where I used to have dreams about hot chicks from school. Ava was never on my mind back then, as she was only seven.

But now?

Damn.

"Hey, Brock, Ava. Good to see you guys." I smile, hoping like hell it looks natural.

"Hey, Brendan." Brock takes a seat at the bar.

Ava sits next to him. "How are you tonight?" she asks.

"I'm good, I'm good." I rub a towel over a glass that's perfectly clean. "What can I get you two?"

"Whatever you've got on tap is great with me," Brock says.

"I think I'll have..." Ava wrinkles her forehead, looking extremely adorable. "I feel like an actual drink tonight. How about a...pink squirrel?"

Pink squirrel? I've heard of it, but what the hell is it?

"I think you're the first person who's ever walked into this bar and ordered that drink," I say. "I may have to look in the bartender guide for that one."

Ava laughs. And oh my God, she sounds sexy. "I'm just kidding, Brendan. I don't even know what's in a pink squirrel."

"If it's truly pink, it must have crème de noyaux in it," I say.

"What's that?"

"It's a liqueur made from the kernels of peach or apricot pits."

She grimaces. "Ooh."

"It's actually almond flavored," I tell her.

"Oh, okay." She smiles, and her whole face lights up. "I love almond flavor. Almond croissants are my favorite, and they're the most popular confection at my bakery."

"Yeah," I say. "Your almond croissants are the tops."

Christ. Did I just say her almond croissants are the tops? What a geek. I've never even tasted them. My favorites are her chocolate croissants.

"So you don't know how to make a pink squirrel?" she says.

"I can make anything."

"Okay, then." Ava smiles. "Make me a pink squirrel."

Now I've stepped in it. I pull out the bartender's book, look up pink squirrel, and hope like heck I have the ingredients for one.

I was right. It calls for three quarters of an ounce of crème de noyaux. Another three quarters of an ounce of white crème de cacao. I have those. Freshly ground nutmeg for garnish.

That I don't have. I may have some upstairs in the kitchen, but without floors covering my joists, I don't really want to look.

The problem is the one and a half ounces of heavy cream.

That I do not have.

But I have vanilla ice cream. That will have to work.

I shove a small scoop of ice cream plus the liqueurs into the blender and let 'er rip.

What comes out is a thick pink liquid.

I pour it into a martini glass, and I have to admit it looks . . . really disgusting.

I set it on top of a bar napkin and hand it to Ava. "Here you go. My very first pink squirrel."

I tap the keg for Brock's beer and slide it to him.

Ava stares at her drink.

"You going to try it?" I ask.

She smiles. "Yeah. Sure. But it's kind of pretty. Almost the same color as my hair."

"That's what I was going for, of course." I raise my eyebrows.

She smiles again and brings the martini glass to her lips.

She takes a sip, leaving a cute pink mustache on her upper lip. She quickly cleans it with a cocktail napkin.

"Well?" I ask.

"You know, it's kind of good. Kind of like an alcoholic milkshake."

"That's what I was going for," I say again.

God, Brendan. Original.

"What in the hell does it taste like?" Brock asks.

Ava sets the drink down and wipes her mouth again. "Kind of almondy. And I don't know how I can even say this, but to me, it tastes pink."

"Well, nobody knows pink better than you, cuz." Brock gives Ava a light punch on her upper arm.

I don't know why, but Ava Steel just became even more attractive to me. How does something taste pink? Damn. I'd like to taste that little pink pussy of hers. I'll bet *that* tastes pink. Nice and sweet and *pink*.

"Have you been talking to Ashley?" Brock asks.

"No, but we should call her. She should come over and tell me if this really does taste pink."

Ashley Steel is Dale Steel's wife, and it's well known around town that she has synesthesia. But as I understand it, to her, sounds have colors and colors have sounds. Is her taste affected too?

Next time I see her I'll ask.

A few townies walk into the bar, so I excuse myself. I'll take the drink orders quickly so I can get back to Ava.

One of them—an attractive brunette wearing a black tank top—points at Ava's drink. "What's that?"

"It's a pink squirrel," I say.

"What *is* it exactly?"

"It's crème de noyaux, which taste like almonds, and crème de cacao—which tastes kind of chocolatey—and vanilla ice cream."

"That sounds fabulous. I'll have that." She peeks down the bar. "Hi, Brock. Remember me?"

Brock turns toward her. "Oh . . . sure. It's Sadie?"

"That's right, Sadie McCall. Who's that with you? Is it Rory?"

Brock lets out a guffaw. Like anyone could mistake Ava for Rory.

Rory Pike is a beautiful woman. In fact, people say she's the most beautiful woman in Snow Creek. And her hair is *not* pink.

Ava Steel is an individual. Her beauty is internal *and* external. Both of these qualities collide to create something absolutely unique. And spectacular.

"No, this is my cousin Ava. Ava, this is Sadie McCall."

Ava pokes her head around Brock. "Hi there," she says.

"Ava!" The platinum blond woman who came in with Sadie looks down the bar. "It's so great to see you. We met at your bakery, remember? You told me about all your hot cousins?"

Ava's cheeks turn the color of her drink. "Hi, Nora."

"Oh wow, I love your hair," Sadie gushes.

"Thank you."

"Does the new hairstylist do that for you?"

"Yeah, I just had it touched up a few days ago."

"It's really fabulous."

"Thank you." Ava goes back to her drink.

Nora and the guy who came in with Sadie order beers.

I grab those first and then prepare Sadie's pink squirrel. I place it on top of a cocktail napkin and shove it toward her.

"You'll have to let me know what you think," I say.

"I already think it's fabulous." She takes a sip. She ends up with the same pink mustache that Ava did, but daintily wipes it away. "It's . . . certainly different. I think I like it."

"Good. I'm glad." I smile. "Does it taste pink?"

Sadie furrows her brow. "Pink? How could it taste pink?"

I chuckle softly. Ava Steel is one of a kind.

"Just wondering." I move back toward Brock and Ava. "So what are you up to tonight?"

"I've been helping Aunt Marjorie plan my parents' twenty-fifth anniversary party. You'll be there, won't you?"

"Absolutely," I say. "I never miss a Steel party."

"Oh, good."

Is that a bit more of a blush on Ava's cheeks? It's hard to tell because she's so naturally pretty and rosy.

My heart flops around inside my chest. What is it about this woman that makes me feel like I'm back in freaking high school?

My cheeks warm. Jesus Christ. I'm fair-skinned—a natural redhead—so anything that happens on my face is more than obvious.

But Ava has turned back to her cousin, and they're chatting about something else.

So I make my getaway. I do my rounds in the bar again, helping Laney out, taking drink orders, and then mixing drinks.

But I'm so hyperaware.

So hyperaware of the woman sitting at the bar, nursing her pink squirrel.

She's too young for you, Brendan.

Too fucking young.

But already I know.

She's the one I want, and no one else will suffice.

"So, Brendan," Sadie says.

I jerk toward her voice. "Hey, you need something?"

"Yes," she says. "I was wondering . . . if you'd like to go out on a date with me sometime."

I stop my jaw from hitting the bar. I know women ask men out these days, but I'm a small-town guy. It's not the norm here.

"Oh?"

Sadie's quite beautiful, with dark hair and a very slim body. In fact, she's usually the type I'd go for. I'm not sure when I began pining over Ava Steel.

I guess I started noticing her when she opened her bakery a couple of years ago. She's the one Steel who actually lives in town, so I see her a lot. She's always so friendly, and I like the way she dresses—despite the fact that her clothes often hide her luscious curves. She definitely has her own style, and as a baker, she's mega talented. I love her chocolate croissants and her baguettes.

And that stainless-steel lip ring . . .

For some reason, I can't get the thought of sucking on it when I kiss her out of my head.

But Ava hasn't ever given me a second look.

She probably thinks I'm too old for her.

Which I am.

I have no idea how old Sadie is, and I don't really care because I'm not actually interested.

But she *is* asking, and for some reason, she chose to ask

me in front of her two friends. So I don't want to embarrass her.

"That would be nice," I say. "What did you have in mind?"

"I don't know. Dinner? A movie?"

"Sounds good," I say. "Do you have any favorite places?"

"Any place but Lorenzo's," Sadie says. "Their food is awesome, but since I work there, I already eat a lot of it."

"There are some nice places in the city," I say.

"Oh?"

"Yeah. There's this new place called the Fortnight."

"I heard that's expensive," she says.

It *is* expensive. And since she asked me out, maybe she's planning to pay. How does this work, anyway, when a woman asks a man out?

"Let's stay in town, then," I say. "I'd offer to cook you dinner myself, except, as you know, my place is kind of out of commission."

"I suppose I could make you dinner," she says, "but I'll have to make sure Nora's out."

"I hear you talking about me," Nora says.

Sadie reddens a bit. "It's nothing, Nora. We'll just go out, Brendan. I'll pick a place."

Good. Sadie's pretty and all, but I don't want to have dinner at her place. It's too . . . personal.

"Sounds good. Just let me know when."

"How about tomorrow night?"

"I think I'm free." I pull my phone out of my back pocket to check my calendar. "I can always get Johnny or Laney to cover me at the bar."

Sadie smiles. "I'm looking forward to it."

"I am too."

Not a lie, exactly. Maybe, if I get interested in Sadie, I'll get Ava Steel off my mind.

Because right now she's knee-deep in a conversation with her cousin, and she hasn't given me a look all night.

CHAPTER THREE

Ava

Brock seems preoccupied, so I sip my pink squirrel, and when the glass is finally empty, I'm kind of sad.

It was pretty good.

Brock eyes the empty glass. "I guess I should've asked for a taste."

"I'll order another one if you want."

"I'm kidding, Ava. I'm not putting whatever was in that glass in my mouth."

"You might be surprised," I say. "It was good."

He finishes his beer and gestures to Brendan with his empty glass.

"Coming right up," Brendan says. "Do you want another, Ava?"

I look at the glass. "You know, I'm not even feeling the first one. So sure, I'll have another. And Brock, you're going to taste this one."

He shakes his head. "Not a chance."

My cousin is clearly distracted. Maybe I can help get his mind off whatever's eating him and get some information on my mystery at the same time.

"You look like you could use a diversion," I say.

"A froufrou pink drink isn't it."

"Well . . . I have a dilemma."

That gets his attention. The Steel men are notoriously protective of the Steel women.

"What is it? Are you okay?"

"Yeah, I'm fine. But I got a weird text message earlier today."

He lowers his brow and wrinkles his forehead. "What kind of text message? Did anyone threaten you?"

I widen my eyes. "No! What would make you think that?"

He sighs. "Just a lot of shit going down."

"At least I don't *think* it's a threat." I grab my phone, pull up the text, and show it to Brock.

Darth Morgen is alive.

He glances at it. "Darth Morgen? Who is Darth Morgen?"

"I have no idea. It came right as I was ending a chat with my tarot group."

Brock does me the courtesy of not rolling his eyes. My family doesn't share my interest in the tarot, but they're nice about it. Another reason to love them. They let me be me.

"Do you think it has something to do with your tarot group?"

"It's not a number I recognize. And of course I searched it, and nothing came up. But I know you and your dad can get numbers traced."

"Yeah, we can take a look at it for you," Brock says. "But have you considered that—"

"It was a wrong number?" I nod. "Yeah, I've considered it."

"Sounds kind of like a *Star Wars* thing."

"That was my thought at first too. I may be a nerd in most things, but I've never been into *Star Wars.*"

"Yeah, but Dave and I are."

"Right. Which is why I thought I'd ask you. Is Darth Morgen someone in the *Star Wars* universe?"

"Not that I know of. But Dave's a bigger *Star Wars* geek than I am." He fiddles with his phone. "I'll text him."

The bells on the door jostle, and—

"Speak of the devil," I say.

"I was just texting you." From Brock.

David Simpson—the third of our trio and second son to Aunt Marjorie and Uncle Bryce, and resident pretty boy of the Steel family with his dark hair and bright-blue eyes—sits down on the other side of me.

"Yeah? What about?"

"Ava got a perplexing text."

I shove my phone into Dave's face. "Does this ring a bell to you?"

He stares at it for a moment. "Darth Morgen."

"Who the fuck is that?" Brock asks.

"He's not in the *Star Wars Legends* universe, but I suppose he could be a character in some fan universe."

"What do you mean?" I ask.

"Fan fiction. Sometimes fan universes go viral, but this doesn't ring a bell to me."

"So it's not a *Star Wars* reference?" I ask.

Dave shakes his head. "Not that I know of. But the name could easily be in some fan universe I don't know about. Disney ruined *Star Wars,* by the way."

"Oh my God." Brock rolls his eyes. "You never miss a chance to bring that up, you big nerd."

"Hey, I don't remember being alone in the line when the Snow Creek Cinema was showing the revamped version of *The Empire Strikes Back.*"

"For the life of me," I say, "I do not see how you two are so popular with the ladies."

"Easy," Dave drawls. "We don't talk about this shit with them."

"Unless we find out they're fans as well," Brock adds.

"So you haven't enthralled Rory with your tales of the *Star Wars* universe?" I ask.

"Negative." Brock grabs his beer right as Brendan places it on the bar and takes a sip.

"Here you go, Ava." Brendan smiles as he hands me my second pink squirrel.

Brendan is incredibly good-looking—and maybe it's because he doesn't look anything like a Steel. Most of the Steels have dark hair and dark eyes, although Dave and I are exceptions with blue eyes.

The only blonds in our family are Dale, Donny, and Henry—none of whom have any actual Steel blood. They're all adopted members of the family.

Brendan? He's not dark or blond.

He's a redhead, but not an orangey redhead. It's more like a dark-strawberry blond or light auburn, and he wears it long like my cousin Dale does.

Right now it's pulled back in a low ponytail, his signature look. His complexion is fair but not overly so. He never looks pale. Just like fine porcelain.

Which is not something I ever thought I'd say about a man. But the guy has a peaches-and-cream complexion, though he's not feminine in any way. He's tall, broad-shouldered, with an incredible sculpted jawline and a straight Grecian nose.

Despite his hair being on the lighter side, his eyebrows and eyelashes are darker brown.

He's way too old for me though. He went to high school with my cousin Dale, so he's eleven years my senior.

Besides, I'm not really looking for a relationship. I date every now and then, but I'm so young. I have so many goals for my business that I want to accomplish. I keep hearing that if you work your butt off in your twenties, it's smooth sailing for the rest of your life.

Of course, it could be smooth sailing for me regardless, with my Steel trust fund and all.

That's not to say that my cousins don't work for their success. They do. They all work incredibly hard. Brock works with his dad, Jonah, on the beef ranch. Dale works with my father, Ryan Steel, at the winery. In fact, he's taken it over now that my dad retired as master winemaker.

Donny went to law school, got himself a partnership track at a Denver firm, but then came home to Snow Creek at the request of his mother, my aunt Jade. Now he's the city attorney here in town.

My cousin Brad, Brock's brother, along with Dave's brother, Henry, run the Steel Foundation, which is the charitable arm of our company.

Diana, Dale and Donny's sister, is now in Denver for an architect internship.

That leaves only the youngest Steels—also known as the awesome foursome. They include my cousin Brianna Steel, my sister, Gina, and Uncle Bryce and Aunt Marj's twins, Angie and Sage Simpson. They're all seniors in college.

We may each have trust funds, but we all learned the value of hard work living on a ranch.

When I was a little girl, Dad used to take me out into the vineyards with him. I think he was hoping I would learn his love of wine, but it's not really my thing. It doesn't seem to be Gina's either. Thank goodness for Dale, though. He was Dad's right-hand man even then, when Gina and I were just kids.

Dale was an adult by the time I was seven years old.

Which means Brendan Murphy was also an adult.

Not that the age thing bothers me. It really doesn't. I just know he would never look at me that way.

Like I said, I'm not looking for a date anyway.

But if I were…

I'd be hard-pressed to find someone better looking, nicer, and more personable than Brendan Murphy.

Dave and Brock are still discussing the *Star Wars* universe, so I interrupt them.

"Hello?" I wave my phone in front of their faces. "I don't think this is a *Star Wars* reference. So what does this text mean?"

"I agree," Dave says. "It's not a *Star Wars* reference, unless it's from someone who thinks he knows the universe but actually doesn't."

"The geek's probably right," Brock says.

"Right."

"Does it have any reference in your world of tarot cards?" Brock asks.

I shake my head. "Nope."

"But you said it came through right as you were ending a chat with that group, right?"

"Yeah. I know the tarot pretty well, and I've racked my brain. I don't think it can possibly be a tarot reference."

Brock takes another sip of his beer. "I'll get our people to trace the number for you. But it most likely came from a burner phone and can't be traced."

"Why do you say that's most likely?" I ask.

Brock wrinkles his forehead. "Honestly? I'm just assuming. With all the shit that's gone down lately, we've come across several untraceable numbers. But this is completely different, so I suppose it could be an actual number."

"*Is* it completely different though?" Dave asks.

"Well . . . yeah," Brock says. "How could this have anything to do with everything else that's going on with the family?"

"You mean with the stuff that you guys found at Brendan's place?" I ask.

A month or so ago, Brendan found some documents relating to our family in his apartment above the bar. His place was trashed soon after, so if there was anything else hiding, it's gone now.

"Partially." Brock clears his throat. "But there's some other stuff going down."

"What?" Dave and I ask in unison.

Brock clams up.

It's funny. Dave, Brock, and I grew up together. We were all born around the same time, and we were all in the same class at school, so we're close. We always have been. Does Brock really think Dave and I are going to let this go?

Dave speaks first. "You know, I've kept my mouth shut. When you and Rory needed someone to watch the Pikes' dogs—"

"Wait a minute," Brock says. "That was because Frank had a heart attack. You know that. The Pikes were in Grand Junction at the hospital."

"Yeah," Dave says, "which didn't explain why *you* couldn't watch the Pikes' dogs."

Brock closes his mouth and inhales loudly through his nose. "There's shit going down. It's not something I want to talk about in public like this."

"Look," I say. "You, Dave, and I have been each other's sounding boards since we were toddlers. This keeping stuff from us? It's not going to fly." I take a sip of my second pink squirrel.

If possible, this one's even sweeter. And pinker. And more pink tasting.

"I need to talk to my dad first," Brock says.

"No, you don't," I counter.

"Actually, Ava, I do. It's some heavy shit."

I take another sip of the sweet drink. Now I'm starting to feel it. "Whatever."

"Yeah, whatever, dude." This from Dave. "Ava, feel like a game of pool?"

I laugh. "Sure. It's a guaranteed win for me."

We Steels all like to play pool, and Dave's not bad, but he's the worst of all of us.

"You're just going to leave me here at the bar?" Brock says.

"Absolutely," I say. "Since you don't want to talk to us about whatever's going on."

"I will. I just need to check with my dad."

"Cool. In the meantime, Dave and I can have a pool game."

I hop off my barstool and follow Dave to the back. It's a weeknight, so the pool tables aren't too crowded, and the third one is free.

"Rack 'em up, Dave," I say
"You got it, Ave." He laughs at our rhyming names.
He racks, and then I shoot first.
It's an unwritten rule with all the Steels.
Ladies always shoot first.

CHAPTER FOUR

Brendan

I do my rounds again and then settle myself behind the bar. Sadie is trying to have a conversation with me, but I'm only listening with one ear. I keep my eyes fixed on Ava but make an effort to look at Sadie every now and then. I can't have Ava see me watching her.

Ava's a good pool player—all the Steels are—and every once in a while, I join them when I'm off duty.

But tonight I'm on duty until twelve, when we close on weeknights. On weekends, we stay open as long as people are here drinking and playing pool. Sometimes it's the wee hours of the morning before I close.

"Don't you think so, Brendan?"

I jerk back to Sadie.

"I'm sorry. What did you say?"

"I said Brock Steel and Rory Pike make a beautiful couple."

"Oh, yeah. Sure they do."

Are we really talking about Brock Steel and Rory Pike?

"I had quite a crush on Brock when I first moved here," Sadie says.

"Oh?"

Am I supposed to care?

"But I don't think you're any less handsome," she says. "You're just as good-looking as he is, but in a totally different way."

Great. I seriously don't care.

Which means I probably should not be going out on a date with this woman.

"You know what, Sadie?"

"What?"

"I just remembered. I have plans tomorrow night."

She frowns. "But you just said you'd get somebody to cover your shift?"

"I do need to get someone to cover my shift...because I'm... I'm having dinner with some friends." I shake my head. "I can't believe I forgot. Laney!"

Laney hustles toward me. "Yeah, Brendan?"

"Can you cover the bar tomorrow night?"

"Tomorrow's my night off," Laney says.

"I know. And I'm sorry, but I totally forgot I made plans with some friends who are coming into town."

She shrugs. "It's okay. I could use the extra cash."

"Perfect. You're the best, and sorry again for the short notice."

"No problem." Laney sets her pad of paper in front of me. "I need a couple martinis, a margarita, and a Tom Collins." She rips the piece of paper off and hands it to me.

"Coming right up."

"So which friends are you going out with tomorrow night?" Sadie asks.

"Some guys from high school are coming into town." I smile, trying to ease the tension that's making my neck stiff.

I don't like lying. But I also just don't think it's fair to Sadie to lead her on. I'm not at all interested in her.

I've never been one to go out with a woman to just go out. I'm not one of the Rake-a-teers, as Donny, Brock, and Dave used to be called.

That old term is fading away, now that Donny and Brock are spoken for.

"Oh? Who?"

Man, she's really going to make me work for this, isn't she? She just moved here. She didn't go to high school here. She won't even know who I'm talking about.

"Some old friends. You wouldn't know them."

"Oh." She takes a drink of her pink squirrel. "I see."

Okay, now I feel like a piece of shit.

"We could go out another time," I say.

Her eyes light up at that one. "Sure, I suppose so."

"What if I give you a call?" I say.

"It's okay, Brendan." She drops her gaze to her nearly empty martini glass. "You and I both know you're not going to call me."

Now I feel like shit times two. Make that times two thousand.

"That's not true."

"You haven't taken your eyes off Ava all night."

"Sadie—"

"It's okay." Sadie attempts a smile. "She's cute. The pink hair and lip ring work for her. Even those awful baggy jeans work on her. She has her own style, and I appreciate that. Plus, she makes amazing sandwiches."

"She does. But I'm not interested in her in that way."

What an acidic lie.

"Then you might want to stop staring at her." Sadie turns to her companions. "If it's okay with you guys, I'm going to take off."

"Okay," Nora says. "See you tomorrow at work."

Sadie opens her purse and pulls out her wallet.

I place my hand over hers. "No charge tonight. It's on me."

"Is that a brush-off? *I don't want to go out with you, but I'll pay for your drinks?*"

"It's just something I do for friends sometimes," I say.

"Okay." She shoves her wallet back into her purse. "See you around, Brendan." She hops off her stool and leaves the bar.

And now I feel like complete crap. Times two million.

Though I still can't take my eyes off Ava's ass as she bends over to make a shot. Even in those baggy boyfriend jeans, it's amazing.

"What a fine ass," I say under my breath.

I don't even realize I've spoken aloud until Nora meets my gaze. "So you *do* like Sadie, then?"

"Oh? Sure, Sadie's a nice girl."

"I mean you like her ass." Nora laughs.

Great. She thought I was watching Sadie go out the door.

"I didn't mean to be disrespectful," I say.

"I didn't think that," Nora says. "Sadie will be thrilled. She really likes you, Brendan."

"I like her too."

I look around for a minute to make sure I'm still thirty-five and still tending bar. For a moment, I felt like I was at a locker in middle school with a girl asking me who I like. Or *like* like.

This has to stop.

"If you'll excuse me," I say to Nora as I set my towel down and step out from behind the bar.

I walk to Ava.

Enough is enough is enough.

Yes, she's young.

Yes, she's shown no interest in me at all.

But damn it. I'm going to ask her out.

Because this has gone on long enough. Dave is in the middle of a shot, so I tap Ava on the shoulder.

She jerks around. "Oh, hi, Brendan."

"Ava, I was wondering if you . . . would like another pink squirrel."

God, I'm such a fucking coward.

She widens her eyes just a touch. "Oh, no, thank you. I started to feel that last one."

Dave attempts the shot. Misses.

"You need anything, Dave?" I ask.

"Yeah, another beer would be great." He laughs. "I actually play better when I'm a little drunk. Thanks, Brendan."

I head back to the bar. "Chicken shit," I say under my breath.

Then I turn around quickly.

Back to Ava.

She's getting ready to make her shot, so I stay quiet until she's done. She misses.

"Crap," she says.

"Ha," Dave says, "and everyone thinks I'm the worst Steel pool player."

"You are," Ava says dryly.

"Ava," I say.

She turns around again. "What is it, Brendan?"

"Can I talk to you for a minute?"

"Sure. What's up?"

"I mean, alone."

She sets her pool cue down. "Yeah, sure. I don't need to watch Dave blow this shot."

I lead her to the corner of the bar. "I was wondering..."

"Yeah?"

"If you'd like to have lunch with me. Tomorrow."

"Well"—she looks down at her feet and then up to me—"I work lunches."

Of course she does. She owns a damned bakery and sandwich shop. *Nice move, Brendan.*

"Dinner then?"

She reddens.

Is that a good or bad sign?

I think good, right? She's blushing?

"I'd like that," she says.

I stop myself from sighing in happy relief, but I can't help a broad smile. "Great. What kind of food do you like?"

She laughs. "I'm a Steel. I like *all* food."

"You mean you're not...like...vegan or anything?"

She gives a cute little laugh. "Why? Because I have a lip ring and color my hair pink? No, I'm not a vegan. You've attended many Steel parties, Brendan. Haven't you seen me down my share of hamburgers?"

I'm an idiot. Of course I have. Because my eyes never stray from her.

"So...tomorrow then?" I say.

"Sure. I close the bakery at six. Then I need to go upstairs and clean up a little. About seven?"

"Great. I'll pick you up at seven at your place."

"Sounds good. I'm looking forward to it."

I smile. "So am I."

Boy, am I ever.

CHAPTER FIVE

Ava

"What was that about?" Dave demands when I return to the pool table.

"I just couldn't bear to watch you miss that shot," I say.

"Joke's on you, then, because I made it, and the next two plus the eight ball. I win."

I glance at the pool table. Sure enough, Dave has sunk all the balls.

"Wait a minute," I tease. "How do I know you didn't just put all the balls in the pockets while I wasn't looking?"

Dave places his hand over his heart in mock surprise. "You think I'd actually cheat?"

I punch his arm. "Nah. Steels don't cheat."

"You're right. You and the rest of our clan are going to have to stop making fun of my pool skills eventually. I made those shots, didn't I, Laney?"

Laney Dooley, a gorgeous sandy blonde nearing thirty and a Murphy's staple, looks over at us and giggles. "Don't drag me into this. I saw nothing."

Dave gives her a flirtatious grin. "Fat lot of help you are, sweetheart." He turns back to me. "Guess you're going to have to take my word for it, cuz. I made the shots."

I pick up my pool cue. "Congrats. Drinks are on you, then."

"You going to answer me?"

I lift my eyebrows. "About what?"

"About what Brendan wanted?"

I open my mouth, but for some reason, I don't want to tell my cousin I'm going out with Brendan. Not because I'm freaked out about the age difference or anything, but because . . .

I'm not sure why.

It seems personal. Private.

I find myself . . . kind of excited about it. I rub my arms against the shivers that have erupted.

I haven't been this excited about a guy in a while.

Maybe ever.

"He wanted to order a pumpkin pie for Thanksgiving. His mom asked him to, and he forgot to come into the bakery today."

"Oh."

Good. Dave seems to buy my little white lie.

"So drinks are on me," he says. "What'll you have?"

I need to go home.

I don't want another drink.

I want to go back to my place and pull a tarot card. Maybe see what dinner with Brendan Murphy has in store for me.

"I think I'll pass," I say as I hang up my pool cue. "I'm going to head out."

"You want me to walk you home?"

"I'm fine. It's only a couple of buildings down, as you know."

"Okay, but I'm going to watch you from the door."

The Steel men are notoriously protective of their women. It's cute, really. My father and my uncles, the original Steel brothers, are quite the chivalrous bunch.

True to his word, Dave walks me to the door and doesn't take his eyes off me until I let myself into the bakery building and lock the door behind me. I walk through the dark bakery to the back and then unlock the door to the stairway that leads to my apartment above.

It's bigger than it looks from the outside. It has two bedrooms, a decent-size living room, and a decent-size kitchen—which I had remodeled to meet my specifications so I could bake here as well as downstairs—and a small bathroom with a bathtub and shower.

It's decorated in early American Ava.

Lots of daisies—my favorite flower—and wall art and odds and ends from flea markets and antique shops. Very bohemian, which is also how I dress most of the time. Flowing dresses and loose jeans are comfortable, and I need comfort when I'm on my feet and baking all day.

I love to cook. Baking is my passion, but I like all of it. And boy, it's been a long time since I've cooked for anyone but myself—other than my customers, of course, and that's always baking. Sure, I slap items together on a sandwich, mix up a batch of cumin mayo sometimes, but it's not the same as cooking a big meal.

Perhaps I should cook for Brendan tomorrow night.

"No," I say aloud.

That would send the wrong message.

We'll go to dinner. We can't have dinner at Brendan's place because it's still a wreck.

And it apparently all has something to do with my family.

I do love my family, but things are getting so strange.

I pour myself a glass of water and pull out my tarot deck. I keep it wrapped in an old scarf that once belonged to my mother. She gave it to me when I was little, said it belonged to her mother. I only have limited memories of my Grandma Diamond.

Yes, her name was Diamond. Diamond Lee Thornbush.

She passed away when I was around eight or nine and Gina three years younger.

Her voice was low and raspy from years of smoking cigarettes, and she lived with us for a little while, but that was so long ago. She died of lung cancer. Mom and Dad, of course, saw that she had the best care their money could buy, but she was too far gone.

Which is why I will never smoke a cigarette in my lifetime.

The scarf is made of silk, and the color is a soft warm pink.

Eerily similar to the color of my hair.

I've always loved the color, and scattered across is a pattern of daisies.

I love the simplicity of daisies. The simple yellow center, the simple white petals.

A friendly flower. An unassuming flower.

While my sister and cousins adore roses and lilies, I prefer the minimalism of the daisy.

I unwrap the tarot deck, shuffle it once, twice, three times, and then I clasp my hands around the deck, close my eyes, and hold it to my heart, infusing it with my own personal energy.

When I do a reading for someone else, I let them hold the deck. Infuse it with their energy, so that I may give them a good reading, and so the cards will display themselves accurately.

But tonight I want a reading for me.

I don't normally do a large display when I do readings for myself. I prefer pulling one card as I did earlier when I got the text message.

I choose to do the same now. I pull one card off the deck and lay it down face up.

Hmm ... A gallant knight holding a chalice. He's sensitive. A poet. He adores all things romantic and refined, but he has a tendency to get lost in love and romance. His energy must be used with caution. If it's hurting your situation, you need to exercise restraint.

The knight of cups.

A bit on the nose, but at least I didn't draw the lovers card.

I need to be cautious because the knight of cups seems to want to take me on an exhilarating ride.

A ride I'm totally not ready for.

This card seems to urge caution for me. I can't get swept away.

I'm not the type to get swept away, but the knight makes me think there's something about Brendan that could make me want to dive in.

I need to watch myself.

Yeah. I'm definitely not making dinner for him here at my place.

No way.

Brendan Murphy is attractive, but I'm not getting swept off my feet by anyone.

I have too much else going on.

In fact ... maybe I should cancel the date.

Is it even a date?

I mean, sure, it's a date. It's dinner. I'll just make sure he understands that I'm not looking for anything serious. That I'm not the kind of woman who will jump into bed with him.

That's not my style. It never has been.

I lost my virginity when I was an old maid of twenty. Hell,

Gina lost hers before I lost mine, and she's three years younger than I am.

I was in college at the time, and I had been dating this guy for a couple of months. I'm kind of ashamed to say that I slept with him just to get it over with. To surrender my V-card.

I wasn't all that into him. He was a nice guy, but I didn't feel a spark.

I've never felt that spark.

With Brendan?

There might be a spark.

I've suppressed it, to be honest. He's just way too old for me, and I've never given him a second thought.

But you never know...

★ ★ ★

I'm taking a turn behind the counter while one of my employees takes a quick break. The lunch crowd has died down, so I have a moment to breathe.

Until the bell dings and someone walks in.

It's Callie Pike, assistant to her fiancé, Snow Creek City Attorney Donny Steel.

"Hey, Callie. Late lunch today?"

"Yeah. Donny and I are swamped over at the office. I just came to pick up a few sandwiches. I called them in earlier."

"Yeah, let me see. Luke just took a quick break." I turn my gaze to the shelf where we keep the takeout orders. I grab the bag with Callie's name on it. "Here you go. Looks like it's all paid for."

"Yeah. Should be. Thanks, Ava." She turns but then looks over her shoulder. "You look different today. Did you do something with your hair?"

"I don't think so." I absently touch the hairnet on my head. How can she even tell what it looks like? "Oh, I did have it colored a few days ago. The first time with Willow. The color came out slightly different."

"I like it. It's ... warmer."

"I like it too. Raine said she left the formula with Willow, but it didn't turn out exactly the same."

"Willow may use a different product than Raine. Apparently all the products are a little bit distinctive."

"Oh?"

"Yeah, I remember Raine telling me that. Back when she and Rory were together."

"Oh? I like it." I fidget with the hairnet again. "I honestly didn't think I'd ever let anyone touch my hair except Raine, but Willow is quite good."

"I'm glad to hear that," Callie says, "because I have an appointment with her next week."

"You don't color your hair, do you?"

"I just highlight it a little," Callie says. "I like a little depth to it. My hair is kind of a plain mousy color. It's not that deep brown like Rory and Maddie have."

"I think your hair is gorgeous," I say in truth.

"Well, thank you." She looks at me again. "Except ... it's not your hair that's different, Ava. You're a little ... flushed."

"It's warm back in the bakery."

"That must be it. Unless ..."

"Unless what?

"Is there something new in your life? Like ... a guy maybe?"

Now I know I'm blushing. The warmth hits my cheeks with a blast. "I have a date tonight."

"Oh? With who?"

"You're not going believe this, but—"

"Brendan Murphy," she says.

I drop my jaw. "How did you know?"

"Ava, everyone knows he's been crushing on you for months."

I drop my mouth open again.

"So . . . I assume that means you didn't know."

"I was completely clueless. He's so much older than I am. I never really gave him a thought. But he is very good-looking."

"Right? Put a kilt on the man and—"

"Oh my God." Tingles scoot across my flesh. "Brendan Murphy in a kilt."

That spark I've been trying to feel?

It just landed between my legs.

Yeah. He'd look like he walked straight out from the Highlands.

"Except I think he's Irish, not Scottish," I say.

"Same difference." Callie smiles.

"I'm looking forward to it. It's been a while since I've been on a date with anyone."

"You'll have fun. Brendan's a great guy."

"How well do you know him?"

"Not that well, but I talk to him a lot when I go to the bar. That's how I know he's got the hots for you."

My skin is on fire. "Am I seriously the only one who doesn't know this?"

"I know, and Rory knows. But that's probably it."

"So none of the guys know."

"Oh, God, no. Men are clueless."

I laugh at that. "Hey, you're engaged to one of my favorite cousins."

"You have a favorite?"

"Yeah, all of them. That's why I said *one* of my favorites." I give her a smile.

She laughs. "Oh."

"Anyway, I have no idea what I'm doing. But he's picking me up tonight at seven."

"Just be yourself. He already likes you."

There goes that flush to my cheeks again. I feel like I'm on fire.

"I better head back to the office." Callie grabs the bag of sandwiches. "Donny and I are swamped now."

"Hey, did anything ever materialize on Brendan's case? About who broke in?"

Callie shakes her head. "I think Hardy's going to close the case. There's nothing."

"That's a shame," I say.

"I know. At least Brendan's insurance paid up."

"Yeah."

"I'll see you soon, okay?"

"Right. Bye, Callie."

Callie walks out the door, the bell ringing once more.

And only then do I realize my heart is pounding.

At the thought of Brendan Murphy.

In a kilt.

And nothing else.

CHAPTER SIX

Brendan

"Where are you going?" Mom asks.

"To see some friends," I say.

"Okay. I thought you were working tonight."

"Laney asked if she could take my shift. Said she needs some extra cash."

"Everything okay with her?"

"Yeah. Just expenses, you know. The economy and all."

"Okay. Have a good time."

I leave the house.

Man, am I ever ready to get back to my own place.

My mom wants to know where I'm going all the time, and I can't say anything because I'm living here for free while my place gets rebuilt.

If things go well tonight... It's not like I can bring Ava back to my place.

But there's always her place above the bakery.

"No," I say aloud.

I'm getting way ahead of myself.

Ava Steel is not the kind of person to jump into bed on the first date. That's part of what I like about her.

No need to take a car tonight. I walk the several blocks from my parents' residential neighborhood into town and stop at the bakery.

The sign on the door is turned to the closed side.

And I realize...

I don't have Ava's number, so how will she know I'm here?

I walk around to the rear of the bakery and knock on the back door.

A few seconds later, Ava answers.

"Hey," I say. "How are you?"

"I'm good." She walks out.

She looks lovely. Her warm pink hair is down, and it falls in soft waves around her shoulders. She's wearing a long dress in muted browns and pinks. The top of it hugs her curves, but the skirt flows, leaving her ass and legs to my very good imagination. On her feet are a pair of brown boots. They look kind of like army boots, laced up, and she's wearing brown socks.

And it all works for her.

For Ava.

She is as unique as a snowflake.

"I'm glad you answered the back door," I say. "I wasn't quite sure how to get up to your place."

"You can't get up to it from outside." She glances at the open door. "I should probably change that."

"Actually, no, you shouldn't. You're much safer without an outside entrance."

"You sound like my father. Snow Creek is the safest town ever."

"I suppose so."

In the back of my mind is always the story of my great-uncle, who my father was named after. The original Sean Murphy, who died here in Snow Creek. Well, not exactly Snow Creek, but on the Steel ranch. At the wedding of Brad and Daphne Steel, Ava's grandparents. And then later, Daphne Steel's friend, a young woman named Patty, who disappeared while shopping in this small town. Neither mystery has been fully solved.

We know my great-uncle died of a drug overdose. But it was also well known that he didn't do drugs. Which means someone dosed him.

At the Steel patriarch's wedding.

My father, Sean Murphy the second, came to Snow Creek years ago to try to solve the mystery of his namesake uncle.

He found nothing but became so enamored with the small town that he never left. He bought the bar and opened it, met my mother here, and eventually brought his sister, my aunt Ciara, out as well. She still lives here, as does her daughter, Carmen.

Granted, that all happened fifty years ago, but I still don't think a young woman can be too cautious.

I want to enjoy tonight, though, which means I need to stop thinking about half-century-old mysteries.

"Anything particular sound good to you tonight?"

"How about Lorenzo's? I love their eggplant parmesan."

Italian does sound good, but not Lorenzo's. That's where Sadie works. She probably won't be working, since she asked me out for tonight, but still . . .

"Maybe Mexican?" I suggest.

"Sure, whatever." She casts her gaze downward.

"You want Italian, don't you?"

She looks up at me and smiles. "I've kind of been craving it all day."

Her smile makes my heart skip. I want to please this woman. "Then Italian it is. Let's walk over to Lorenzo's."

After all, Sadie's probably not working.

We arrive, and Lisa Lorenzo herself, the owner, is playing hostess tonight. "Brendan," she says. "And Ava. How nice to see you both. Two for dinner?"

I nod. "Yeah, thank you, Lisa."

Lisa grabs two menus. "Follow me."

She takes us to a table in the back, which I didn't ask for. We have a secluded little corner to ourselves.

I'm not complaining.

I hold the chair out for Ava, and she raises her eyebrows at me.

What? Has she never been out with a gentleman before? I happen to know all the Steel men practice chivalry.

She takes a seat, and I gently scoot her in. Lisa hands her a menu.

"Thanks, Lisa," she says.

I take the seat across from Ava, and Lisa hands me my menu.

"Your server will be with you in a moment." Lisa whisks away.

"So you like the eggplant parmesan here, huh?" I say.

"I do. I already told you I'm not vegan or vegetarian, but it *is* nice *not* to eat meat once in a while."

"Maybe I'll try it." I scan the menus. "I don't mind going veggie now and then."

"It's fab." Ava glances down at her menu.

The shadow of our server casts over the table.

I look up and—

Of course. Brown hair up in a high ponytail, slim figure, and a look of consternation on her pretty face.

"Good evening, Brendan," Sadie McCall says. "Plans with your friends fell through?"

"Yeah," I say.

"Right." She turns to my companion. "Hello, Ava."

"Have we met?" Ava asks.

"Yeah. Last night at the bar. It's nice to know I'm so forgettable." She shakes her head slightly. "To both of you."

Ava blushes. "I'm so sorry. I remember you now. You were sitting a couple of seats away from me with some friends, right?"

"Yes."

"Sadie?"

"You remembered my name." She looks away from me. "More than I can say about some people at this table."

Ava cocks her head and meets my gaze. "What is she talking about?"

I'm not sure how old Sadie is, though I'm pretty sure she's older than Ava. Is she really going to turn this into some kind of high school drama? Like I'm sitting with the wrong people in the cafeteria?

I sigh. This is my fault anyway for lying to her. I should've just said I wasn't interested in going out. That I accepted for the wrong reasons.

Or . . . I should've thought of a better excuse.

Or better yet . . . I shouldn't have come to Lorenzo's.

But I wanted to please Ava. And I truly thought Sadie was off tonight.

Man, I'm off my game. I should've seen this entire situation coming from a mile away.

I clear my throat. "Would you be more comfortable if we moved to another table? Somewhere outside your station?"

Ava raises her eyebrows. "Brendan, what is your problem?"

"No. I'm a professional." Sadie smiles sweetly. "Would the two of you like to order a cocktail?"

Ava looks up at Sadie. "Not a cocktail, thank you. But I would like a glass of Chianti with my dinner."

Sadie smiles and makes a notation on her pad. Then she turns to me. "Cocktail for you, *sir*?"

God, yes.

"Bourbon. Double. Neat."

"Any particular brand?"

"I don't rightfully care. Jack Daniels is fine."

Of course, Jack Daniels isn't technically bourbon. It's sour mash whiskey, but I'm betting Sadie doesn't know this.

"Jack, double." She makes a note on her pad. "I'll get that out for you right away. Would the two of you like water?"

"Yes, please." Ava gives her a smile.

"I'll be right back with all of that." Sadie walks away.

As soon as she's out of sight, Ava looks back to me. "What was that all about?"

I pause a moment, but Ava's raised eyebrows indicate she's not going to let this go.

I sigh. "It's a long story, and I come off bad in it. Do you mind if we skip it?"

Ava shakes her head. "Oh, hell no. You're going to tell me why our waitress seems to have it out for you."

"Sadie asked me out last night. For tonight."

"Oh, and you turned her down. So she's a little put off by it."

"Not exactly…"

"Then exactly what *did* happen?"

"I originally said yes, but then I changed my mind." I look down at the silverware on the table. Pick up my fork. Fidget with it. "I'm not really interested in Sadie, and I thought going out with her would give her the wrong impression."

"Good. But she's still upset by it."

"Well . . . she's probably upset because I'm here with you."

"If she likes you, I suppose I understand that."

I could stop the story now. Ava has accepted it, and it's doubtful that Sadie will clue her in.

For some reason, I don't want to leave Ava Steel with a half-truth. I don't want our relationship starting out on that foot.

"Actually, what happened is that I broke the date and told her I had plans to go out with friends tonight."

"Uh-oh," she says. "And here you and I are."

"Right."

"Is that why you didn't want to come here?"

"Partially." I shrug. "Okay, definitely. I mean, I figured she wouldn't be working since she asked me out for tonight. I thought it was her night off. But either she planned to get someone to cover her shift, or she picked up a shift."

"I see." Ava pauses a moment, slides her napkin into her lap. "So basically none of this would've happened if you'd been honest with Sadie in the first place."

"When you're right, you're right." I glance at my menu.

"Brendan . . ."

I look up at Ava. "Yeah?"

"You shouldn't have lied to Sadie."

"Trust me. I know."

She smiles then, and my heart rate goes nuclear.

"I'm flattered, really," she says. "Flattered that you'd rather go out with me than with Sadie. She seems nice—or rather, she did at the bar. Tonight, not so much, but she has her reasons. Plus, she's gorgeous."

I return Ava's smile. "All that is true. But choosing you over her? That's a no-brainer."

She drops her gaze from mine. "So why did you accept Sadie's invitation?"

"I don't know. I guess I figured you wouldn't be interested."

She looks back at me. "Why wouldn't I be interested in going out with you?"

I draw in a breath. May as well go for broke. Be honest. "Because of our age difference, Ava. I'm eleven years older than you are, remember?"

She says nothing for a few seconds, and I can't read her. Does the age difference bother her?

Finally— "You know my aunt Marj, right?"

"Of course."

"Did you know that she's thirteen years younger than Uncle Bryce?"

I raise my eyebrows. *Did* I know that? That's funny. The people in the generation above us always seem to be the same age.

"Is she?"

"Yeah. She was twenty-five when they got married, and he was thirty-eight. Same age as my uncle Joe."

"So the age difference doesn't bother you."

"No. Not in *that* way, anyway. I never thought about you that way because you're so much older."

Damn. Brick to gut.

She smiles then. "But I figure what's going to happen will happen."

A grin splits my face. "That's a great attitude, Ava. A great attitude for sure."

CHAPTER SEVEN

Ava

It's not a lie, either. To be sure, our age difference *was* something that concerned me . . . until I drew that tarot card right before our date. The knight of cups.

It's telling me not to get swept away.

Which means I'll be tempted to get swept away, despite the age difference or anything else. I'll be cautious. Or try to be, anyway.

Brendan's so funny. He got a little red when he was talking to me about how he canceled the date with Sadie last night.

I'm not angry with him. Sure, he shouldn't have accepted the date if he wasn't interested, but at least he didn't keep it. He just should have told her the truth right away. But that would have hurt Sadie's feelings. He was trying to be nice.

Of course, Sadie ended up finding out anyway, so her feelings *were* hurt.

Honesty is *always* the best policy. That's what my family always says.

So I'll be honest with myself. There's a spark here. A spark with Brendan Murphy that I haven't felt in a long time, if ever.

And I'll keep the tarot card in mind. I'll try not to be swept away.

But my God, he's handsome. Handsome in such an unconventional way.

Sadie returns then. "Here are your waters and your bourbon, Brendan."

Brendan smiles. A wide smile that shows off his perfectly straight teeth and full lips. Dark-auburn stubble graces his jawline.

"Thank you," he says.

"Yes, thank you, Sadie," I agree.

"Are the two of you ready to order?"

"I think we'll both have the eggplant parmesan," Brendan says. "Sound good, Ava?"

Normally, I would be a little miffed that a guy ordered for me, but when Brendan does it? It just seems gentlemanly. I'm not upset at all. After all, I told him what I wanted.

"Yes," I say. "It's my favorite."

"Anything else? Some garlic bread?"

Brendan looks at me with his eyebrows raised.

"No, thank you."

"Right," Sadie says. "You're the baker, aren't you?"

"Guilty," I say.

"Lisa makes her bread from scratch, from one of her ancestors' recipes. I can see why you wouldn't want to try it."

I wrinkle my forehead. "I love Lisa's bread. I just don't want any garlic bread."

"Oh," Sadie says. "I'll bring you a breadbasket, then."

Once Sadie's gone, I regard Brendan. "You sure pissed her off."

"I know. This isn't turning out to be a very good date, is it?"

"I think you need to apologize to her," I say.

"Ava..."

I dig in my heels. "Just go. Take her outside. Tell her

you're sorry, that you shouldn't have accepted the date when you were interested in someone else."

"God." He sighs. "This is something I really have to do, isn't it?"

"That's really your own call," I say. "But it's what *I* would do."

Honesty is *always* the best policy.

How many times have my mother and father drummed that into my head? It was a mantra growing up in the Ryan and Ruby Steel household.

"I'll do what you ask," Brendan says. "But she's working."

"I know that. It doesn't have to be right now. You just need to apologize to her. If you notice that she goes on break, you can do it then. Otherwise you'll have to call her or go to see her outside of work."

Brendan nods. "You're right. I'll take care of it."

I smile with satisfaction. Brendan Murphy is a good man. I've always known that. The fact that he was trying to let Sadie down easily isn't really a problem. The problem is that he shouldn't have accepted the date in the first place.

He takes a sip of his bourbon and smiles.

A wave of warmth settles over me.

Oh boy…

I *do* need to heed the warnings of the card.

A busboy arrives with a basket of bread, and then he pours some olive oil on a small plate for dipping and sprinkles some salt and pepper on top of it.

I grab a slice of bread. I wasn't lying when I told Sadie that I love Lisa's bread. It's like a French baguette, only softer. I have no idea why Sadie thought I wouldn't eat anyone's bread but my own. She's probably just being pissy because I'm here with Brendan.

Brendan moves to take a piece as well when his phone rings.

He pulls it out of his pocket and takes a look.

"Do you mind if I take this? It's Hardy. Maybe something new on my case."

"No, that's fine."

He smiles at me and then puts the phone to his ear. "Hey, Hardy. What's going on?"

Pause.

"I'm kind of in the middle of something."

Pause.

"All right. Hold on for a moment." He turns to me. "Hardy's got some stuff at the station that he needs me to look at. He says it's important that I look right away."

"Oh." I try not to let my disappointment show too much. "I assume it's involving your case, so I understand. Go."

"Tell you what."

He places his hand over mine, and a spark surges through me.

"I'll head over to the station. But before I do, I'll tell Sadie that we need to take our food to go. Can you stay here until it's ready? Then just bring it to me at the station. And we can maybe eat in the park or something."

"It's not a bad night"—I look out the restaurant window—"but it's dark. It's the middle of November, Brendan."

He sighs. "Crap. You know I'm staying at my parents' house."

I pause, nibble at my lip ring. "It's fine. We can eat at my place."

Good thing I straightened up this morning.

"Are you sure?"

"Of course."

"You're the best, Ava." He puts the phone back to his ear. "I'll be right over, Hardy."

He shifts the phone in his pocket and pulls out his wallet. He takes out several bills and lays them on the table. "This should cover dinner plus tip."

I nod. "Okay."

He leaves the table, stops to talk to Lisa briefly near the door, and then heads out.

About ten minutes later, Sadie comes by with a to-go bag. "Here you go. Sorry you guys can't stay tonight."

"Brendan got a phone call. Something about his case."

"So he didn't break the date?"

"No, he didn't. I'm taking this food over to the station and meeting him there. We'll eat at my place later."

"So somehow he got to your place already."

"Sadie..."

She shakes her head. "None of this is your fault, Ava. Brendan and I..."

I rise. "None of my business. See you later, Sadie." I grab the bag and leave.

CHAPTER EIGHT

Brendan

Hardy Solomon went to high school with Dale and me, so he's my age. He's a good guy, and I know he tried to find information about who trashed my place.

"What's the good word?" I ask as I walk into the police station.

Hardy's out of uniform, wearing a felt cowboy hat and blue jeans, but his officers aren't.

"Hey, Brendan," Hardy says. "The guys called me in. Looks like we might have something."

"Yeah?" My pulse quickens. "Please tell me you can figure it out without roping off my place again. I've got a contractor coming in tomorrow to give me an estimate and to get started."

"Well..."

"Shit. Are you kidding me?"

"I know this is a pain in your ass, Brendan, but do you want to figure this out or not?"

Hardy doesn't know about the documents I found hidden underneath my floorboards. Only Dale and Donny Steel—and whoever they chose to tell—know. Our guess is that there were more documents somewhere in my place, and whoever trashed it was looking for them.

I can't share any of this with Hardy, though.

"We got an anonymous tip," one of the officers says.

"Oh?"

"Yeah. We're hoping you can make some sense of it. Or if you can't, maybe your dad can?"

"Okay. What exactly did you get?"

Hardy clears his throat. Then he hands me a sheet of paper.

"This is an email we got from some dummy account. When we tried to email back, it bounced."

I scan my eyes over the paper. Only two lines.

DARTH MORGEN IS ALIVE.
ASK THE MURPHYS.

"What the hell is this supposed to mean?" I demand.

"We were hoping maybe you could tell *us*."

"I don't know."

"Okay. Then we go to your dad."

"Have you called him?"

"Not yet. Your place was trashed, so we decided to talk to you first."

"What makes you think this has anything to do with my case?"

"It says to ask the Murphys."

"So? I don't have a clue what this means. Get my father in here if you think he might."

Hardy glances at his phone for a few seconds and then sticks it to his ear. "Hey, Sean? Hardy Solomon here. Can you come down to the station? Brendan's here, and we've got a new development." *Pause.* "Thanks."

A moment later, Ava enters the station, carrying the takeout from Lorenzo's.

My whole body reacts at the sight of her. I take the bag. "Hey."

"So what's going on?" she asks.

"We're not sure. My dad's on his way down. He might have some information to decipher what Hardy found."

"Maybe I can help," she says.

"I doubt it. Unless you can make any sense of this." I hand her the paper.

Her jaw drops.

"Ava?"

"This is bizarre. Really bizarre."

"What do you mean?"

"I got a text with this *exact* message."

I keep myself from jerking forward in surprise. "What?"

"Well, not exactly. Just the *Darth Morgen* part. Not the part about talking to Murphy."

"I don't understand. Why would you get the same message?"

"I don't know. It's not like you and I ... I mean, other than tonight..."

"I know. That's what I mean. Whoever this is... they couldn't possibly have known we were going to go out."

She wrinkles her forehead. "I think it's a puzzle."

"Well, clearly."

"No, I mean..." She looks down at the paper and then hands it to me. "Don't freak out on me, but when I got the same message, I drew a tarot card."

"Why would that freak me out?"

"Because not everyone believes in the tarot."

"No, but my mother does. Didn't she come to you for a reading once?"

"I can't tell you that. Anyone who comes to me gets full confidentiality."

I smile. Ava is a woman of integrity. I like that. "I don't know enough about it to say whether I believe in it or not. Tell me what you're thinking."

"The card I drew didn't make a lot of sense for me," she continues. "But when I thought about it more deeply, maybe it did. There's secret knowledge somewhere."

Does she know? About the documents Dale and Donny found at my place?

Maybe. She is a Steel, after all. But I got the impression that Dale and Donny weren't going to blab everything to their whole family until they could research further.

"What kind of secret knowledge?" I ask her.

"If I knew that, Brendan, it wouldn't be secret."

I can't help but chuckle. Ava Steel is something else.

"Did you call anybody when you got this text?"

"The only others I told were Brock and Dave, last night at the bar. Brock's going to trace the number for me, but I haven't heard anything from him yet."

"Should we call him?" I ask.

"Yeah, I can give him a call. Excuse me for a minute."

While Ava's on the phone, my father walks into the station. His own strawberry-blond hair, lighter than mine, is turning silver. "What's going on, Brendan?"

"Honestly, Dad, I have no idea. Hardy?"

Hardy prints another copy of the document and hands it to Dad. "You and your wife are the only other Murphys in town."

"Not exactly," he says. "There's Ciara and Carmen."

"That's right," Hardy says. "I guess if you and the missus don't know what this is about, we'll ask them."

Dad scans the document. "What the hell is this supposed to mean?"

"That's what we're supposed to ask you," Hardy says.

"I'm at a loss. And Brendan, you don't know?"

I shake my head. "I'm flummoxed, Dad."

"I wish I could help you, Hardy," Dad says. "But I don't have a clue what any of this means."

"We're going to have another look at Brendan's place," Hardy says.

"Sounds like I'm staying with you and Mom for a while longer," I say.

"Now that's ridiculous," Dad says. "Brendan needs his own place. There's not any reason to believe this has anything to do with whoever trashed his apartment."

"There's the Murphy reference," Hardy says.

"Yeah, whatever. You guys have already combed the place. What the hell else do you think you're going to find there?"

Hardy sighs. "All right. Go ahead with your contractor, Brendan."

"Thank God," I say under my breath.

Ava returns and taps me on the shoulder.

"Any news?" I ask.

"No. I mean, no good news anyway. Brock says the number was untraceable. Probably a burner phone."

"Can I tell him?" I gesture to my father.

Ava darts her gaze from me to my father and then to Hardy, who has turned away for a moment.

"Can we go outside?"

"Sure."

"Come on, Dad."

We walk outside the station and stand on the sidewalk.

"I'm sorry," Ava says. "I'm just not sure if my family would want Hardy involved."

"Involved in what?" my father asks.

"That Darth Morgen reference," Ava says. "I got the same text. Yesterday." She hands my father her phone.

He glances at it. "And this number?"

"Untraceable," Ava says. "Brock checked it out."

Dad sighs, runs his fingers through his graying hair. "There never seems to be any answers."

"Any answers about what?" Ava asks.

"There's a mystery. A mystery that's never been solved. And it involves your family, Ava."

"You talking about your uncle?" I ask Dad.

"I am."

"And you think this has something to do with it?"

"No. But I'm not going to rule out the possibility. When I came to Snow Creek looking for answers thirty-five years ago, all I came up with was dead end after dead end. No one knew what happened to my uncle. There was the party line of him getting drugged at Bradford Steel's wedding, but I couldn't find out who drugged him. Or why."

"I don't see how this could be related," Ava says.

"It probably isn't," Dad says. "But it's strange that the sheriff got an email telling him to ask *us* about the reference. And you got the same reference."

"It is bizarre," Ava agrees.

"Yes, but think about *how* it's bizarre." Dad runs a hand over his face. "You're part of the Steel family."

"Yeah . . ." Ava says.

"So for some reason, this phrase has to do with us and the Steel family," Dad says.

"Sure you're not stretching that a bit?" I ask.

"Brendan, maybe I am," Dad says. "But I've been trying to solve the mystery of my uncle for over three decades. And now, we have something here—other than my uncle's death—that seems to link us with the Steels."

"But it's some peculiar kind of *Star Wars* reference," I say.

Ava shakes her head. "I asked Dave about that. He knows all things *Star Wars*, and he's pretty sure this is *not* a *Star Wars* reference."

"What is it, then? What does Darth mean?"

"It's not a word in the English dictionary," Ava says. "It was the first thing I checked."

"And Morgen? With an *e*?"

"I found a couple of things. Spelled with an *e*, it means morning in German, but Darth isn't a German word. It can refer to Morgan with an *a*, the sorceress in King Arthur lore, and it's a unit of land measure equal to about two acres or about two thirds of an acre, depending on the country it's used in."

"Land measure..." Dad scratches his head.

"Well, you Steels have a lot of land," I say.

"Yeah. True." Ava rubs at her jawline. "So we have two possibilities for Morgen."

"One," I say. "I doubt this has anything to do with King Arthur."

Ava smiles. "Don't be so sure. Legends have a lot they can teach us."

Dad shakes his head. "No offense, Ava, but I'm betting that if this means anything, it has something to do with the land."

"What about Darth?" I ask.

Dad shakes his head again. "I don't know, son. I just don't know."

The takeout bag weighs heavy in my hand. "Our dinners are getting cold, so we'd better go eat."

"All right. I'll go back and tell Hardy you're leaving. I'm not sure what any of this means, but it is odd that the sheriff got the message. If he was told to ask the Murphys, why didn't the message just come to one of us?"

I sigh. "I don't know, Dad. But I have a feeling we've got another mystery to solve."

CHAPTER NINE

Ava

We arrive back at my place, and I pull out some plates and silverware, setting my small table quickly.

Brendan eyes my red-and-white-checkered tablecloth and smiles. "We could be sitting in Lorenzo's."

"I found it at a yard sale and fell in love with it," I tell him. "As you can probably tell, I like eclectic things."

Brendan looks around my apartment, and I follow his gaze as he rests it on the burnt-sienna steamer trunk I use for a coffee table, my lamp made of conch shells, the carved wooden box where I keep my tarot deck, and the black-and-white photo of Lucille Ball and Desi Arnaz hanging above my television.

"Frankly? I like your taste. I like that you're just so... uniquely *you*, Ava."

My cheeks warm. "I think that's one of the nicest things anyone's ever said to me."

He trails his finger over my cheek.

I burn at his touch.

And honestly? It's the first time I've ever burned when a man touched me.

As if in slow motion, he brings his lips closer. Brushes them lightly over mine.

And there it is.

The spark.

That damned spark.

Take a chance, Ava. Take a chance on this man.

No. Can't get swept away. Listen to the cards.

"The food…" I say. "It'll get cold."

"You got a microwave?"

"Of course."

"Then who cares?"

His mouth comes down on mine again, harder this time.

The soft point of his tongue probes my mouth open…

And I'm lost.

Lost in this kiss. Lost in his soft tongue swirling around mine.

Lost in…

No more thoughts.

Only feelings.

Only Brendan. Only me. Only this kiss.

He wraps his arms around me, and it's a good thing, too, because I'm not very steady on my feet.

He pulls me into his body, and I melt against him, and then—

I pull back, breaking the kiss with a loud smack.

I felt it.

It.

His hardness. His erection.

"Ava?"

I bite my mouth. "I'm … sorry."

"No. *I'm* sorry. I wasn't thinking. I just…" He shakes his head. "I'm very attracted to you, Ava. I guess that's pretty obvious."

HELEN HARDT

I can't help myself. I drop my gaze to his crotch.

Brendan is tall. As tall as my father, at least. With a lean build and a butt that looks delicious in the jeans he's wearing.

"Maybe we should have our dinner," he says.

I nod. "That's a great idea."

But I don't move.

I've already set the table, so Brendan takes charge. He pulls the containers out of the takeout bag and plates our dinner.

"You have any olive oil?" he asks, holding up the bread.

"Yeah. In the cupboard above the sink."

Brendan grabs the olive oil and pours some onto a plate from my shelf. Then he finds the salt and pepper above the stove and brings them to the table.

"I should've brought a bottle of wine from the bar."

"Yeah, I don't have any wine. I'm sorry. I'm a poor winemaker's daughter, to my father's chagrin."

"It's okay. We'll just have water." He smiles, and then he goes to the sink, pours two glasses of water, adds ice from the freezer, and brings them back, setting one in front of me.

I grab it and drain half of it in one gulp.

My God, I'm on fire.

It must be so obvious too. I'm not a virgin, but I may as well be for the way I'm feeling right now.

Brendan takes up the room. It's like he owns the place, even though it's mine, not his.

I swear to God, if he told me to get on the bed so he could tie me up, I would let him.

Remember.

The knight of cups.

I picture the card in my mind. The handsome knight on

73

the white horse. The gold chalice he carries. He holds it up, as if in warning.

I can't get swept away.

But my God ... already ...

How did I never notice Brendan Murphy? I mean, I noticed him, of course. I just never considered ...

He's so much older ...

"Is it warm enough?" Brendan asks. "I can heat your plate in the microwave."

I shake my head. "Honestly? Most stuff from Lorenzo's is better the second time. I order takeout from Lisa at least once a week, and it's always too much for me to eat at one sitting, so I put it in the fridge and eat it later. I never reheat it."

"A woman after my own heart." He smiles. "Is it too much to hope that you like cold pizza too?"

"It's only the best breakfast ever." I return his smile.

My nerves are still a little on edge, but I'm getting more relaxed. It's easy to relax around Brendan. But I'm not exactly sure why.

I'm wildly attracted to him, and that kiss ...

My God, I was already getting swept away.

The knight of cups.

The knight of cups.

The knight of cups.

Easy, Ava. Don't let your emotions go wild.

Although it's not emotion at this point. I like Brendan. I always have. But right now? This is purely physical. I'm getting swept away by his attractiveness, by his amazing kissing abilities.

By his ...

God, that bulge in his jeans.

He's sitting down, so I can't see it. It's probably gone down anyway.

But my God, I remember it.

The hardness pressing against my belly.

Just a little lower . . .

It could've flicked my clit through my jeans, and then . . .

Knight of cups.

Knight of cups.

Knight of cups.

Breathe in. Breathe out. Breathe in. Breathe out.

"Ava?"

I glance at Brendan. "Yes?"

"You haven't touched your dinner."

I draw in a breath. "Right. How is it?"

"Delicious." He smiles.

"Good."

I take a forkful of the eggplant, bring it to my mouth. It smells robust and cheesy, but I know I won't taste it. All I can taste is Brendan Murphy's mouth on mine.

I take another bite, chew, swallow.

And then another.

My heart is stampeding, and I'm still warm all over, and I have to hold back a shudder.

Knight of cups.

Knight of cups.

Knight of cups.

This is going to be a long evening.

CHAPTER TEN

Brendan

I went too quickly.

I knew it when I kissed her, but I couldn't help myself. Her lips, that lip ring.

I wanted so badly to tug on it with my teeth, but I didn't. That would've been too much.

I guess it was all too much for Ava. So much that she stopped the kiss.

Did she not enjoy it as much as I did?

My fault. I should've waited. This is our first date, and we've never even flirted before tonight.

Ava's not the flirting type.

I finish my eggplant, and she's left about half of hers on her plate.

I'm not sure what to do, because this is her place, not mine. Should I let her take the lead? Should I ask if I can clear the plates?

And then what?

I'd love to take her to bed, but she has to make the first move.

Before I can decide, she rises and takes my plate to the sink. Then she wraps her own unfinished portion in foil and sets it in the fridge.

"You want something for dessert? I have some ice cream."

That's not *exactly* what I want for dessert, but it will do for now. Although the idea of licking it off her hot body . . .

Down, boy.

"Sure. What kind do you have?"

"French vanilla. It's my favorite."

"You're not a chocolate girl?"

"I know, crazy, right? I've always loved plain old vanilla."

"I like vanilla too. But I also like chocolate. And strawberry."

She chuckles softly. "Sounds to me like you just like ice cream."

"I do. When I was little, my mom used to make homemade ice cream. It was the best on a hot summer afternoon. She doesn't do it so much anymore."

"Oh yeah? Aunt Marjorie makes the best brown sugar vanilla homemade ice cream. It's even better when she flavors it with bourbon."

"That sounds great. How come I've never had any of that at one of the Steel parties?"

"It has to be made in small batches. Not really party material."

I nod. "I guess that makes sense."

Ava takes out the carton of ice cream and scoops two portions into a couple of bowls. She puts a spoon in each and brings them back to the table, setting one in front of me.

"You need more water?" she asks.

"Yes, please."

She fills both of our waters, adding ice, and then sits back down next to me.

She takes a spoonful of ice cream, brings it to her lips, and runs her tongue slowly over it as she puts it in her mouth.

And I'm about to burst out of my jeans.

I take a bite of ice cream myself. Maybe it'll help me cool off.

Not likely.

"Brendan?"

"Yeah?"

"Could you be honest with me about something?"

There's a loaded question. Will she ask how I feel about her? What I'm looking for? How much experience I've had?

I brace myself for anything.

"I'll try," I say.

She takes another spoonful of ice cream and swallows. "Something's going on with my family. I know it has something to do with what happened to your place."

"Oh?"

I'm not sure how much I'm supposed to tell her. Dale and Donny asked me to keep everything to myself while they worked it out.

But Ava...

She's asking me straight out, and the stuff was found at my place, so why can't I talk about it?

"Have you talked to your cousins? Dale and Donny?"

"No, not really. They're so much older than I am and—" She stops abruptly, her spoon halfway to her mouth.

"Right. They're my age."

"I didn't mean it that way. It's just that... I'm not as close to them as I am to Brock and Dave."

"I believe Brock has an idea of what's going on. Dale and Donny brought him in."

Why is this such a big secret? Especially from Ava? Her

father was specifically mentioned in the documents—in a quitclaim deed transferring all the property specifically to Ryan Steel, signed by his father, Bradford Steel.

Of course, it was never recorded.

"I guess I could ask Brock," Ava says.

"No, Ava. You can ask me. I honestly don't know what all of it means, but I do know a few things. Apparently your family has a lien on my property. The bar."

"We do?" Her eyes open wide.

"Yeah. I didn't know, because technically it's not my property. It's still in my father's name, even though I run it now. And I live there. It will be mine eventually."

"I don't know a whole lot about liens. I guess we could call Donny or Aunt Jade."

"It's no big deal," I say. "It hasn't hampered our ownership or stopped us from getting anything done on the property. But I would like it removed."

"I understand. How did you find out?"

"I found some documents under the floorboards of my place."

"You did?" Another spoonful of ice cream stops midway to her mouth.

"Yeah, and I'm pretty sure that's why my place was trashed. Someone was looking for more documents."

"And did they find anything?"

I look down at my ice cream. A pool of vanilla has melted around it. "Honestly, I don't have a clue. They trashed the place so badly that if there was anything to find, they probably either found it and took it, or it got ruined."

"What else did you find?" Ava asks.

"A birth certificate."

"For whom?"

"Someone named William Elijah Steel."

She wrinkles her forehead in that adorable way. "I've never heard of him."

"Neither had your cousins," I say. "Another weird thing is that there was a father listed on the birth certificate, but no mother."

"How can that even be?" she asks. "Everyone knows who the mother is. Someone had to watch the baby come out of her."

"Exactly. So the birth certificate has probably been doctored."

"And this was all found underneath your floorboards?"

"Yep."

"Why would they be at your place?"

"You got me. All I know is that my father bought the place from some dude named Jeremy Madigan."

"Madigan? I don't know the name."

"Your cousins seemed to. Maybe it's best if you talk to them."

She fidgets with her lip ring. With her tongue. And damn, she looks sexy.

"I wonder if it has something to do with that message I received. Because you and your dad received the same message."

"True. It is definitely a puzzle."

"You know? I love a puzzle." She smiles.

"Ava, so do I."

CHAPTER ELEVEN

Ava

I'm intrigued by what Brendan told me, but in all honesty, I'm only listening with one ear.

The rest of me is imagining his full lips on mine again.

I like this guy. If I go jumping into the sack with him—which is a totally un-Ava-like thing to do—where will that leave us?

Is he a love 'em and leave 'em kind of guy?

I don't think so. I don't know Brendan well, but I don't think he's had a serious relationship in a while.

But then again . . . I haven't paid that much attention to him.

My bad.

Brendan Murphy is definitely worth paying attention to.

I just never let myself think of him that way. He's Dale's age.

I can't help but chuckle. Dale's wife, Ashley? She's only a year older than I am.

What is age anyway, except a number? After all, I gave Brendan the example of Aunt Marj and Uncle Bryce. Thirteen years apart.

"You got quiet," Brendan says.

"Just thinking. Wondering how it can all be related."

"I suppose it's possible that it's not."

"I suppose," I agree. "But why would you and I have received the same message? Whatever *Darth Morgen* refers to, it seems you and I are both involved."

"We'll figure it out, Ava."

"Yeah, we will."

I have excellent intuition, and right now it's telling me that the message I received has something to do with all the papers Brendan found in his place. And maybe with other stuff too. Brock has been preoccupied lately. Something's going on with him, and I know it's not personal, because he's very happy with Rory. Which means it has something to do with the Steel family.

I finish my ice cream, and then I take both of our empty bowls from the table and put them in the sink.

I turn around and—

"Oh!"

Brendan is standing right behind me, and when I turn, only inches separate us.

My body heats, and my nipples tighten.

Sizzles shoot through me.

"Ava..." His voice is low and raspy.

"Yes?"

"I like you a lot, and I don't want to fuck this up."

I open my mouth to speak, but nothing comes out. I'm not sure what to say to that.

"And I'd really like to see you again."

I nod this time, and I open my mouth, hoping my voice won't crack. "I'd like that. To see you again, I mean."

"Maybe we can figure out this puzzle between the two of us."

I keep myself from frowning. Is that what he means? We're to see each other again just to figure out what's going on? Or is he talking about the puzzle of our budding connection in light of our age difference? Or both?

"Oh. Sure."

"So . . . tomorrow night?"

"Sure. We can get together . . . to work on the puzzle."

He smiles and then trails a finger over one of my cheeks. "That's fine, but it's not what I meant."

"What did you mean?" I'm trying to sound coy but failing miserably.

I've never been the flirtatious type. No wonder. I suck at it.

"I mean I thought we could go out again."

"Okay." I cock my head and smile, attempting to be coy again. Then, realizing I must look like a moron, I realign my neck and meet his gaze. "Tomorrow's Saturday, and the bakery's open until seven on Saturdays."

"So it's a date, then."

"Okay. And we're closed on Sundays."

Why did I just say that? He's going to think I'm inviting him into my bed tomorrow night.

Which is not a bad idea.

My God, that card was right on target.

The knight of freaking cups.

I *so* want to get swept away in this man.

"We could go to Grand Junction," Brendan says. "Try a new place there."

"Why don't I make you dinner here?" I say.

Did those words just come out of my mouth?

I'm a good cook, and I love to do it. But my God . . .

He smiles, pushing my hair behind my ear. "I'd like that."

"What kind of food do you like?"

"Any kind."

"Okay. Liver and brains it is." I can't help an impish grin.

"Honestly, I'll eat anything you make for me. It's the company I'm after, not the food."

My cheeks warm. I must be red as a candy apple.

"My God." He pushes my hair behind my ear on the other side. "You're so beautiful."

My lips part.

Beautiful?

I'm not beautiful. Gina is beautiful. She looks just like my dad with dark hair and light-brown eyes. My mother is beautiful. Diana and Brianna are beautiful.

I'm just Ava.

And I'm okay with that.

"I'm not," I can't help saying.

"But you are. Those high cheekbones, full pink lips. And that lip ring is sexy as fuck."

I shudder. I don't even try to suppress it.

"And your hair ... It works for you. Makes you look so unique, striking. Mysterious, even."

This time my jaw drops.

"You look surprised."

"I know I'm not horrible-looking," I say. "But as far as the Steel women go, I'm pretty average."

"Only in your own eyes, baby." This time he trails his finger over first my lower lip, bypassing the lip ring, and then my upper.

My nipples are so hard.

So freaking hard.

How long has it been since I've had a man's lips on them? Years. Not since college.

I've had a few dates now and then, but none of them ever went anywhere. I don't fall into bed with just anyone, especially not after my first time was so lackluster.

"You..." I say.

"What?"

"You're beautiful too."

He smiles. "First time anyone's ever called me that."

"Oh, but you are." My fingers itch to touch his face, scrape against his stubble, but I keep my arms pinned to my sides. "So handsome, in a nontraditional way. And one of the only guys I know—other than Jesse Pike and my cousin Dale—who can pull off such long hair."

"Thank you for the compliment, Ava."

"It's not a compliment. It's the truth."

"Then you need to accept that what I've told you is the truth as well," he says. "You are beautiful. In my eyes? You're the most beautiful of all the Steel women."

I can't help myself then.

I stand on my tiptoes, wrap my arms around his neck, and pull him down to me, our lips meeting.

CHAPTER TWELVE

Brendan

I try to keep the kiss gentle. I truly do try.

But within seconds, my tongue is invading Ava's mouth.

She kisses me back, entwining our tongues together, and she tastes like vanilla ice cream.

I pull back slightly, run the tip of my tongue over the lip ring, and give it a tiny tug.

A soft sigh escapes her throat.

Good. She likes that. I give it a slightly harsher tug.

I stop myself from jerking when I feel a pull on my ponytail.

I'm totally turned on.

I want her to pull my hair. I want everything from her.

I deepen the kiss then, drawing her even closer to me.

My dick is hard as a rock, and I press it into her, making her gasp softly.

My God, I could kiss her forever.

Her lips feel so perfect beneath mine, and I—

She pushes my shoulders back, breaking the kiss.

I widen my eyes. "Ava?"

"Sorry. I just..."

"What is it?"

"I... I can't get carried away, Brendan. The cards..."

"What? What are you talking about?" If those damned tarot cards told her not to get involved with me, I may die an untimely death right here in her kitchen.

"I know you'll think it's stupid, but the tarot cards... They warned me. They warned me that I could get swept away in you. My God, they were right."

I resist the urge to grin.

I love the fact that she wants me as much as I want her.

"Is getting swept away such a bad thing?"

"No. But I..." She looks down but doesn't pull out of my embrace. "You're so much older, and I'm sure you're more experienced, and I just... I don't want to disappoint you."

I close the distance between us, stroke her cheek once more. "That's not possible."

"But I..."

"Ava, baby. I respect your feelings. I will never ask you to do anything you're uncomfortable with."

"I know that. What's uncomfortable is that I'm *not* uncomfortable with anything as far as you're concerned. I need to watch myself. I can't get sucked in."

Again, I resist a large grin. She's as attracted to me as I am to her. That's a good thing from where I'm standing.

"Why worry about getting sucked in? We like each other. We're attracted to each other. I promise you I won't do anything you don't want me to."

"What do you want to do?" she asks.

"Right now I'd really like to kiss you again."

She smiles. "I'd like that too."

"All right, then." I lower my mouth. I brush my lips lightly over hers, and then I lick first her top and then her bottom lip, giving special attention to the lip ring.

When she parts her lips, I dive between them with my tongue.

She wraps her arms around me tightly, and without meaning to, I lift her.

Now she wraps her legs around me, and my dick is so hard. I know it's poking at her. Right between her legs.

She moves against me, and damn... I want her.

She wants me too. I can tell. But I'm determined to go slowly so she doesn't feel like she's getting swept away. I'm not sure why that's important to her, but I respect her wishes.

I certainly mean her no harm.

Was she hurt in the past? If she was, I don't know about it. In this small town, everybody knows everything about each other.

I move forward slightly so that she's sitting on the counter. Her legs remain clasped around me, and I want so much to grind into her—grind my hardness against her.

But she has to make a move first.

Now that she doesn't need to have her arms clasped around me to hold herself up, she loosens a bit, and then she cups one of my cheeks, caressing the stubble.

She trails her other hand down the buttons on my shirt. She unbuttons one, and then another, and then—oh my God...

Her hand is on my chest.

I'm going to have a burn in the shape of her small hand for all to see.

God, her touch.

I'm so hard. So fucking hard.

Her flowing skirt is wide enough that she's able to wrap her legs around me. And now, the fabric is wrapped around her hips.

Already I can smell her. The ripeness of her pussy.

What I wouldn't give to drop to my knees and slide my tongue between her legs.

And why not?

She's touching my chest. Shouldn't I get to touch her?

I break the kiss. "Ava," I growl in her ear.

"Your chest," she whispers. "So hard. All muscle."

"I want you," I say.

"Oh, yes," she says in a whisper. "Please."

"Tell me," I say gruffly. "Tell me what you want."

"I want..."

"Say it."

"I want to get swept away... I want no regrets..."

"No regrets?"

"I mean... it doesn't have to mean anything, Brendan."

She just squeezed the air out of my lungs with those words. But I'm feeling bold. "What if we *want* it to mean something?"

"I just want..."

"Tell me."

"I want to feel. I just want to *feel*."

This time I do drop to my knees. I remove her boots and socks, and then I slide the skirt all the way up her legs, relishing the smooth softness of her supple limbs. When I get to her panties, I look up, meet her gaze.

"Okay?" I ask.

She bites on her lip and nods.

God. I'm fucking throbbing.

I grasp the cotton of her panties, slide it over her hips and down her smooth legs.

Simple white cotton.

Simple white cotton bikinis.

But I may as well be holding satin and lace for as turned on as I am.

I spread her legs. Kneel between them. Her plump pussy glistens. I close my eyes and inhale—take in her succulent scent.

"When's the last time you had your pussy licked, Ava?" I open my eyes and meet her gaze.

"I don't know…"

"You don't?"

"It's been a long time, Brendan. A long, long time." She arches her back, closes her eyes.

My God, she looks amazing.

I move toward her, spread her legs wider, and I press a kiss to her beautiful pussy lips.

She gasps.

I move away for a moment. Is she going to tell me to stop?

When she doesn't, I delve back into the delectable feast.

I swipe my tongue from the bottom all the way up her slit. Then I nibble at her clit, already swollen and engorged.

She tastes of springtime. Even in the middle of November, Ava tastes like springtime. Like the first burst of nectar from the trees and flowers.

I've never tasted anything so delicious.

I try to go slowly—truly I do—but before long, I'm devouring her, shoving my tongue inside her cunt, pushing her thighs over my shoulders so I can get closer.

The soft moans and her delicate voice fuel me. Make me want her even more.

"My God," I rasp against her flesh. "I could eat you all night."

"Please," she says.

"Please what, baby?"

"Please...just...make...me...*feel*..."

Come. She wants to come.

"I can make that happen."

I slide my tongue around her swollen lips and then skim it over her clit while I thrust two fingers inside her heat.

I find her G-spot quickly, massage it as I lick her clit.

"Oh, yes," she sighs. "Like that. Please..."

I tease her a bit, massaging the G-spot and then sliding my fingers in and out of her slowly as I continue to gently lick her. All I need to do is suck her clit between my lips and she'll burst.

But I don't want this to be over that quickly. I haven't yet had enough of her taste.

I move from her clit for a moment, kiss and suck on the flesh of her inner thighs. That smooth skin.

Then I go back to her clit.

In and out of her pussy my fingers slide, and then—

I poke her G-spot and suck on her clit.

And she erupts.

Sweet Ava Steel erupts into flames underneath my tongue.

"Yes! Yes, just like that! My God, Brendan, I'm flying!"

Good, good, good...

I suck on her clit some more, prod at her G-spot, until the contractions of her pussy begin to subside.

I release her, slide my fingers in and out of her wet heat slowly, slowly, slowly...

Until I remove them.

I rise, pull her close to me, kiss her lips, and let her taste her own flavor on my tongue.

She groans into my mouth.

I groan into her mouth.
We kiss hard and passionately.
Until she pulls away and gasps.
"Brendan, please. Take me to my bed."

CHAPTER THIRTEEN

Ava

The knight of cups.

Screw the knight of cups and his pretentious chalice!

Brendan Murphy just gave me the best orgasm I've ever had.

And you know what?

I'm ready to take a chance.

To get swept away.

Swept away to another dimension.

I bet his dick is huge—huge with a gorgeous ginger bush.

I'm the kind of woman who likes her men to look like men. When I touched his chest, I felt a smattering of hair. He's not hairy by any means, but he has just enough. Just enough to get my pulse moving.

The knight of cups.

Darth Morgen.

All of it is erased from my mind.

All I know is now.

This moment.

This man.

He's so tall, and his shoulders are so broad. His face is sculpted and masculine with that auburn stubble, and . . .

It all takes my breath away.

My pussy is still pounding from that orgasm. Does he feel it pulsing against him?

He's hard. So hard. And judging from the size of his bulge, I'm not going to be disappointed.

"Which door?"

"First one," I pant.

Did I make my bed this morning? Who cares? We're going to mess it up anyway.

And God, do I want to mess it up.

He sets me on the edge of the bed, and I stand, pull my dress over my head, and toss it. My shoes, socks, and panties are already gone, and I'm not wearing a bra tonight. My boobs are small enough, perky enough, and I can get away without one.

So I stand.

Offering myself to Brendan Murphy on a silver freaking platter.

My nipples are hard, my breasts flushed.

My pussy is still throbbing, and though I usually shave my bush into a nice triangle, I haven't in over a week, so it's not particularly enticing.

But I don't care.

And from the smoldering look in Brendan's heavy-lidded eyes? Neither does he.

"You're so beautiful, Ava." He moves toward me.

"I need to see you," I say. "I need to see you naked, Brendan. My God . . ." I lick my lips. "I can't *wait* to see you."

He doesn't grin. Instead he narrows his eyes slightly, and the bright blue of his irises begins to burn.

"I tried not to get swept away," I say. "But I need to take this chance. I need to . . ."

Words fail me then.

Words fail me because Brendan Murphy is unbuttoning his shirt, and with each button, I see more of his ivory flesh.

When his shirt is in a puddle on the floor, I can't help myself. I gawk at him. I gawk at his chest.

We've both lived in Snow Creek our whole lives, yet I've never seen him without a shirt. Surely he must go swimming. Why haven't I seen him at the pool or at the gym?

Because he definitely works out. His muscles are the size of trucks.

His chest hair is just as I imagined. Auburn scattered over rock-hard pecs in the perfect amount.

Part of me wants to reach out and touch him all over.

But part of me resists. Part of me doesn't want to destroy the feast for my eyes just yet.

Because my God, I could look at him all night ... and he hasn't yet taken his jeans off.

He kicks off his shoes. Then he unsnaps his jeans.

I suck in a breath.

I'm going to see it.

In just seconds, he's going to free his cock, and I'm going to see it.

I bite my lip, twist my lip ring with my tongue.

The lip ring.

Men love it.

Apparently it feels really good when I suck their dicks.

Except I've never been a big fan of sucking dick. It doesn't do much for me, and I find it very uncomfortable.

But damn ...

I want to suck Brendan's dick.

I haven't even seen it, and already I know it's massive,

given the size of his bulge. It won't be an easy blow job, but my God, I want it in my mouth.

He peels his jeans and boxer briefs off his muscular legs, and then he stands before me. Naked. Naked and glorious.

My gaze drops to his cock.

In all its freaking splendor.

Nine inches of glory, and a diameter of . . .

I don't know. It's not a beer can, but it's close.

No way will I be able to fit my mouth around it.

Except I will be able to because I want to so badly.

What would he think if I dropped to my knees right now? Took that giant cock of his between my lips?

My God.

Who the hell am I?

I force my gaze upward, and I'm rewarded with the sight of his perfect shoulders, chest, abs.

I can't help myself.

I walk toward him, reach out, touch his pecs.

I expect him to do the same, to cup my breasts.

But he doesn't.

He stands there. Lets me touch him.

I get it. He wants to go slow with me. He's already said as much.

Fuck the knight of cups. I'm done with slow.

I take one of his hands and place it on one of my breasts.

This time *he* sucks in a breath.

I swear to God, my nipples harden even tighter.

"My God, Ava."

I gasp in another breath, and then I grasp his dick.

"Oh my God . . ." he growls.

"I can't believe how magnificent you are," I say on a sigh. "You're absolutely perfect."

"So are you." He squeezes my breast and thumbs my hard nipple. "I always knew you'd be beautiful."

"I'm nothing compared to you."

I'm kind of making myself sick with the way I'm fawning over him, but my words ring true.

Brendan Murphy is a magnificent specimen of a man.

"Tell me what you want," he says.

"I want you. You made me feel so ..."

"You make me feel the same."

I widen my eyes. "No. I'm talking about when I came."

"You don't think I felt that?"

"How could you?"

"Ava, baby, giving you an orgasm gave me a lot of pleasure."

"Oh my God ..."

I nearly lose my footing, but he steadies me. He lifts me in his muscled arms and sets me gently on the bed.

"I can't wait to get inside you," he says. "You deserve a night of slow lovemaking, but if I don't get inside you soon, I think I'm going to go crazy."

"Please," is all I say.

"I don't have a condom. I didn't plan ... I didn't expect ..." He wipes at his forehead. "Christ, I fucked up."

"I'm on the pill. So just tell me I have nothing to fear from you and let's go."

"Nothing," he growls. "I swear to you I'm clean."

Then he thrusts his cock inside my pussy.

The burn. The delectable burn.

I cry out at the invasion because he's so damned massive, but my God, the *burn*.

"You okay?" he rasps.

"God, yes. I'm more than okay."

"Thank God, because I have to fuck you." He pulls out and thrusts back in.

The burn lessens slightly, but it's still there, like a torch boiling through me.

I love it.

Such a good burn.

I'm not all that experienced, but I'm experienced enough to know that I like a larger cock.

And Brendan Murphy?

He's perfection.

He slides out of me once more and then thrusts back in. Already I'm nearing the precipice once more. His gorgeous auburn pubes hit my clit with each thrust. Just a few more, and—

"Oh my God!"

The climax rips through me, surprising me. I knew I was going to come again, but this one caught me completely off guard.

"That's it, baby." He plunges harder, faster. "You come again. Come for me."

Harder and faster still.

The burn... Oh, the burn...

My orgasm continues, and just when I think I'm ready to stop, he thrusts into me, I feel him release, and he hits my clit at another angle, starting a third orgasm.

We come together.

Together we soar.

And for just a moment, I am *completely* swept away.

CHAPTER FOURTEEN

Brendan

She's so tight.

So perfectly tight and sweet.

And coming inside her?

As amazing as I always knew it would be.

What is it about this woman?

What is it about Ava Steel?

I don't know, but she's my perfect match.

Already I feel like she is the last person I'll ever come inside. I'm gone. Completely pussy-whipped, except it's much more. I don't want to scare her, so I can't tell her this.

But I know. Deep within my soul, I'm positive.

She pulls me close to her, wraps her legs over my hips.

"My God . . ." she says.

"Amazing," I reply.

"That's not even enough to describe it."

"We're not even close to done," I tell her. "There's so much more I want to do with you."

"Oh?" She closes her eyes and smiles. "Tell me. Tell me what you want to do to me."

"I want to kiss every inch of your body. Every fucking inch. I want to slide my dick between your sweet lips. I want to eat you again. I want to turn you over and slide my tongue between the cheeks of your ass."

She gasps.

Have I gone too far?

Hell, she asked.

"But Ava . . . I won't do anything you don't want me to do."

"I want it, Brendan. I want it all."

"We'll get there. I promise."

"Mmmm . . ." She closes her eyes. "I can't wait."

Then a soft snore.

She's fallen asleep with me still embedded inside her.

Oh, sweet Ava. I slowly detach myself from her and cover her flushed body with her blankets.

Should I stay?

I can't just leave. Not without waking her up, and I don't want to do that. I suppose I could leave a note, but that's so impersonal.

I don't want anything about this encounter to be impersonal, so I won't wake her up. Something tells me she needs this sleep. This pure relaxation.

I'll stay here. Sleep beside her. If she wakes up in the middle of the night and asks me to leave? Then I'll leave, of course. But I won't leave without her knowing I'm leaving.

This woman means something to me. Something very special, and I don't want to screw it up.

I give her a chaste kiss on the cheek and then make myself comfortable on the other side of her queen-size bed.

I've got a king-size bed at my place. I'm a big guy, and I like to move around.

Correction. I *had* a king-size bed at my place. Before it was trashed.

Being so close to Ava Steel on a queen-size bed isn't a horrible thing. It's kind of nice. I'm not a cuddler, but part of me wants to pull her to me, snuggle into her.

But I don't know if she would want that, so I turn away from her, slide my arm underneath the pillow, and settle in.

Usually I can fall asleep easily after an orgasm, but for some reason, sleep eludes me tonight. I'm a bit nervous, which is unlike me. I haven't dated a lot in the last year, but I certainly know my way around a woman.

I've been crushing on Ava Steel for months now.

I hope I didn't ruin the possibility of something more with her. I know the rules. Never sleep with a woman on the first date—unless you don't want a second date.

I ruminate. Relive the beauty of our joining and hope like hell I haven't screwed up something amazing.

Until I finally drift to sleep an hour later.

★ ★ ★

I wake up to the sun streaming through the window in Ava's bedroom.

She let me spend the night.

Maybe she's not awake yet. I sit up in bed and rub the sleep out of my eyes.

To my astonishment, the bed is empty.

"Ava?"

I get up and find my underwear on the floor. I pull them on and pad out of the bedroom to Ava's kitchen.

Nothing.

No pot of coffee made. Maybe Ava doesn't drink coffee. She doesn't sell it at her bakery.

"Oh, of course," I say out loud.

Ava's at the bakery. It's Saturday morning, and she's

working. She has to get up early to get the day's bake started.

What time is it anyway? I head back into the bedroom, find my jeans, and grab my phone out of my pocket. Damn. It's nearly ten a.m.

I don't normally sleep this late, even though I don't begin my own work until the afternoons. I'm usually up by eight o'clock and out on a run.

I stretch, enjoying the feel of my capillaries bursting.

What should I do?

I need a shower for sure. I don't really want to go to my parents' house and explain where I've been. Not that I owe them any explanation, but Mom will ask, and I'll feel obligated to say something.

Nope. Best thing to do is to shower here at Ava's place and then head over to the bar to get things ready for the day. Exercising will have to wait until later. I can always hit the gym for a quick cardio workout. I prefer running in the open air, but the Snow Creek gym is a good alternative, and I use it when the weather is bad.

Today though? On this mid-November morning? The weather is gorgeous. The Indian summer has been beautiful this year. Yes, the snow will come. Possibly even before Thanksgiving. But today is gorgeous. Colorado blue sky and the Rockies to the east. Picture perfect.

I gather my clothes and head into Ava's small bathroom. Just a simple sink, toilet, and shower, with some requisite Ava-eclectic decor, including a porcelain toothbrush holder in the shape of a golden retriever. I smile. So very Ava.

I start the shower. How did I not hear Ava this morning? I'm not usually that heavy of a sleeper, but after that orgasm inside her?

I'm not sure a freaking army could've awakened me.

I don't have my toothbrush, and I don't want to use hers, so I simply slide toothpaste over my teeth with my finger and then rinse well. Good enough until I can actually brush my teeth.

I step into the shower and squeeze some of her shampoo—it's an unmarked bottle—into my palm. And I inhale.

Smells just like Ava.

I can't quite place the fragrance. Woodsy with a touch of spice and a dash of sweetness. Kind of like citrus and peppermint.

I rub it into my scalp—definitely peppermint with the tingle—and through the ends of my hair. When I'm thoroughly cleansed, I turn off the shower, and—

I don't want to use her towel, but I wasn't thinking far enough ahead to get one out for my own use. Plus I don't want to be too nosy around her place. So I dry off with her towel. It's still slightly damp from when she took her own shower this morning. I borrow her brush, bring it through my hair, and then clean the red hairs I left in it. My hair falls in wet strands around my shoulders.

I walk back into the bedroom, dress in the clothes I wore last night, and then I pull my wet hair back with a leather band.

I need to go down to the bakery to see Ava. I want to tell her goodbye, tell her what a nice time I had.

Which means...walking down there and possibly confronting her employees. Plus, it's a Saturday, and people will be in buying their bread for the weekend or a Saturday morning pastry. Eating lunch. Or brunch.

Yeah...

The whole town of Snow Creek will know I spent the night at Ava's place.

Does she want that? I don't want to sneak away, but it may save face for her.

I walk down the stairway, open the door that leads into the back of the bakery, and as I suspected, it's bustling. I sneak out the back way, nearly knocking over a garbage pail as I do so.

I hate doing this, but what other choice do I have? I don't want to embarrass Ava.

I begin walking toward the alley, when—

"Brendan?"

I turn.

Ava stands there, her pink hair pulled back into a hairnet. She wears a black apron smudged with flour.

"Hey."

"You weren't going to say goodbye?"

Shit. I did the wrong thing. "I wanted to. I just wasn't sure you would want me to. I didn't want to embarrass you or anything by coming into the bakery."

"Are you kidding me?" She points to her hair. "I don't get embarrassed. Besides, it probably would've just looked like you came in the back way."

"Oh." Warmth hits my cheeks. "I'm sorry, then. Thank you for last night. I had a great time."

She smiles. "I did too. Are we still on for tonight?"

"Absolutely."

"Good." She glances at the back door. "I'd better get back to work."

"I understand. I'll see you tonight at eight."

"Yep. Just show up here at the back door like last time."

I nod.

Then I walk, unaware that I'm whistling a bright and happy tune, toward my parents' house.

CHAPTER FIFTEEN

Ava

Saturdays are ridiculously busy at the bakery.

I called Brock earlier, asking him to come in for lunch so we could chat. He's waiting for me now at a table in the back. I finish up a sandwich, wrap it up, and then turn to Maya.

"I'm going to take a break to have lunch with Brock. I'll take this over."

"Got it." Maya turns to the next customer in line. "May I help you?"

I grab the sandwich—roast beef and cheddar on rye—and head toward the table where Brock sits.

"Here you go." I set the plate in front of him.

"Thanks." He takes a drink of his spring water. "You sounded pretty serious on the phone. What's going on?"

"Remember that weird text I got?"

"With the *Star Wars* thing? Yeah."

"It turns out that Brendan got the same message."

Brock lifts his eyebrows. "What?"

"Yeah. Only it didn't come to Brendan or to his dad. It came as an email to Hardy Solomon at the sheriff's office. It was the same message. *Darth Morgen is alive.* And then underneath it said *Ask the Murphys.*"

Brock frowns. "Okay."

"So I need to ask you. What do the Murphys have to do with all of this?"

Brock attempts to open the small bag of kettle cooked potato chips that came with his sandwich. The bag tears, and chips go flying.

"Crap. Sorry about that."

"Nice save. You going to answer me?"

Brock shoves a chip into his mouth. Crunches noisily and swallows. "The Murphys? Honestly, we don't really know yet."

I inhale, let it out slowly. "Okay. Don't be mad at Brendan, but he told me a little bit about what you guys found under his floorboards."

"What *he* found under his floorboards. Before he called Dale and Donny in."

"Why Dale and Donny?"

"Probably because they're the closest to his age. You know he and Dale were in the same high school class, right?"

"Right." Of course I know that. I've been deliberating on our age difference, and apparently so has Brock.

"Then I got involved because they went to my father."

"Why not go to their own father?"

"I don't know. Because my dad's the big patriarch and all? Whatever."

"I guess that makes sense. Sort of." I cock my head. "But seriously, what's going on? I know you and Uncle Joe have been researching ever since Uncle Talon got shot."

Brock nods. "I'm not sure how much I can tell you."

"Why not?"

"Because we haven't actually talked to your dad about it yet."

"Why not?" I say again.

"I don't know. Your mom and dad are getting ready to have their twenty-fifth anniversary. Nobody wants to rain on their parade, you know?"

"So you're sure nobody else knows?"

"Uncle Bryce knows because he and my dad tell each other everything. And Uncle Talon knows because he's the one who got shot. And Dale and Donny know."

"Aunt Marjorie?"

"I doubt it. Uncle Bryce probably hasn't wanted to unload this on her."

"Unload what?" I shake my head and huff. "I'm sick and tired of being kept in the dark here. And I'm pretty sure I can speak for my dad. He's not going to feel great that his brothers left him out of this."

Brock wrinkles his forehead.

"Brock?"

"What?"

"What *aren't* you telling me?"

"Nothing."

Except he's lying. I love my cousin. I'm closest to him and Dave of all my cousins because of our age. Having grown up with him, I know him almost as well as he knows himself.

So I know he's lying to me.

But I also know he wouldn't lie to me unless he had a good reason.

"Brock . . ."

He clears his throat. "You need to talk to your father. And your mother."

"What? Why? You just said they don't even know what's going on."

He munches on another chip and drops his gaze to his

barely eaten sandwich. "Right. Yeah, I wasn't thinking. I'm not at liberty to say anything more."

I stand. "Enjoy your lunch, Brock."

Brock reaches a hand to me. "Ava, come on. Sit back down."

"Why? So you'll tell me you can't talk to me? You, Dave, and I have been talking to each other since we were in diapers."

"If it's any consolation, I haven't let Dave in on this either."

I roll my eyes and sit back down across from him. "That's no consolation at all."

"Let me talk to my dad. Okay?"

"No. Not okay." I stand again and walk back to the counter. "I need to take a quick break," I tell Maya. "I'll be upstairs if you need me."

I strip off my apron, throw it in the hamper full of dirty aprons to wash later, and head toward the door that leads to my place. I unlock it quickly, walk up the stairs, wash my hands in the sink, and then go to my mahogany bureau. On top sits the wooden box where I keep my cards.

I unwrap my grandmother's scarf, shuffle the cards, and then clasp them to my heart.

I close my eyes, picture a pink cloud of warmth surrounding me and the cards, infusing my spirit into them.

I want to know what's going on, and I need some guidance.

I sit down at my small table and prepare to do a spread.

The Celtic cross spread is the most common spread used in tarot readings, but it's not the one I use the most. It's a complex spread of ten cards. I do use it, but only when I have at least an hour to do a detailed interpretation.

I don't have that kind of time right now, so I choose a less complex spread—my favorite, which is the three-card mind, body, and spirit spread, which I also interpret as past, present, and future.

The three cards are all right side up, which is odd in itself. Of course it also makes them easier to interpret. When cards show up in reversed positions, the interpretations differ slightly.

The first card in my spread—the one that represents mind and the past—is the two of wands. A wealthy man literally holds the world in his hands. The card makes me think of having control over my surroundings. It shows contemplation and assessment of direction in life.

Interesting.

Interesting because I feel absolutely no control over what's happening to me at the moment. Not with the bizarre message about Darth Morgen, and not with my budding relationship with Brendan. What did I do? I got completely swept away. But Brendan is not why I drew these cards today.

I expected to see a card that was a little more questioning. Instead, the two of wands in relation to my mind and the past seems to indicate there's something I need to assess. Is my life moving in a different direction?

Perhaps it is, with my new involvement with Brendan Murphy.

But again, that isn't why I chose to consult the cards today.

I wanted guidance on my family, on the strange text.

Of course . . .

Brendan got the same bizarre message, albeit in a different way.

So he *is* involved.

Whatever direction my life is taking with regard to that text I received, Brendan is most certainly involved. So that means my relationship with Brendan is involved as well.

The next card—that representing body and present—is the five of swords. A swordsman stands against a stormy sky.

Hostility.

That's the first word that spears into my mind as I contemplate this card.

Which makes sense. I'm feeling a little hostile toward Brock at the moment, as if he's playing some kind of mind game with me. This card indicates the truth in that.

The third card then. Spirit and future.

Also the action I must take—and it's the only card in this reading from the Major Arcana.

It's the card of judgment, and the image depicts humans rising before a trumpeting angel.

And as I stare at the image, at the humans hoping the angel will take them to heaven, I feel as though something new is coming.

A rebirth of sorts, or a new phase in my life.

And the strange text has something to do with it.

But viewing each card individually is like reading the lyrics without hearing the music.

What do these cards say when put together?

Something new is coming.

And it may not make me happy.

I bite my lip, fiddle with my lip ring.

Not exactly the result I was hoping for—but that is the guidance I'm getting from the cards.

I draw in a deep breath, stare at the spread once more. Then I grab my notepad and make notations of the spread in my tarot journal.

Then I note how I'm feeling right now.

Which is…confused. Or…not confused so much as

slightly fearful that I'm going to find out something I don't want to know.

But I can't allow myself to fear the future. I must fight that fear.

These cards tell me two things.

First, Brendan Murphy is going to be a part of my life—at least for now, and at least with regard to the message we both received.

Second? Something is changing. Something that may test my limits.

And I need to be ready for it.

CHAPTER SIXTEEN

Brendan

Mom is out back working in her garden when I get home, and I don't know where my father is. I walk to my bedroom, strip off my dirty clothes from yesterday, and get into a new pair of jeans and a simple T-shirt. I'll change before my date with Ava this evening.

Then, I walk to the door of my closet, open it, and pull out the small safe I keep on the floor. After entering the combination, I click the door open.

Inside are the originals of the three documents I found in my apartment above the bar.

The birth certificate for William Elijah Steel.

The lien on our property held by the Steel Trust.

And the quitclaim deed, signed by Bradford Steel, transferring all Steel real property to one Ryan Steel.

Ava's father.

Why would Brad Steel ever sign this document? He had *four* children—four children who did indeed inherit his fortune in equal shares when he passed away twenty-five years ago.

But at some point—assuming the signature isn't forged— he signed this deed transferring it all to *one* of those children.

Ryan.

Why Ryan?

Ryan was the third born, the youngest son of Brad and Daphne Steel.

Why the third child?

Why not the first child or the last?

What is different about Ryan?

The Steel brothers are icons in our town. I've heard the stories of when they were younger. Ryan was always considered to be both the best looking and to have had the best personality of the three brothers.

Ava doesn't look much like her father. She looks more like her mother, Ruby. But her creativity? That comes from her father.

Ryan Steel is the most creative of the Steels. His wines are legendary, and apparently some of the grape combinations he used were frowned upon by most vintners, but he made them work. He has a gift that allowed him to spin straw into gold—at least in the art of winemaking.

He was the last of the Steel brothers to get married. His wife—Ava's mother—is a former police detective. When she married a Steel, she no longer needed to work, but she did use her knowledge as a private investigator sometimes. She still does.

Which makes me wonder . . .

Why hasn't Ava asked her mother what this text message might mean?

Perhaps she has.

The biggest question is . . . why did she and I get the same message?

What is the connection?

I smile at the word *connection*. Ava and I definitely have a connection, and it has nothing to do with some peculiar message.

My God . . .

Last night was—in a word—nirvana.

I can't wait for tonight.

But in the meantime, I'm going to try to figure this out. I pull out my laptop and fire it up, typing in *Darth Morgen*.

Nothing except some *Star Wars* references, and I'm not a fan of the franchise.

Morgen.

Lots for that. Most notably Morgan le Fay from Arthurian lore—the sorceress who seduced and betrayed her brother.

I smile. Ava is certainly no sorceress, and she doesn't have a brother to betray, but she does read tarot cards. Though Ava wouldn't admit it to me, my mom has asked for a reading on occasion and told me that Ava doesn't charge anything. She does it for the love of the art. And while I'm not sure my mother takes it seriously, she does say it offers some peace of mind sometimes.

Maybe my mother is as good a place as any to start with these questions.

I leave the house and walk outside to her garden where she's digging up some bulbs for the winter.

"Hey, Mom."

She's on her hands and knees, her graying blond hair pulled back in a bandana, and she looks over her shoulder.

"Brendan. When did you get home?"

"Just a little while ago. Do you have a minute?" I crouch down to her level.

"Of course. If you want to grab some work gloves from the garage, I'd love some help."

I just showered, but what the hell? I am living here free of charge. I'll shower again before I meet Ava tonight.

"Sure, I'll be right back."

I grab some work gloves and another handheld spade from the garage, and then I return and sit down beside my mother.

"What did you want to talk about, honey?"

"Did Dad tell you about the email Hardy got?"

She nods. "I have to say I'm stumped."

"Me too. Apparently Ava Steel got the same information in a text."

"Ava? That's strange."

"I know. There doesn't seem to be any connection between our two families. Except for Dad's uncle."

"Yeah," Mom says, "and that was so long ago. This can't possibly have anything to do with that."

"That's what I was thinking. So you have no idea?"

She shakes her head. "I don't. I wish I did. I know how much things like this are going to eat away at you and your father. The two of you are like cats, you know?"

"Cats?" I let out a laugh. "I'm not sure I see a connection there. You know we're both dog people."

"I mean like the old saying. *Curiosity killed the cat.* Not that I think this is going to kill either of you. But you're both so curious. You just can't let a puzzle lie."

"I know it always bothered Dad that he couldn't find any answers about his uncle."

"You're telling me. He still talks about it to this day."

"Are you saying there are no stones left unturned with regard to Great-Uncle Sean?"

"Nope. Your father's done all he can. He traced it as well as he could. There's nothing left. He's gone through all the medical records, everything."

"He must've missed something."

"No. This is your father we're talking about, Brendan. You know he doesn't miss anything."

I sigh. Mom's right. Dad's focus on something gives new meaning to the phrase *beating a dead horse.* He's loath to let anything go.

"The big issue that I see with this new development," Mom says, "is that it has opened up the whole Uncle Sean thing for your father again."

"Maybe there *is* something he missed," I say.

"There absolutely can't be, Brendan. Your father picked it to death." She sighs, removes one of her gardening gloves, and rubs her brow. "It almost cost him his marriage."

I drop my jaw. "You can't be serious, Mom."

"He and I met here, as you know. I've been a small-town girl my whole life, and I fell hard and fast for your dad, a big city boy. That handsome red hair of his that you inherited. He had a personality to match his hair color, and I would follow him anywhere. But he made himself sick over his uncle, Brendan. I finally told him to stop."

"You did?"

"I did. Because there was no more information to be found, and I wanted to have a marriage."

I nod. I always thought my parents had a good marriage.

"We've been so happy," she says as if reading my mind. "But now that this is all coming up again . . ." She puts her glove back on, pulls out another bulb, and shoves it in the pile.

"Mom, Dad loves you."

"I know that. I've always known that. We're as in love today as we were thirty-five years ago, but I don't want to go back to that place, Brendan. That place where your father is so focused on something to the detriment of anything else."

"He's retired now, Mom. He has the time."

"For sure," she says. "But you've never seen your father that way. I have. It's not a pretty sight."

"But if there's information out there..."

"I'm not going back to that place. I'm going to do my damnedest to make sure he leaves the past in the past."

I don't reply.

My father's older now, and perhaps he'll be content to let this lie.

I, on the other hand? This is a puzzle, and like Mom said, I'm as curious as my father is.

I will find out what it all means. Ava and I, together, will figure it out.

CHAPTER SEVENTEEN

Ava

Brendan loves Italian food, so I choose to make chicken piccata and a side of pasta with lemon and olive oil. It's an easy enough recipe, one I learned from Aunt Marj when I was still a teenager. It's simple and makes a lovely presentation.

I grabbed a bottle of my dad's Pinot Grigio from the liquor store that will go perfectly with the meal. It's in the refrigerator chilling.

Everything is set, but I'm still in my bathrobe after having taken my shower when I got back from the bakery. I head to the bedroom to choose an outfit for tonight.

Last night I wore a flowing dress. It's kind of what I'm known for, but tonight?

I want to look a bit sexier for Brendan.

My God, this is so not me.

But I choose a tank top—a tight-fitting one—made of simple stretchy cotton.

No bra.

My nipples poke through the fabric, but that's okay.

Then a denim miniskirt and simple flip-flops on my feet.

I leave my hair down in soft waves around my shoulders, and I add some large hoop earrings.

Not too bad, I say to myself.

Then I jerk at the loud knock on the door. I go down the stairs, let Brendan in the back way. He looks gorgeous, of course, in jeans and a blue button-down that brings out his bright-blue eyes. His hair is usually tied back, but tonight he wears it down, and I desperately want to run my fingers through it.

He looks me over.

And his mouth drops open.

"My God, Ava. You look like a dream."

"I know it's not my normal look."

"I mean, you're always sexy."

I open my mouth too, but then I close it quickly.

Brendan is attracted to me for whatever reason. Why should I tell him not to be?

I've always felt like the ugly stepchild of the Steel family. Even though I'm not a stepchild. I'm a full-blooded Steel. But even those of us who aren't Steel blood—Dale, Donny, and Henry—are all incredibly good-looking.

I'm the ugly duckling of the bunch.

But Brendan doesn't think so.

"Come on up." I smile.

He follows me up the stairs, and when he gets to the top, he inhales. "Wow. Smells amazing in here."

"I'm glad you think so."

"I smell garlic, lemon. What are you making?"

"Chicken piccata with a side of pasta." I open the refrigerator and take out the bottle of Pinot Grigio. "Would you like a glass of wine?"

"Yeah, sounds great."

I fumble with the corkscrew, and he takes it from me. "Allow me. I'm a professional."

I smile.

His hair falls right below his shoulders. I think it's actually longer than mine.

I grab two stemmed glasses out of my cupboard and set them on the counter. Brendan fills them both and hands one to me. He picks up the other and clinks it to my glass.

"To a memorable evening."

Warmth flies to my cheeks.

"Yes, to a memorable evening," I echo.

I take a sip of the crisp white wine. Much to my father's chagrin, I've never been a huge wine drinker—or any kind of alcohol drinker—but I do like his Pinot Grigio. While most of the Steel family favors red wine, I prefer white. My father only makes a few white wines, not counting the sparkling varieties— this one, a Chardonnay, and a white Rhône blend.

Funny how I still think of him as the winemaker. He's retired, and Dale has taken over. But I can't see my father ever truly retiring. Just like my mother never truly retired from her—

"Oh my God!" I say.

Brendan jolts. "What? Are you okay?"

"Yes, I'm fine, but why didn't I think of this before? My mother is a *detective*. I need to ask her about that text."

Brendan laughs. "I was thinking that to myself this afternoon. I'm surprised you haven't asked your mom."

"It's funny. I consider myself a member of the Steel family, and I love my parents dearly, but living here in town instead of on the ranch, with my own business independent from their money, I forget about the amazing resources I have available. My mom is one of them."

"The bakery's closed tomorrow. Why don't we go see your mom?"

"We?"

"Sure, if you don't mind. I basically got the same message via Hardy Solomon."

I chew on my lip, play with my lip ring. "That's true ... but ..."

He trails his finger over my cheek. "But ... you don't really want to explain to them what you're doing with me."

"No. It's not that. Not really." I stare at my wineglass. "It's just ... This is private between us, Brendan. I'm not ready to make it public yet."

"Make *what* public, exactly?"

"That we're ..." My face is on fire. "Going out, I guess?"

"We *are* going out, Ava."

"Well ... yeah ... but ..."

"It's okay to take a chance." He closes the short distance between us, fingers a lock of my hair, and tugs it a little. "I'm serious when it comes to you."

I bite my lip again. "I ... I'm serious too."

Why is that so hard for me to say?

I didn't go looking for Brendan. He came to me. But my God ... last night ...

I didn't follow the advice of the cards.

I let myself get swept away.

The card was urging caution so I wouldn't get hurt.

Is Brendan going to hurt me?

I can't ask him that. What guy in his right mind would say *Yes, that's my plan. To hurt you*"?

"You know what?" I say. "I'd love it if you would come with me. Let me text my mom and see if she's got some free time tomorrow to talk to us."

I grab my phone, which is hooked up to a charger in the kitchen, and send Mom a quick text.

> *Hey, Mom. I'd like to come talk to you
> tomorrow. Do you have any time?*

She texts back almost immediately.

*For you? Always. Why don't you come
have lunch with Dad and me?*

I bite my lip. Ponder what to say.

> *I kind of just want to talk to you alone.*

Is everything okay, sweetie?

> *I'm fine. But Brendan Murphy and I need
> to talk to you.*

Brendan Murphy?

> *I'll explain it all tomorrow. Maybe you
> should come into town.*

I can do that.

> *Perfect. I'll make your favorite sandwich.
> See you around noon?*

It's a date.

"Okay," I tell Brendan. "My mom's coming here tomorrow. To the bakery. So you come over at noon, and I'll make us all some sandwiches. We can talk to her then."

CHAPTER EIGHTEEN

Brendan

The food smells so good, but I hardly taste it. All I can remember is the taste of Ava's pussy.

I would love to take her to bed again, but I'm not sure it's the right thing to do.

I like this woman. I like her more than I've liked anyone in a long time—and *like* isn't even the right word, but I can't quite say the other L-word yet—and I don't want to screw it up. Even if it means the inevitable blue balls.

Taking a woman to bed on the first date is never a good idea, but I did it anyway.

I did it because I wanted her so much.

I take another sip of the crisp white wine. "Your dad does know how to make a good wine," I say.

"Yeah, he has a gift." Ava swishes the light-amber liquid around in her wineglass. "My uncles all think it's funny because none of them have any creativity at all. Seems my dad got all of it."

"Not just your dad. Marjorie, as a chef, must be very creative."

"True. But Uncle Joe and Uncle Talon have no artistic talent of any kind."

"You do, though." I raise my glass. "Obviously you got

creativity from your dad and your aunt. I mean, you're an amazing baker."

"Thank you." Redness creeps to her cheeks.

"Everyone talks about it in town," I continue. "How you make the best baked goods they've ever tasted. And how you've done it all on your own without using your family's money."

"Everybody knows about that?"

"Yeah, pretty much. Is that an issue?"

She shakes her head. "I'm used to the whole town talking about me. That's what they do when you're a Steel." She shifts in her chair.

"I didn't mean to make you uncomfortable."

"You didn't. Like I said. I'm used to it."

I twirl pasta around my fork, trying to get it to stay on without strings hanging down.

Ava smiles at me. "I gave that up years ago. Just cut it with your fork first."

I laugh. "That's what I normally do, but I wanted to impress you with my Italian food prowess."

"You don't have an ounce of Italian blood in you, Murphy."

"No. I don't think I do. I'm all Irish on my dad's side. And there's a little Irish on my mom's side, along with some Scottish and English. Totally a son of the British Isles." I chuckle.

"You know what's funny? I've never really thought about where the Steels come from." Ava sets her fork on her plate.

"Steel sounds like it's a British name too."

"Maybe. We could ask my mom tomorrow. But she wasn't born a Steel, so she may not know."

"Maybe it'll be a good way to break the ice," I say.

"Yeah, in fact... I've been thinking. I don't want to worry my mom."

"Why would she worry?"

"Because she's my mom. I know the text doesn't seem to be a threat or anything, but it came from an unknown number, and I don't know what it means."

"True. I don't want to worry your mom either, but I got the same message. I agree it doesn't seem like a threat. Do you think it could be some kind of warning?"

Ava sighs. "Mom *is* the person most likely to be able to help us decipher it. She was a police detective and private investigator for years."

"Yeah."

"In fact, she's the one who helped Dale come out of his shell when he first came to the ranch. By letting him in on the investigation."

I drop my jaw. "You mean Dale came out of his shell long ago?"

"Yeah." Ava smiles. "I can understand why you think he didn't. But that's the story. I have no recollection of it, of course, because I wasn't born yet. But apparently my mom brought him in on an investigation back then, and he was able to help her a little. And that really got him talking. Apparently he didn't talk at all when he first came."

"He never has been that chatty," I say. "He's a good guy, though. He and I were never friends because Dale didn't really have friends. But everyone liked him."

"Probably because he was a Steel," Ava says.

"I'll admit your name doesn't hurt, but although he was kind of a recluse, everyone knew he was a good guy. Ashley has really helped. I've seen him laugh and smile more in the last year than I have since I've known him. And I've known him since we were ten, when he first came here."

Ava laughs nervously. "You've known my cousin longer than I've been alive."

My heart drops into my gut. There it is. The age thing again. Why does it bother her so much? Perhaps she's not truly ready for a serious relationship. In which case I need to slow it down. I will *not* take her to bed tonight, no matter how blue my balls get.

God, that's going to be hard.

No pun intended.

"So I drew some tarot cards," Ava says, "asking for guidance about the text." She looks down at her plate.

"You don't have to be embarrassed about that, Ava."

"I'm not embarrassed. I'm just used to others not taking me seriously."

"I'm not most others. I know you take the tarot seriously. What did you find out?"

"Thank you," she says.

"For what?"

"For not rolling your eyes."

I grab her hand across the table. "Maybe you should do a reading for me sometime."

A gorgeous smile splits her face. "I'd be happy to."

"But first, tell me what you found out about the situation we both seem to be in."

"It does seem that you are part of the situation. And I'm not talking about the two of us on a date tonight. I'm talking about the two of us getting the same message."

"That makes sense."

"The feeling I got from the cards I drew was that something new was coming into my life and I may not like it."

"I hope you don't mean me on that count." I force a smile.

"Oh, no. That's not the feeling I got it all. It has more to do with my family. I'm feeling very hostile toward my cousin Brock right now because he's keeping information from me. Brock and I, along with Dave, have always been very close because we were all born only months apart. We were in the same grade at school, and my uncles started calling us Huey, Dewey, and Louie after Donald Duck's nephews. I never thought about the fact that they were all boys and I was the lone girl. We were simply Huey, Dewey, and Louie. Our genders didn't matter."

"And now you feel like Brock is pulling away?"

"Not pulling away so much as . . ." She draws in a breath. "I guess you have to have a big family to understand. But Brock, Dave, and I—even though we're cousins—have always felt more like siblings."

"And you're feeling hostile."

"I am. And I don't like feeling hostile, especially toward Brock, who, like I said, is more like a brother to me than Gina's a sister."

"I understand. At least I think I do, not having any siblings of my own. So that's why you seem a little off tonight."

"Do I?"

"Yeah. Not in a bad way. Just like you're a bit distracted."

"I admit the reading took me back a bit. I don't like thinking badly about my family. And I sure don't like thinking that something's going to happen with my family that I'm not going to like."

"Yeah, I understand that. Reminds me of a conversation I had with my mom earlier."

"Oh?"

"Yeah. Apparently this new development—this weird text—has got my dad thinking there might be something he missed all those years ago when he was trying to figure out the mystery behind his uncle's death."

"The one he was named after. The original Sean Murphy."

"Yeah. Apparently my dad got really focused on that when he was younger. And my mom doesn't want him to go back to that place."

"Why would she think this has anything to do with that?"

"Honestly? I don't really know. My guess is he said something to her about it."

"Do *you* think it has anything to do with that?"

"No."

I'm not sure how much I can say to Ava about the documents. Not much more than I've already said. My guess is it has something to do with those documents. Which is more likely than it having anything to do with my great-uncle.

"Well, I'm hoping my mom can shed some light on it."

"Yeah. Me too."

We finish our dinners, and Ava clears the table.

"I didn't have time to make any dessert," she says, "but I still have ice cream."

"Sounds perfect."

She dishes it up, and I take a spoonful, letting the richness flow over my tongue.

As delicious as the confection is, Ava's richness would be even better.

But no.

I have *got* to hold back tonight.

"How about that reading?" I say.

"You mean a reading for you?"

"Yeah. I'd like that."

"Do you have a specific question you'd like answered?"

"Is that how it works? Can't you just do a reading?"

"I can, but it's more helpful if I know what I'm looking for."

"Okay, then. I'll ask the same question you did. What is the meaning of this message that we've both received? How does it factor into my life?"

"Okay."

We finish our ice cream, Ava clears the table, and then she pours us each more glasses of water and wine.

"Let me get my cards."

She walks over to a bureau and opens a wooden box. She pulls out what appears to be something bound in silk.

"I'm going to shuffle the cards." She sits back at the table and unwraps a scarf to show me a deck of cards. "And then I want you to hold them to your heart with your hands touching them. You need to infuse your energy into the deck."

"Okay."

I have no idea what she's talking about, but I will do my best. I want to respect her feelings on this matter.

She shuffles the cards once, twice, three times. Then she hands them to me.

I clasp them in my hands, hold them to my heart.

"Close your eyes," she says. "Feel your energy flowing from your body and into the cards."

I obey, closing my eyes. As far as feeling my energy? I'm not exactly sure what she wants me to do, so I just think the words.

Energy flow to the cards. Energy flow to the cards. Energy flow to the cards.

Then I open my eyes.

"Hand the cards back to me," she says.

I do, and she sets them in front of her. "Now cut the deck."

I do.

She sets the second pile on top of the first, and then she holds the cards for a moment, closing her own eyes. Then she opens them.

"What were you doing just then?"

"I was infusing them with my energy so that I might give you a good reading."

"Okay."

"I'm going to do my standard three-card reading," she says. "The Celtic cross reading is the most common, but it's a ten-card spread, and I think three cards is better for a specific question."

"Whatever you say."

She lays three cards on the table. The images are vivid and bright, and my gaze falls on the first one that faces me. A naked woman kneels by water, and above her shines a large yellow star surrounded by smaller white stars.

Ava stares at the cards for a few moments, twisting her lips.

"Ava?"

CHAPTER NINETEEN

Ava

"Give me a minute," I say. "I'm thinking."

The cards I drew are a little disturbing, and I need a moment to process.

The first card I drew for Brendan is the star. It's normally an amazing card, meaning hope or calm, essentially a good omen.

But it's upside down, in the reverse position.

Which indicates the opposite. Darkness.

This is his mind and his past.

I don't feel that Brendan has a past of darkness, and I'm not sure there's anything going on in his mind that's dark.

So I need to think about the card for a moment in relation to the other two cards.

The second card, representing the present and his body, is the two of swords. A blindfolded woman sits in front of water, balancing two swords. Behind her, a crescent moon shines. This card is upright, not reversed, and is normally a card that indicates indecision about something. The suit of swords is a suit of masculine energy, so I'm not surprised that I drew a sword for Brendan. It's also a suit of intellect and thought. Logic.

Again, I'm perplexed.

How these two cards work together and then in tandem with the third, which is the devil—a horned beast with bat wings. Two naked demons serve him.

The card is in reverse position.

While the devil normally indicates some kind of destructive pattern, the reversal of its position indicates freedom. Sounds good, but what does it mean for this reading as a whole?

"Ava?" Brendan says.

"Give me a moment."

"You're freaking me out a little here."

"Some readings take longer than others," I tell him. "There's nothing to be concerned about. I just need to see the cards as a whole. Figure out what they mean."

"Can you at least tell me what they are?"

"Of course. Your first card is the star, but it's in reverse position, meaning it's facing you and not me."

"Okay."

"The star is a good card. Usually it's a good omen."

"A good omen for what?"

"Well, that depends. Depends on your question, depends on the rest of the cards in your reading. But it's in reverse position, so it means—"

"A bad omen?"

"No, not really. But it does have a darker feeling to me. The star is usually an inspiring card. It signifies hope, inspiration. Its reversal doesn't necessarily mean the opposite. But it does mean that you're possibly feeling adrift. Uninspired."

"I suppose that's true," he says. "I have no idea what the message means, no idea where to start."

"That can make sense."

"What's my second card?"

"The two of swords. All the sword cards have a very masculine energy, so I'm not surprised that I drew one for you."

"So is that the meaning of this card then? I'm a guy?" He smiles.

"It's a card of balance in some senses, but sometimes it can indicate feelings of nervousness and uncertainty. Possibly difficult choices ahead."

He drums his fingers on the table. "O . . . kay. Still freaked."

"Don't be. We have to take the reading as a whole. But I admit your next card is a challenge."

"And it is?"

"It's the devil, also in reversed position. The star and the devil are considered opposite cards in the tarot. Normally the devil means—"

"Evil?"

I smile. "No, of course not. But it does mean you may be focusing on material things, or you're trapped in some kind of mental bondage."

"Great."

"But it's reversed, which can mean freedom from bondage, but that's the easy answer. And with the tarot, you should never accept the easy answer." I close my eyes, breathe in, breathe out.

My intuition has never failed me, and I won't allow it to fail me now.

Adrift. Difficult choices. Freedom from bondage.

What does all of this have to do with the message that Brendan and I received? What does it mean for him specifically?

I open my eyes. "I feel like this mysterious message is

going to lead to some perplexing choices for both of us."

"I don't understand."

"Honestly? I don't either. The tarot doesn't always give us a straight answer. In fact, it rarely does."

"What might these difficult choices be?"

"I don't know, but I feel a real family element from both our readings."

"So someone from both of our families is involved in this?"

"It could mean that. I'm not clairvoyant, Brendan. All I have is my intuition and the guidance of the cards. But that's what I'm feeling. My family is involved. Your family is involved. Something is going to be revealed that's going to lead to some difficult choices."

"Okay."

"It's not something we can run away from," I say. "I knew that as soon as I got that text. Even then, I felt it would have some kind of life-changing effect for me. I just don't know what."

"Life-changing effects don't have to be bad," Brendan says.

"Absolutely not, and I choose to think of this as a positive."

"Then I will too." He smiles.

I stare at the cards a little longer, hoping I'll get some more insight.

The card that draws my gaze is the last card, the devil in reverse. The horned king sits on the throne, a reversed pentacle above his head. His right hand is raised. He's bearded, definitely male. And he's challenging me.

Or he's challenging Brendan. Or perhaps challenging both of us. In the reverse position, he's challenging our faith.

And then it comes to me.

Exactly what this card means—and I know it was meant for me as well as for Brendan.

The devil is challenging me to hold tight to who I am.

To not let anything question that.

Which means...

Something is coming that's going to *cause* me to question it. Something is coming that's going to cause Brendan to question something about himself as well.

And it's coming quickly.

CHAPTER TWENTY

Brendan

My nerves are jumping under my skin.

Hell, I asked for this. I wanted this reading. Do I believe in this stuff? Not really, but I want Ava to know that I respect her feelings and beliefs.

But now that she's read the cards for me?

Icicles are poking at the back of my neck.

There's a certain rightness to everything she said. And I don't mean right in the sense of yes, something's going to happen. I mean right in the sense of something inside me *feels* what she's saying.

Something inside me believes what these cards are telling me.

She's staring at them right now. Playing with her lip ring with her tongue, fidgeting with her fingers.

Does she always stare at the cards this long after she draws them?

I almost feel like she's in some kind of trance.

Finally she draws in a deep breath and looks up, meeting my gaze. "I'm not sure I did the best job on your reading."

"Why would you say that?"

"Because when I infused the cards with my energy, instead of focusing on your question, I was focusing on *our* question."

"Except it's the same question," I say.

"True. But this reading . . ." She glances down, stares at the spread. "I feel like it's not just for you. It's for both of us."

"Is that a bad thing?"

"Not in the way you mean," she says. "But as the interpreter of the cards, I can't allow my own questions to get in the way of interpretation for someone else. I'm afraid I did here."

"If we both have the same question . . ."

"Right. We do. But the way this affects both of us could be very different. I'm not sure I did you justice with this reading."

"Maybe you did. Maybe the reading *was* for both of us." I trail my finger over her forearm.

"That's the feeling I'm getting," she says, "but we're two different individuals, Brendan. So these cards could—*should*—have two different meanings for both of us."

"But that's not what you're feeling?"

"No. It's not what I'm feeling at all."

"I'm trying to understand, Ava."

"I know you are, and I appreciate that. You're a good friend, Brendan."

Uh-oh. Heart to gut again.

The F-word.

Surely, after last night, she doesn't think of me as merely a friend.

I try to put that in the back of my mind for now.

"So you're as adrift as I am," I say.

"In a way." She stares down at the spread again. "But as I look at all three of these cards together, and especially the devil in reverse, what I'm seeing is a challenge. A challenge to our vision of ourselves."

"I'm not sure what you mean."

"Do you know who you are, Brendan?"

I hold back a chuckle. "Yeah. I'm Brendan Murphy. I've been Brendan Murphy for thirty-five years."

"Right. Brendan Murphy. And I'm Ava Steel. And I feel like I've always had a very good idea of who I am. I'm not the typical Steel."

"That's what I like about you," I say.

"You mean you don't like the Steels?"

"God, no. I love the Steels. You're all great. But you... You're not afraid to be yourself, Ava, and not only do I respect the hell out of that, I also think it makes you unique. I like unique. I like *you*."

She blushes then. "I like you too, Brendan. Exactly as you are."

I lift my eyebrows. Maybe we are friends. Friends are good, and friendship is a solid basis for something more. "Then we seem to have a mutual admiration society."

"I think we need to be confident in who we are," she says.

"I can't recall a time when I wasn't."

"Me neither. But I'm concerned." She looks into my eyes for a moment but then breaks her gaze away. "I'm concerned about this hostility I'm feeling toward Brock. It's not like me."

"I'm concerned as well," I say. "About my mother and father. My mother's freaked out that my dad's going to go off the deep end searching for answers about his uncle again, and now, after this reading? I'm kind of concerned about that too."

"So you see what I'm saying?" Ava says. "Already we're having new feelings about our families. And that could lead us to question who we are at our very core."

"I don't see how it could lead that way."

"Good. Don't let it." She finally picks up the cards, adds them to the deck, shuffles them, and wraps them in the scarf.

An odd feeling of calm settles over me. Relief, almost. Relief that the cards are no longer on the table.

"You don't let it either," I tell her.

"I won't," she says. "Or I'll do my damned best anyway."

She rises, walks back to the bureau, and places the cards back into the wooden box. Then she makes some notes in a leatherbound journal.

"I kind of put a downer on this evening," she says when she returns to the table.

"I asked for the reading," I say. "If it's anyone's fault, it's mine."

"I think we both need to understand," she says, "that this *isn't* a negative reading. No reading is either positive or negative. It's simply guidance from the cards and from the reader's intuition."

"Right. I understand that. I think the guidance here is that whatever is behind this mystery may lead us to question who we are. We need to work against that."

She nods. "Exactly."

I'm quiet for a moment. Ava looks so beautiful, but the mood for any kind of sexual encounter has been broken.

Just as well, since I decided I wasn't going to fuck her tonight anyway.

"I think we could use a walk," I say. "Would you like to take a walk through town?"

She smiles. "Brendan, that's a great idea. I think walking would help clear both of our heads."

I glance out her window. "You'd better grab a jacket. It's pretty cool in the evenings."

"Yeah, I'll change into some jeans. Give me a moment, okay?"

I nod, and she goes to her bedroom.

I try not to think about her taking off her skirt.

She returns a few moments later, wearing jeans—tighter than her usual boyfriend jeans, and her ass looks amazing— and a gray blazer that looks like it might've come out of her father's closet.

It's very Ava, and it works on her.

"Shall we?" she says.

We walk down the stairs, through the door into the bakery and out the back way.

It's Saturday night in Snow Creek. Hardly a thriving metropolis. Most of the businesses closed at six, but the restaurants are open. And of course my bar is open, with Laney tending tonight again with help from Maryanne and Nicholas waiting tables.

I take Ava's hand, small and warm in my own, and she blushes a bit but smiles up at me.

Good.

I guide her out of town, through the small park, and then we walk a few blocks through a residential area.

We don't talk much, and I figure Ava is thinking about the tarot reading. Maybe about meeting with her mother and what the message might mean.

And while I'm concerned about all of that, I'm mostly thinking about my dick, which is hard, because I'm walking next to Ava Steel.

But damn it, I will not bed her tonight.

We walk back through the main drag in town, and just as we're passing my bar, Brock Steel and Rory Pike exit.

Ava goes rigid.

"Hey, guys," I say.

"Brendan, Ava," Rory says. "Nice to see you."

My gaze drops to Rory's left hand. She's wearing a ring with a giant pink stone.

Ava grabs Rory's hand. "It's gorgeous!" She then gives Rory's hand to me.

I glance down. "So it's official."

"Sure is," Brock says, "so hands off her, both of you."

Rory laughs and pulls her hand away. "He's just kidding."

"That's what you think." But Brock smiles.

Rory Pike is gorgeous. All the Pike girls are. But Ava Steel is the most beautiful woman in town in my eyes. In her own exceptional way.

"Brock," Ava says.

"My cousin's a little mad at me, if you can't tell," Brock says.

"Yeah, I've heard the tale."

"Ava, you want to go into the bar with us?" Brock asks.

"Aren't you just leaving?"

"We were, but what if I buy you a drink?"

"No. I had two glasses of wine with dinner," Ava says.

"Okay." Brock grins. "But you can't be mad at me forever. I'm just too damned charming for that."

Rory grabs his hand. "Come on, Brock. I think they're on a date."

"He's taking a date to his own bar?"

"Ignore him." Rory looks over her shoulder.

The two of them walk hand-in-hand down the street.

"Sorry about that," I say.

"Why? You didn't do anything wrong. He's the one I'm mad at."

I glance at the door leading into my bar. "You want to go in? Maybe we could both use another drink. And since you're with me, you don't have to pay."

"No," she says. "I think I'd just like to go home now."

"Okay. Let's go."

We walk by the bakery, and I take her through the alley to the back door. "Good night, Ava."

She lifts her eyebrows. "Don't you want to come in?"

"Well, of course. I was just going to ..."

"Going to what?"

I let out a heavy sigh. "I was determined not to go to bed with you tonight, Ava."

She frowns. "Why? Didn't you enjoy it the last time?"

"Are you kidding me?" I cup her soft cheek. "It was fucking spectacular."

"Then what would be a good reason for not doing it again?"

"I don't want you to think I'm only after one thing."

"Why would I think that?"

"Because ... you're better than this, Ava. You're better than going to bed with a guy on the first date."

Her gaze darkens, and not in a good way. "What the hell is that supposed to mean, anyway?"

"Oh, hell if I know." I trail my fingers through my long hair, tugging on the ends. "It came out all wrong. You know what? I would love to come upstairs with you. I would love to make love with you all night. But I would also love to just talk.

I want to get to know you, Ava. I like you. I would like for this to . . . lead somewhere."

She smiles, still holding my hand. "I think I'd like that too. The universe seems to be pushing us together right now, sending us both the same message."

I rake my fingers through my hair once more with my free hand. "Damn it, Ava. That is not at all what I meant."

"I know." She squeezes my hand. "I like you too, Brendan. Our age difference throws me off a little, but I can handle it. I just always would wonder if you could."

"How can you ask me that?"

"Because I'm so young. I have so much less experience than you—and I'm not just talking about sex. I'm talking about . . . everything."

"That doesn't matter to me. None of that matters to me."

"Not now, but what about the future?"

I grin. "So you're saying we have a future?"

"I'm saying I'm open to it. But I want us to be friends, too. I don't want anything that happens between us to affect our friendship. Especially because of these messages. Clearly we're going to have to work together to solve this mystery."

"I'll always be your friend, Ava."

And I mean it. At least I hope I mean it. If something happens between us and we don't work out as a couple, I'm not sure if I could remain friends with her.

Because honestly?

I don't feel like there's anyone else for me. I'm already half in love with this woman.

I have been for a long time. It makes no sense, but since when did love make sense?

"I promise," I tell her, hoping like hell I can keep the vow

I'm about to make. "No matter what happens, you and I will always be friends."

"Good. I'm glad." She fingers a lock of my hair. "You said you wanted this to lead somewhere. Right now, at this moment, I'd really like it to lead to you following me up to my apartment."

My groin tightens. "I would love to."

CHAPTER TWENTY-ONE

Ava

As soon as we're inside the bakery, Brendan grabs me and crushes his mouth to mine. I open for him instantly, letting him devour my mouth with his teeth, lips, and tongue. The bakery is dark, and the scents of yeast, almond, and fresh-baked bread drift around us, sweeter, to me, than any perfume or flower.

He said it was okay if we didn't make love. It was okay if we just talked.

But I'm glad he's kissing me. I'm glad he didn't want to just talk. Because frankly I don't want to talk right now. I want to *not* talk.

I want to not *think*.

If I have to think, all I want to think about is Brendan's lips on mine, his mouth between my legs, his dick inside me.

I need to feel right now.

I need to turn my mind off and just *feel*.

Somehow we make it through the door and up the stairs to my place.

His mouth still fused to mine, Brendan brushes my jacket from my shoulders until it's on the floor.

A soft breeze from my heating vent brushes over me.

He breaks the kiss and stares down at me. "You're so beautiful, Ava."

"And you're magnificent, Brendan. Just gorgeous."

He takes his shirt off, unbuttoning it slowly, and I savor each new inch of flesh that's exposed.

My gaze goes straight to his left bicep, to a Celtic knot tattoo. It circles his upper arm, and on the back of his left shoulder is another Celtic tattoo. I noticed his ink last night, but I was way more focused on his musculature. Now I want to take in these images.

"Turn around," I tell him.

"Okay."

I touch the tattoo. "The triquetra."

The Celtic symbol for mind, body, and spirit—just like the reading I did for both of us. The three-card spread, representing mind, body, and spirit plus past, present, and future. Indeed, the symbol represents anything that comes in a three.

The triple goddess—maiden, mother, crone.

In Christianity—father, son, holy spirit.

Land, sea, and sky.

Birth, life, and death.

Three is everywhere.

"Yes," he says.

"But you're Irish, not Scottish."

"I'm a little Scottish, but that doesn't even matter. Celtic symbolism is important in Irish and British culture too. Besides, it's a common misconception that the triquetra is Celtic in origin. Some say it's Germanic or Norse."

"Which you aren't either."

"No, I'm not, but I love the symbolism of it. The power of three."

I run my fingers over the beauty of it. "It's very nicely done."

"Cyrus over at the tattoo shop did it for me years ago."

"How did you choose it?"

"It's the first one I got, right after high school. I was looking for balance in my life, and it reminds me that to have balance, you need to pay attention to mind, body, and spirit equally. If you become strong of body but neglect your mind and spirit, you may live a long life, but you'll only be existing."

I smile and kiss him, outlining the triquetra with my tongue.

He shudders.

"I've been thinking about getting a tattoo. I love my ear piercings, and of course my lip. But I don't have any ink yet."

"Cyrus does an amazing job. He did all my tats."

"You have more than these two?"

"Boy, you really weren't paying attention last night, were you?" He chuckles and unbuckles his jeans, unsnaps them, and then kicks off his shoes before he pulls his jeans over his hips. He keeps his boxer briefs on—that bulge is still apparent—and folds his jeans in half and hangs them over a chair.

Then he moves toward me again, turns around, and gives me an incredible look at his amazing ass.

But I draw my gaze downward, to his left calf.

And oh my God.

It's a merman. Sort of. He has horns...and my God... he looks a lot like the devil on my tarot card. Except he has a fishtail, of course. He's holding a trident, except...it's not a trident. Instead of having three prongs, it's actually another triquetra.

"Wow." I kneel and touch his calf.

"Murphy means sea warrior."

"Does it?"

"It does. So this is my tribute to my name."

"It's awesome." I run my fingers over the sea king's tail. "Maybe I will go see Cyrus. But I don't know what I'll get. That's been my issue the whole time. I love ink. I always have. But I've never found an image that just quite suits me."

"You'll know it when you find it."

"I've considered the triquetra," I say. "But I want to make it unique in some way."

Brendan turns to face me and pulls me to my feet. "Now that is classic Ava. Unique. You don't want just a regular old triquetra."

I shrug. "What can I say? When you're right, you're right."

"You know?" He brushes my hair over my ear. "I'm standing here in my underwear, and you have entirely too many clothes on."

He's right, of course. I tug on my tank top, ready to pull it over my head, but he touches my hands to stop me.

"Please," he says, "let me."

I smile, gazing into his searing blue eyes.

Everything about Brendan Murphy is spectacular—from his porcelain warrior's body to his gorgeous auburn hair. But those eyes, fringed in dark-brown lashes, so big and blue and full of fire. They set me ablaze.

His fingers trail a burning path as he lifts the tank top off me. He sucks in an audible breath as my boobs fall gently against my chest.

"You should never wear bras, Ava," he says.

I open my mouth to say something, but what do you say to that? Hell, I'm ready to throw out all my bras just because he told me to.

He skims his hands up my sides and over the tops of my

breasts to my shoulders, caressing me gently.

My nipples are hard and taut, but he hasn't touched them. Is he waiting for permission?

He trails his fingers to my jeans, unsnapping the snap and then unzipping the zipper. He brushes them over my thighs.

I stand before him now.

He kneels down, removes my shoes, and then pushes my jeans down my legs, and I step out of them.

We stand before each other now only in our underwear.

His boxer briefs are skintight, and the strong muscles of his thighs protrude beneath them. His underwear is blue, a similar shade to his eyes but not nearly as vibrant, of course. No fabric can mimic the color that nature provided Brendan.

My underwear is camouflage cotton bikinis.

I don't own any sexy panties. It may be time to drive to Grand Junction and go to Victoria's Secret.

I stop myself from laughing out loud at that thought. That is *so* not me.

I like to look nice. I even like to look sexy when I can pull it off.

But sexy underwear? Not my thing.

Brendan's gaze drops to my pussy. I'm already wet for him. I have been since we walked back to my place.

When he said good night and I thought he didn't want to come up, I was so disappointed.

Even though I know we're moving quickly.

Even though I know...

I'm being swept away.

I'm ignoring the guidance of the cards. The damned knight of cups.

It's not the first time I've ignored what the cards told me. The problem is? Every time I do so, I end up regretting it.

But how can I regret this? How can I regret being with Brendan? He showed me so much pleasure last night, and it's been a long time.

I don't go looking for sex. I never have. But it found me this time.

I didn't go looking for Brendan Murphy. He came to me.

Is it possible to continue to enjoy the physical parts of this budding relationship without getting swept away?

I'll think about that tomorrow.

Because I'm so done with thinking tonight.

I just want to feel.

I want to feel beautiful, and Brendan does that for me.

And I want to feel...

I want to feel...

Damn it.

I want to feel loved.

Sex is not love.

Words of wisdom from my mother when I came of age, and I've always kept them close to my heart.

And I realize now what that knight of cups was trying to tell me.

Don't get swept away by the sex and confuse it for something it's not.

It's okay to feel.

Just don't mistake the feeling for love.

Good enough.

I jump into Brendan's arms.

151

CHAPTER TWENTY-TWO

Brendan

Ava's legs are wrapped around me, her pussy grinding against my hard cock.

Her little titties are squished against my chest, and her lips—those full and beautiful lips—are sucking at my neck.

Oh my God.

If we didn't have our underwear separating us, I could plunge into her right now.

If only...

So much I haven't yet done to her. I haven't licked and sucked on those cute little nipples. I haven't kissed every inch of her body. I haven't made slow sweet love to her.

But slow isn't in the cards for tonight.

I'm aching right now. Literally aching. My cock is so hard, and my balls are scrunched up to my body...

If I don't get into her pussy soon, I may explode.

Damn, what she does to me.

"Ava," I whisper in her ear.

"Yes?" she says against my neck.

"I need to take you to bed. I need to get inside you. God, I need you more than I need air."

"Yes. Please."

I turn then, she still safe in my arms, and carry her to her bedroom. I set her on the bed, ease her panties off her, and toss them on the floor.

Then I inhale the fragrant scent of her pussy.

"God," I growl.

"I want you," she says. "I want you so much, Brendan."

"Oh, Ava, you have no idea ..."

I spread her legs, needing to taste the secret treasures between them.

I clamp my mouth onto her pussy, licking, sucking, chewing on her labia.

My cock beats against my body. Ready. So ready.

"Ava," I say against her wet thigh. "I'm going to fuck you quickly. Quick and hard and fast. But I promise next time will be slow. Next time will be everything you deserve."

"All I need is to *feel* right now, Brendan," she says. "Feeling you inside me—that huge-ass cock—how you burn through me—it's exactly what I need. So please, Brendan. Fuck me. Fuck me now."

"God," I groan.

I move away, quickly rid myself of my offending boxer briefs, and within another second I'm inside her—my cock embedded deep inside her wet, tight pussy.

I stop for just a moment. A solemn moment to enjoy the complete joining of our bodies.

But then I can no longer wait. I pull out and thrust back in.

In.

In.

In.

In.

In.

And—

I release. It happens even faster this time. The second time. I don't know how it's possible, but she feels even better tonight.

And I'm a complete heel.

I didn't make this sweet woman come first.

What a selfish lover I am. But I can take care of that.

I allow myself a few moments, relishing the feeling of being inside her as I release, but then I withdraw.

"Your turn," I say.

She's lying on her back, her eyes closed, her arms above her head. Her pink hair is fanned out on her pillow, and she looks so relaxed.

She looks like… She looks like she's already had an orgasm.

"Baby?" I say.

"Mmm?"

"I want you to come."

"Mmm…okay."

"You look so relaxed."

"I am. You gave me what I needed."

"I did?"

She opens her eyes then, and a soft smile curves her lips.

"I just wanted to feel, Brendan. And you inside me? It's an amazing feeling."

I lift my eyebrows. "I can make you feel way better than that."

"I know you can. But believe me, what you did was perfect."

"Are you saying you want me to stop?"

She widens her grin. "That's not what I'm saying at all."

"Okay."

"Do what you need to do. What I *can* tell you is that if you chose to do nothing at this point? I'd have all the satisfaction I need right now."

Women are so interesting. They truly can be satisfied without an orgasm. Men are so much more carnal.

But you know what?

I have the capacity to give her an orgasm. Maybe two or three. If she thinks she feels good now? Just wait.

I hover above her for a moment, taking a few seconds to appreciate her flushed beauty. Then I kiss her, dive between those beautiful lips, and tangle my tongue with hers.

She groans into my mouth, and I meet it with a moan of my own. We kiss for a few timeless moments, and then I break it, trailing my lips over her jawline, her neck, her shoulders. Her skin is like silk, and I flick out my tongue to lick her, kiss her, give her a few little sucks. Until I get to those beautiful little tits.

"My God, Ava, you have the most perfect tits." I kiss the top of one and then the other, and then I go in for that beautiful little nipple.

It's hard as a berry when it meets my tongue, and I suck. I suck, fueled by the eager moans coming from her throat.

I've always loved tits. I've been infatuated with them since I was a little boy. And when I came of age? All I could think about was getting my hands on girls' breasts.

I'm still a boob man to this day, which doesn't explain why I've waited until now to touch and suck these wonderful nipples.

Except with Ava it's different. I'm not attracted to her tits. I mean, I am, but her tits are just one part of her. I'm attracted to *every* part of her. Her tight little body. Her beautiful full lips. Her lovely blue eyes and yes, that pink hair. That pink hair that works for her and only her.

I tug on a nipple while I trail my fingers to the other one, twisting it.

Ava arches her back, soft sighs easing from her throat.

"Do you like it? Do you like when I suck on your little titties?"

Her answer is a moan.

And then a breathy, "Yes."

"I could suck on these all day," I say. "My God, you're beautiful."

I close my lips over her nipple once more and suck it. I suck it and I suck it and I suck it. Then I close my teeth around it and bite it. Tug on it.

"Oh God, yes!" she gasps.

I could easily spend another hour just on these beauties. I drop one from my mouth and move to the other one, replacing my lips on the first one with my thumb and forefinger and giving it a good pull.

She's undulating her hips, which means she needs more.

So I remove my fingers from her nipple while I continue to suck on the other and trail them over her soft belly down to her wet pussy.

I circle her clit, and then I move lower, thrusting one finger inside her.

She moans beneath my attentions, spurring me on. I find that spongy G-spot and push on it.

She responds with a gasp.

I continue, and with my thumb, I nudge her clit. I stuff another finger inside her and then withdraw them and push them back in.

"Oh, Brendan..."

Damn.

My cock is responding.

How can I be ready again so quickly?

I'm going to make her come.

And then I'm going to make her come again.

All while sucking on this beautiful nipple.

I work her pussy, and I work her clit, my tempo in tandem. Clit, G-spot, a few thrusts of my fingers.

I get a good rhythm going, and—

"Oh my God, Brendan. So good...so good...so—"

Her pussy contracts against my fingers, and wetness flows over me.

"That's it," I say against her nipple. "Come. Come for me, Ava."

I relish the contractions of her pussy around my fingers, and I continue sucking on her nipple, and when the contractions begin to slow, I begin the movements again.

I pull out another climax from her. And then a third.

Then I remove my fingers from her, and even though I'm hard, I resist the urge to thrust inside her again.

I want her to remember those orgasms.

I want to show her that I can be selfless. That I can give as well as take.

She's lying limp on the bed, her body flushed all over, her lips glistening and parted. I brush my mouth over hers in a chaste kiss.

"You're amazing," I whisper against her mouth. "Beautiful and amazing."

"Brendan..."

My name comes out of her like a sigh.

"Wow."

I can't help but smile. I love giving a woman pleasure, but tonight? I think I enjoyed her orgasms more than I enjoyed my own. That's never happened before.

I gasp when something grips my cock.

It's her warm hand.

"Please," she says. "Come back inside me."

Well, since she said *please*.

I push her up onto her side, and then I slide into her from behind. She's so wet and tight and ready. Again I hold myself inside her for a moment, just savoring the completeness that she makes me feel.

And then I slide in and out of her slowly. Because it's my second time, I can take my time.

Slow and steady wins the race.

Except...

This is Ava Steel, and slow doesn't seem to work with her.

After the first couple of slow glides, the urge to go faster consumes me.

And I pump—pump into her.

Take her with a vengeance, and after five more thrusts, I'm coming again.

Exploding inside her.

Giving a little piece of my heart to Ava Steel.

Is she ready for that?

Doesn't matter.

Ready or not, here I come.

I've given it to her. And now I have to live with the consequences.

CHAPTER TWENTY-THREE

Ava

Sunday is my one day to sleep in, but still I have to get up. Brendan is sleeping beside me, and it feels totally normal.

I rise, wrap a robe around myself, and head into the kitchen to make a pot of coffee.

Does Brendan like coffee? I have no idea. I know so little about this man who I've slept with twice now. And I mean *literally* slept with.

Though that normally might freak me out a little, it doesn't this time. Not at all. I like waking up next to Brendan Murphy.

After I start the coffee, I walk down to the first floor to check out the bakery.

Good. I have enough day-old baked goods that are still fresh enough to make sandwiches for Mom, Brendan, and me today. I don't need to do a small bake.

I go back up, and Brendan is still asleep.

I don't want to wake him, so I get in the shower, and when I'm done, I go back out to the kitchen and pour myself a cup of coffee.

Will he want breakfast? It's eight a.m. Late for me but early for him.

Does he even eat breakfast? Again, so much I don't know.

Well, I want some breakfast. I throw a few slices of the

day-old bread into my toaster, and then I grab some eggs out of the refrigerator.

I don't have any breakfast meats, as I don't like them. I hope that won't disappoint Brendan.

I do have some of Aunt Marjorie's delicious spiced Palisade peach jam. Perfect for toast.

The smell of toast and eggs doesn't rouse Brendan, so I eat breakfast alone, do some quick chores around the apartment, and leaf through a magazine and take the monthly quiz. Turns out I don't put sex before work.

Shocking.

Eleven rolls around, and I have to wake him because we're meeting my mother in an hour.

I walk back into the bedroom and—

He's just getting out of bed.

"Hey, sleepyhead," I say.

"Man. I slept hard for someone who didn't work last night."

"You worked." I smile.

"Glad you enjoyed the efforts."

"I can't think of any time I've enjoyed a man's efforts more." So much truth in those words.

Brendan Murphy is a magnificent lover. Maybe his age is a benefit. No man my own age has ever made me feel like that. He's got a lot more experience. That must be what it is. What else could it be?

I'm certainly not having feelings for him.

At least that's what I keep telling myself...

I can't get swept away. Sex is not love. I must remain in my own head.

He rises, naked, his dick semihard.

I have to stop myself from salivating at the sight of it.

He's such a beautiful specimen of a man. Absolutely majestic with that long hair. He could be royalty.

Then I laugh out loud.

"Something funny?" he says. "I'm standing here naked. You're going to give me a complex."

"If you must know, I was thinking about how you look like royalty. But then I thought about the fact that a lot of actual royals aren't always that good-looking."

"Okay. I'll accept that explanation."

"You look like a highland warrior, Brendan. With that Irish red hair."

"The Highlands are in Scotland."

"I know that. But still…"

"I don't suppose I could convince you to join me in the shower," he says.

"God…" My flesh heats. "That *is* tempting, but I've already showered, and we're meeting my mom soon."

"I understand."

"Do you want anything to eat? I had some breakfast… three hours ago."

He stretches his arms above his head. "No. I can wait until lunch."

"Coffee, then?"

"That I will take you up on."

"Okay. I'll just bring a cup to you in the bathroom."

"Sounds great."

I go back to the kitchen, and of course the coffee is now cold. I heat a cup in the microwave and take it to Brendan, leaving it on the counter in the bathroom. I can't resist taking a quick peek at him through the shower doors.

I leave the bathroom before I'm tempted to strip and join him.

★ ★ ★

"I'm stumped," Mom says, after looking at my text and Brendan's email.

"But you don't seem concerned," I say.

Mom strokes her medium-brown hair, which is the same hue as mine—if I didn't color it. She uses a henna rinse to cover her few gray strands. She's wearing jeans and a gray Mesa College sweatshirt, where Gina is a senior. "No. I have pretty good intuition from all my years doing detective work. I don't get the feeling that this is any kind of threat. But I *am* going to make sure you're safe."

"Meaning?"

"I'll have your father get security set up for you. The family's in the process of hiring a new security company anyway. We'll just add this to that contract."

"Mom, no."

"Ava, sweetheart, this is important to me. Your day-to-day life won't be affected at all."

"I don't need some huge piece of muscle sitting in my bakery all day watching me. It will scare away the customers."

"No, I don't mean an actual bodyguard. Just security keeping watch on you. They're very unobtrusive."

I let out a heavy sigh. "And again . . . my answer's going to be a no on that, Mom."

"Ava," Brendan says, "I think your mom may be right."

"*Et tu*, Brendan?"

"I just think—"

"You just think I'm young and can't take care of myself," I finish for him.

"Ava, don't put words in my mouth," he says. "But if there's any chance that this could be some kind of threat, I agree with your mom. You should be safe."

I roll my eyes. "I'm a grown woman. I can take care of myself."

"No one is saying you can't," Mom says. "But just on the off chance—"

"No."

"Ava…" Mom sighs. "You know what your father's going to say."

"Which is why we're not going to tell him," I say.

"I don't keep secrets from your father, Ava," Mom says. "You know that."

"I'm asking you to keep this in confidence," I say. "At least for now, Mom."

"But he may have some insight into this."

"Dad's not a detective."

"No, but he's a Steel. The Steels have been watching their own backs for decades."

"Why not let your dad in?" Brendan asks. "My dad's in on this."

"The message came to your dad—to you and your dad."

"The message came to the Murphys," he says.

"Right. My message did not come to the Steels. It came to me. Ava Steel."

"Fine," Mom finally relents. "We'll keep this to ourselves for now, but I'm going to need to do some thinking. It may be a puzzle, or a riddle."

"I drew cards for it."

"Did you get any guidance?"

Mom doesn't believe in the tarot, but she understands that I do, and she respects it. I've always loved her for that. Some of my cousins used to give me crap about it, but most of them have come around, usually after I asked them to sit for a reading, and they appreciated—even if they didn't believe—my interpretation.

"The biggest feeling I got is that it has something to do with family. Some kind of change in my family dynamic or some kind of new knowledge."

"Hmm." Mom cocks her head. "Then I'm going to suggest again that we talk to your father. He knows this family as well as anyone."

"But there's also your side of the family, Mom."

"My mother and father are both dead and buried," she says. "I don't have any siblings. You know all this."

"So you think it has to do with the Steel side of the family."

"Most likely. If it has to do with the family at all."

I resist the urge to argue because my mother is ultimately right. My interpretation of the cards does not mean it's the truth. I can only offer guidance based on my own intuition.

In fact, this could have nothing to do with family at all.

"What about numerology?" Brendan says.

I nearly drop my jaw to the table. "You believe in numerology?"

"I didn't say that. It doesn't matter what I believe. What matters is what whoever sent this believes."

"There aren't any numbers in it," Mom says.

"That doesn't matter," I say. "Letters can still be interpreted using numerology. Each letter has a number assigned."

"I had a feeling you'd know about numerology." Brendan smiles.

"It's not a discipline I practice," I say, "but I know of it. For example, I can't tell you which numbers each of these letters correspond to. I would have to look it up."

"It might be worth looking up," Brendan says.

"Sure, I can do that."

"My best guess," Mom says, "based on what I know from my years as a detective, is that it's a code of some sort. Each letter represents another letter. There are computer programs we could use to crack it. That's what I would do first."

"Let's do it, then," Brendan says.

"I can get on that right away." Mom holds up the copy of Brendan's email. "May I keep this?"

"Sure," he replies. "I have a couple more copies."

"Thanks." She folds the paper, tucks it in her purse, and then rises. "The apps are on my computer at home."

"Is there anything else you think may be of significance?" I ask.

"Only the number the text came from, and the email address."

"Brock already checked the number for me. It's untraceable. Probably came from a burner."

"Same for the email address in my case," Brendan says. "When we tried to reply, everything bounced back."

"Okay," Mom says. "Whoever's sending these messages doesn't want to be recognized. Or found. At least not yet."

"What do you mean *not yet*?" I ask.

"The messages were sent for a reason," she says, "and at this point, I think we can assume that they were sent by the same person. Or at least on behalf of the same person."

"I don't understand."

"What I'm saying is, whoever sent these messages will

most likely reveal him or herself. Otherwise, why would they send them? What would be the point?"

I rise and begin gathering the empty sandwich plates. "Well, they could send it because it's something they think we should know."

"If that were the case," Mom says, "why send it in code? If someone were just trying to give you information they thought you needed, they would just give it to you."

"I suppose you're right."

"Someone is setting us up to solve a mystery," Brendan says.

"I'm not sure it's a mystery," Mom says. "Because again, if that were the case, someone would just give you the information. This is a game."

"What do you mean by *game*?" he asks.

"I mean whoever's sending these messages has decided that the two of you—and perhaps your father too, Brendan— are going to be players in a game in which someone is hoping to engage you. And while I understand your curiosity, and I do think you should try to figure out who sent this and what it means, please be cautious."

"Why?" My heart beats rapidly.

"Be aware that you can get sucked into it," Mom says. "I've seen things like this. I've seen people led on wild chases, running around like rats in a maze at the behest of some unknown entity who simply likes to watch."

"You're talking about a sociopath," Brendan says. "In fact..."

"What?" I ask.

"Nothing. Or maybe it's not nothing. My mom was telling me how my dad got sucked into the mystery surrounding his uncle's death at the Steel wedding fifty years ago. He followed every lead and eventually came up with nothing. So I wonder... Was there a sociopath who was sending him on a chase?"

Mom doesn't answer right away, which disturbs me. It's a yes or no question, but she seems to be thinking about it.

"Mom?" I finally say.

"I don't know, Brendan. It's possible."

Strange. My mother rarely says *I don't know*. Even if she doesn't know, she usually puts forth some kind of theory based on her years as a detective and investigator. Her intuition.

"You're freaking me out, Mom."

She smiles, though it seems forced. "Just thinking about sociopaths. The Steel family has had its share of run-ins with them over the years."

My skin goes cold. Goose bumps erupt on my forearms despite my long sleeves.

"Mom, you just said that you got the feeling there was no threat."

"And I still have that feeling, Ava. But I don't put all my faith in a feeling. Just because I don't feel my blood run cold when I read this? That doesn't mean you shouldn't take adequate precautions."

"Security," I say.

"Yes. Please rethink your stance on security," Mom says.

"I'm going to agree," Brendan says. "If your mom and dad are willing to offer you security..."

"We'll offer it for you as well, Brendan, if you want it."

Brendan's brows rise. "No, I'll be fine."

I chuckle, shaking my head. "You know? That's great. I will consent to security... on the condition that you do too, Brendan."

"There's a difference between you and me, Ava."

"Yes, there is. Eleven years and a Y chromosome. That's it. You're no more bulletproof than I am."

"Bulletproof? Ava, there's no reason to believe our lives are being threatened. It's just a good idea to have someone watching."

"I agree," Mom says. "It's never a bad thing to be prepared."

I sigh, throwing my hands in the air. "Fine. But no bodyguards. If you want to have someone sitting outside in the car watching the place, that's one thing. But they better not interfere with my customers and their enjoyment of this establishment."

"I'll make sure," Mom says. "Thanks, honey. This is for the best."

"Wait, wait, wait," Brendan says. "I can't take you up on this offer, Mrs. Steel."

"Please, call me Ruby. And yes, you can."

"No. I understand that you want to protect your daughter, and she's an heiress to your fortune. But the Murphys. No. Just no."

Ava touches my arm. "Brendan, security for you and your father is nothing to my family."

"That's not the point, Ava. The point is that we don't do that. We pay our own way."

"Fine. Then pay my family back for the security."

"With what? I run a bar."

My cheeks warm. How could I have been so rude to Brendan? I'm the one Steel who doesn't live off her family's money. I should know better than to assume Brendan can pay for high-priced security.

"I'm so sorry," I say to Brendan. "Please accept my apology."

"Of course."

Then I turn to my mom. "No security. For either of us."

CHAPTER TWENTY-FOUR

Brendan

That's not the result I wanted. I feel strongly that Ava should have security, but I have to accept her choice as well.

The thing I like best about Ava is that she's her own person. Totally unique.

So I must respect her decisions.

If I want her to have security, I will have to consent to having security as well. And the Steels will foot the bill.

My father will hate it. We have no issues with the Steels now. But I know my father still thinks that their ancestors had something to do with his uncle's death. He'll hate taking money from them, and frankly, I'm not in love with the idea either.

But I need to make sure Ava is protected. I don't feel an imminent threat, but Ava is too important to me to take any chances.

"All right, Mrs. Steel—"

"Please, Ruby."

"Ruby." I clear my throat. "I'll consent to security, but I can't speak for my father."

"Brendan," Ava says. "You don't have to—"

I hold up my hand to stop her. "This is the only way Ava will take security. And I think you should have it, Ava. Not that I think there's anything to worry about, but what if, on

HELEN HARDT

the off chance, someone *does* come after you? I would never forgive myself if I were the reason you didn't have security and adequate protection."

Ava rolls her pretty blue eyes. "Fine. I'll take the security, Mom. But don't make Brendan take it, okay? I changed my mind. I don't think he feels right about it."

An anvil falls off my shoulders. "Thank you, Ava. Ruby, I truly appreciate the offer."

"I understand." Ruby rises. "If you change your mind, it's an open-ended offer."

"Are you leaving, Mom?"

"Yeah. I have some things to do at home this afternoon. But I'm going to check into this. Try to decode the message. In the meantime, I want to know right away if either of you get any more information from anyone out of the ordinary. Even if it seems completely unrelated."

"Yeah, of course," Ava says.

"Make that any message at all that doesn't come from someone you know," Ruby says.

I nod. "Absolutely. We really appreciate your help."

"I would do anything for my Ava."

Ruby smiles, and in that moment, I see a lot of her in Ava. They have the same eyes, the same full lips, the same teeth. Ruby is a beautiful woman, she doesn't wear a lot of makeup, and she dresses mostly in jeans and loose T-shirts. Ava is the same way.

I've heard rumors that everyone in town always wondered how Ruby Lee was able to capture the best-looking Steel brother, Ryan.

But *I've* never wondered.

Because I see in her a lot of what I see in Ava. They're

both gorgeous women, just not in the traditional Steel sense.

But that doesn't make them any less beautiful.

Ruby leaves, and Ava turns to me.

"I'm sorry. I shouldn't have put you on the spot like that about the security."

"It's okay. You were just concerned about me, and I'm touched by that. But I do want *you* to have security, Ava. You live here alone. And not to play the gender card—"

"But you're going to," she says dryly.

"Right. I'm going to. You're a woman living alone."

"Yeah, but in the middle of Snow Creek. If anything happened to me, someone would hear it."

"Not necessarily. Not everyone lives above their place of business like you do."

"You do," she says.

"You're going to make me play the gender card again." I sigh and place my hand on her arm. "Besides, even if I were in my own place—which I'm not at the moment—you're a few buildings down from me. What are the chances I'd be able to hear you if something happened?"

"Maybe Willow would hear me."

"She's closer than I am, above the beauty salon, but what if she did? She's a woman living alone, just like you are."

Ava opens her mouth, but I gesture for her to stop.

"I know exactly what you're going to say. Just because you're a woman doesn't mean you can't take care of yourself, and I agree. But you against three men who are armed?"

"You wouldn't do any better against three men who are armed."

Well, I would, but I'll keep that to myself for now. She knows that as well as I do. In addition, what if someone *does*

HELEN HARDT

hear her? But what they hear is a gunshot? It would be too late to do anything.

But Ava's feeling empowered, and I don't want to discourage that.

"The point is, your family can afford to offer you security, and while I understand and respect the fact that you don't like taking their money, this seems like a no-brainer to me."

"If it's such a no-brainer, why won't *you* take their offer?"

"Because I'm *not* a member of your family, Ava. It's that simple."

She opens her mouth again but then closes it.

I give her arm a squeeze. "So you do understand."

"Yes, I do. I understand. I just want you as protected as I am."

"I own a firearm, and I know how to use it," I tell her.

Her eyes go wide.

"I know your father and mother both shoot, and so do Dale, Donny, and Brock. Did you ever learn how to shoot a gun?"

"God, no. I hate guns."

"I could teach you how to handle a weapon, if you'd like me to."

She shakes her head vehemently. "I'm just not comfortable with that, Brendan. But thank you for the offer."

"Well, as your mother says, it's an open-ended offer. If you change your mind, all you have to do is ask."

"Trust me." She steps back from me, hunches her shoulders. "I will *never* change my mind."

★ ★ ★

"So you found another place to stay at night," my mother says over dinner.

"He's a thirty-five-year-old man, Lori," my father says.

"I understand that, Sean. I'm just making conversation."

Right. I don't believe that for a minute. My mother is trying to get information out of me. But I won't out Ava Steel. She may not be ready to tell anyone that she and I are . . .

What the hell *are* we, anyway?

Dating, I guess.

But dating doesn't usually mean falling into bed the first time you're together. Definitely not for Ava Steel.

"Is that a problem?" I ask.

Mom smiles, handing me a bowl of green beans. "Of course not, honey. I just worry when you don't come home."

"When I'm not living here, you never know when I don't come home."

"I know that." She spreads butter on her roll. "You'll understand one day when you have children. Well, maybe you won't, actually. It's kind of a mother thing."

"It's a mother thing," Dad says. "I love you, son, and I'll always be concerned about you. But I don't worry when you don't come home at night."

"Thanks, Dad."

"Fathers and mothers are different," Mom says. "I always worry, but when you're not living under our roof, I don't know whether you come home at night or not, so while I'm always worrying because you're my son and I'm your mother, it's a little less real when I don't expect you home."

"Would you like me to let you know when I'm not going to

be home for dinner or to spend the night?"

"Lori . . ." Dad says.

"Well"—Mom looks down at her plate—"it would be nice if you'd let me know about dinner. Because then I don't have to make as much."

"Absolutely," I agree. "I'll be more careful from now on. That was rude of me. I should let you know."

She smiles then, takes a bite of her roll.

"Sometimes, though, I don't know until fairly late whether I won't be home for dinner."

"Just do the best you can, Brendan," Dad says.

"Will do." I'm still holding the bowl full of beans, so I serve myself a couple of spoons full and hand it off to Dad.

The three of us are quiet for the rest of dinner.

Afterward, Dad motions for me—quietly—to join him in the study.

"Sorry about your mother," he says.

"It's okay. It's a little annoying, but she's my mom and I love her."

"I do too. When will your place be ready?"

"Insurance paid me an amazing amount," I say. "So I was able to get the whole thing expedited. Less than a week."

Dad raises his eyebrows. "That's interesting. Insurance companies usually try to screw you over."

"I was surprised too, but I'm not going to complain."

"Right. But something seems a little off to me."

"Dad, can you for once just take something good that happens and not try to overanalyze it?"

My father's always been kind of a cynic. He's not depressed or anything, but he's just always sure there's some other morsel of information that we need. It's why he still thinks there's something he missed about his uncle. Just a glass-half-empty kind of guy.

"All right, Brendan," Dad says. "It's your policy, and it's your home."

"True, but you still own the building."

"I do, but it will be all yours when I pass. You just handle this as you see fit."

"I will."

"Now . . . what did you learn from Ruby Steel? Did she have any insight into what these messages may mean?"

"She thinks it's code for something, and she didn't perceive any immediate threat."

"Good. I don't think it's a threat either. I think it's information, and I just have that poking feeling that this has something to do with your great-uncle."

"If that's the case, why would Ava get the same message?"

"Because the Steels have always been involved in what happened to him. I've known that from the beginning. I just couldn't prove it."

The urge to defend Ava and her family hits me hard. "None of the Steels alive today had anything to do with it. They can't be charged with any crimes. They weren't even alive then."

"I know that. But they may have information. Information they're keeping to themselves because they don't want their sainted name tainted."

"I don't have any beef with the Steels," I say. "Ha! No pun intended."

"Puns are supposed to be funny, Brendan." Dad shakes his head, chuckling. "I know you don't. Neither do I."

I liked my beef pun, but I'm relieved the tension has dissipated a little. Still, I know my dad. I know when he's not being completely truthful. He may *think* he doesn't have any issue with the current Steels, but he does. Why else would he use the term *sainted name*? The Steels are hardly saints, and they've never claimed to be.

What is Dad going to think when he finds out I'm involved with one of them? Halfway in love with her already?

I sigh. I don't like keeping things from my father, so no time like the present...

"Dad, there's something you should know."

"What's that?"

"The last two nights, when I didn't come home?"

"Brendan, that's none of my business. You don't owe me any explanations."

"So you're not the least bit curious?"

"Of course I am." He laughs. "But I respect your privacy."

I clear my throat. "Thank you for that. I know you do, and I appreciate it. But you should know... Those two nights? I was at Ava Steel's place."

Dad's eyebrows nearly fly off his head.

"That surprises you, I see."

"Yes. It surprises me that you would date any Steel, but Ava? She's a horse of a different color, no pun intended."

"Puns are supposed to be funny," I mimic dryly.

"Touché."

"Ava is a lovely young woman."

"Did I say she wasn't?"

"Well, you seem to be implying something."

"Brendan, no. I think Ava's great. I love her bread. Everyone in town does. She's just... different."

"Which is why like her," I say. "She's attractive and intelligent and so... insightful."

"Okay." Dad shuffles some papers. "This does put a little kink in my plans."

"I had a feeling it would. I don't want to go after the Steel family. They had nothing to do with my great-uncle, as you know. And if they're holding secrets? They must have a good reason to be doing so."

"Brendan, if their secrets didn't have anything to do with us, why were documents regarding their family hidden on property we own?"

My dad makes a good point. One I've acknowledged but would prefer not to.

"Still," I say, "those documents pertain to things that happened a long time ago."

I consider the documents.

Specifically the one that transfers all Steel property to Ryan Steel—Ava's father.

What does it all mean?

But Dad is right ultimately. Because Ava and I both got the same message, we're connected somehow.

I just don't know how.

"Ruby has apps," I say to my father. "Apps that can help her decode the message. She's going to get back to me as soon as she can."

"All right. Still, I'd like to do our own research."

"Ruby and Ava can be trusted," I say. "I'd stake my life on it."

"I have nothing against Ruby Steel or her daughter," Dad says. "I'm sure they're both very trustworthy individuals. But they are Steels at their core. And if there is something their family doesn't want us to know, they *will* keep it from us."

I say nothing.

I have no counter for my father's statement, because in my heart?

I hear its truth.

CHAPTER TWENTY-FIVE

Ava

I decide to visit my uncle Joe in the evening.

Brendan and I didn't make any plans, and Sunday is my one day and evening off, so I figured why not?

I didn't call ahead of time, but we Steels drop in on each other all the time. No one minds.

I don't know if Brock will be there. He lives in the guesthouse behind Jonah's house. Rory is moving in with him soon, if she hasn't already.

I pull into the long driveway, get out of my car, and walk to the door.

I draw in a breath.

Then I knock.

The door opens, and my aunt Melanie stands there. "Ava, what a nice surprise. We were just sitting down to dinner. Can you join us?"

"I... That's not why I showed up."

Aunt Melanie laughs. "I know that, silly. But Brock and Rory are here. I'm sure they'd love to see you."

She holds the door open for me, and I enter.

After saying a quick hello to the dogs, I walk through to the kitchen, where the other three are seated.

Brock furrows his brow when he sees me.

He's not angry. He's just wondering why I'm here.

"Ava's going to join us for dinner." Aunt Melanie nods to her housekeeper, Patrice. "Could you set another place, please?"

"Right away." Patrice smiles.

Soon I have a place set in front of me, and I'm seated at the table.

"What brings you out this way?" Uncle Joe asks.

"I have some questions, actually." I turn my gaze to Brock.

"I haven't had a chance to chat with my dad yet about that," he says.

"Not yet? It's been two days."

"What's this about, Brock?" Uncle Joe asks.

Brock clears his throat. "Ava was asking me about some of the things that are going on right now. I didn't know if I was at liberty to discuss them."

"You see," I say, "I got this strange text message. Brendan Murphy got the same one. Only his came in an email."

"What?" Brock says, kind of harshly.

"Oh, Brendan didn't tell you?"

"Why would he tell me?"

"I don't know. But he and his dad got an email with the same cryptic message."

"Brock," Uncle Joe says, "what is she talking about?"

I pull my phone up and show him my text message.

This time Uncle Joe furrows his brow. "I don't have any idea what this means."

"I thought it might be a *Star Wars* reference," Brock says, "but Dave says it's not."

"Well," Uncle Joe says, "Dave ought to know."

I stop myself from giggling. "I had my mother look at it,

and she's pretty sure it's not anything threatening. She thinks it's a simple puzzle."

"Why would anyone send you a puzzle?" Uncle Joe asks.

"That's just it," I say. "I don't know. But it clearly has something to do with me and with the Murphys."

"Our family has a bit of a troubled history with the Murphys," Uncle Joe says.

"Yeah, I know all about that." I take a sip of the glass of water that Patrice set in front of me.

"So Brendan told you about his great-uncle," Uncle Joe says.

"Yeah. I mean, I already knew, but he went into a little more detail."

"What kind of detail?" Brock asks.

"Not much. All he knows is that his dad tried to figure out exactly what happened to his uncle and ran into dead end after dead end."

"I admit it's perplexing," Uncle Joe says. "And I've learned, in the recent past, that my own father was not the paragon of virtue the town would like to think he was."

"What?" I widen my eyes.

"Seems our family has kept some secrets from us over the years," Brock says.

"Brock . . ." Rory admonishes him.

Brock shrugs. "She has the right to know. Just like I had the right to know."

"The right to know what?" I ask. "What are you two talking about?"

Uncle Joe sighs.

"Ava," Melanie says, "this is really something your mother and father should talk to you about."

"Oh, no," I say. "You're not opening the door and then slamming it in my face. I came here to get information. Seems like you're telling me there's more information than I even know about."

"I agree with Aunt Melanie," Uncle Joe says. "You need to talk to your parents first."

"Dad," Brock says, "you haven't even told Uncle Ryan everything."

My mouth drops open again. "What the hell is going on?"

"Jonah," Aunt Melanie says, "I agree, but she is your niece."

"Yes, and I'm her uncle, not her father. This is Ryan's call, not mine."

I stand then. "Aunt Melanie, thank you so much for offering to feed me tonight, but I regret that I can't stay."

"Ava, please," Uncle Joe says. "There are things you just don't understand."

"I'm twenty-four years old, Uncle Joe. I'm not a child."

"We know that, sweetheart," Uncle Joe says. "It's just—"

"Don't try to justify anything," I say.

"You need to tell Uncle Ryan, Dad," Brock says.

"I see that."

"Why are you keeping something from my father, anyway?" I demand of Uncle Joe. "He's your brother, for God's sake."

Uncle Joe doesn't reply. He simply twists his lips slightly.

I shake my head. "Thank you for nothing." I leave the kitchen, walk through the living room and entryway, and out the door.

I'm tempted to drive to my mother and father's house, but something stops me.

I need some guidance first.

And that means I'm going home to draw some cards.

★ ★ ★

I choose only one card.

The guidance I seek is some understanding of the conversation with Brock and Uncle Joe. Why they're keeping things from my father.

And I gasp aloud when the card hits the table.

It's the hierophant again. He wears red priestly robes and a crown. Two fingers of his right hand are pointed upward, and in his left hand he holds a triple cross.

In all the years that I've practiced the tarot, I've never drawn the hierophant with regard to myself . . . until a few days ago when I first got the ominous text message.

One difference though.

This time the card is in the reverse position.

The word that comes to my mind as soon as I see the card is *hypocrisy*.

Hypocrisy with regard to whom? Brock? Uncle Joe? My own father?

I'm not sure, but something pokes at the back of my neck.

There is knowledge out there—secret knowledge—and this message I received has something to do with it.

And my family's involvement?

Whatever it is, in some way, I may find that it's hypocritical.

That is what my intuition tells me.

A wave of sadness surges through me.

I may have chosen to separate myself financially from my

family, but I love them without question. I always have. This card doesn't change that fact.

But they are people. Individuals. And no individual is perfect.

Not even someone from the Steel family.

CHAPTER TWENTY-SIX

Brendan

A week later, my place is ready. The insurance money paid for everything, including great-quality new furniture, which has already been moved in. A leather couch and recliner are the focus of my living room, way nicer than what I had previously. Bending Ava over that new couch . . .

Damn. Already the image is seared into my mind.

The hardwood floors are freshly polished, and I nearly slid across them when I first walked into the place.

Hell, this is way better than it was before.

I've missed Ava, but she's been quiet lately. We've shared a few lunches, but the couple of times I've asked her to have dinner, she's said she's busy.

Perhaps we aren't meant to be.

I will have to accept that.

I asked her a few times if she had heard from her mother about the message, and she simply shook her head.

Now that my place is ready, I'm going to try once more. I'll ask her to come over to dinner. I make a mean hamburger.

I walk to the bakery at five fifty-five. That way I'll be able to get into the building through the front door. As it turns out, she's standing right inside the door, turning the sign from *Open* to *Closed* just as I arrive.

"Ava," I say through the door. "I know you can hear me. Come on. We need to talk."

She—somewhat reluctantly?—opens the door. "Hi, Brendan."

"Look, I don't know what I did to upset you, but—"

She wipes her hand on her flour-covered apron. "You didn't do anything. This has nothing to do with you."

"Then why haven't you been willing to have dinner with me?"

"It's not that I don't want to, it's just..." She hangs her head. "I'm afraid I wouldn't be very good company right now."

"Shouldn't I be the judge of that?"

"I've had a lot on my mind." She walks to the counter, grabs a towel, and begins wiping it down.

"Hasn't your mom gotten back to you with any possible solutions to our puzzle?"

"She hasn't, and that's just part of the problem." Ava leaves the rag on the counter and pulls the hairnet off her head. Her hair is tied up in a messy bun. "My mom is a smart woman. Not just smart, but shrewd and clever. An excellent detective and investigator. But if *she* hasn't come up with anything yet? Especially with all the code-breaking apps she claimed to have? Something's rotten here."

I walk toward her. "That does seem strange."

"It's my family, Brendan. Like I said, it's not you at all. I've been ruminating on this for almost a week now, and none of it makes any sense."

"Do you want to talk about it?"

"I would, but there's not really anything to talk about. It's more feelings."

"Then we'll talk about feelings."

"It would bore you to tears."

"Ava, nothing about you could ever bore me to tears."

She smiles then. Sort of. "You know what? I've missed you."

"Good news, then. From now on? I'm only three buildings away."

She smiles. "Your place is done? Already?"

"It's all done. No more sleeping over at my mom and dad's house. I'd love to give you the grand tour of my tiny place. I'll even cook for you."

She tilts her head. "You cook?"

"More like I fry hamburgers on my George Foreman grill, but yeah."

"You know?" This time her smile is genuine. "I'd like that, Brendan. I know I've been blowing you off, and I'm sorry. I haven't wanted to."

"That's some consolation, I guess," I say. "But let me make my position clear on this. I like you a lot, Ava. I'd like to see where this goes. I know we jumped into bed pretty quickly, and believe me, I'm not sorry about that. But I want you to know that you're more than just sex to me."

"I know that. If I thought I were just sex to you, I never would've gone to bed with you a second time."

"Yeah, that was your idea as I recall." I laugh.

"It was, and now that I look at you"—her eyelids flutter—"I have no idea why I have been depriving myself for a week."

"I don't either." I cup her cheek. "Come on. I'll make you some supper."

Ava turns away and grabs something. She hands me a bag of large rolls. "Buns. For the burgers."

I take the plastic bag from her. "Perfect. Thanks."

"I'm a mess. I need to shower first."

"You can shower at my place," I say. "In fact, I think I could use a shower myself."

CHAPTER TWENTY-SEVEN

Ava

He's inside me, fucking me up against his newly tiled shower wall.

Again, the burn. Brendan is so huge, and he tunnels through me like a flaming freight train.

The water sprinkles over us, and my hair is plastered to my face and shoulders, as is his.

He pounds into me and brings me to orgasm. His pubic bone presses against my clit with each thrust.

"Brendan!" I scream out.

"That's it, baby. You come. You come for me."

He thrusts, thrusts, thrusts . . .

Until—

"Yes, God," he grits out.

I feel his release even as I'm knee-deep into my own. It makes me soar higher, ever higher, until finally . . .

He slides out of me, and my feet hit the floor of the shower.

We wash each other's hair then, and I was right. Brendan's hair is even longer than mine, and so silky. I love the feel of it between my fingers.

Once we're both squeaky clean, Brendan turns off the shower. He gives me a large white bath towel and helps me wrap it around my body. Then he takes another towel and dries my hair for me.

HELEN HARDT

All this while he's still standing naked and dripping wet.

Too soon, he covers himself with a towel and dries his own hair.

"You know," I say, "I came over here in my apron and my work clothes. I don't have anything to change into."

He lifts his eyebrows. "I don't think that's a problem at all."

"Do you have a T-shirt I could put on?"

"I was thinking we'd just stay naked tonight."

"You want to fry hamburgers while you're naked?"

He laughs then. "Interesting point. I'll find us both something."

Moments later, he's clad in jeans and a Dragonlock T-shirt, and I'm wearing a simple white T-shirt that falls midway to my knees.

"What can I help you with?" I take a look at his brand-new kitchen. Stainless-steel appliances, white and black tile that contrasts nicely with the hardwood throughout the rest of the small apartment.

"Nothing. You already did your part by making the hamburger buns."

"Seriously, I'm glad to help," I say.

"I know you are, but there's no need. I'm just going to fry up some burgers, throw some cheddar on them, and put them on your buns." His eyes twinkle. "Then later, I'm going to put something else between your buns."

"I could cut up some lettuce and tomatoes," I say, the warmth of a blush coating my cheeks.

"Okay," he finally relents. "There are a couple tomatoes in the refrigerator. There should be some lettuce too. I had groceries brought over earlier."

I open the refrigerator. Two tomatoes sit on the top

shelf along with a head of iceberg lettuce. I use green leaf or butter lettuce on the sandwiches at the bakery. They're more flavorful, but iceberg is good on a burger. Adds some crunch.

Once I have the tomato sliced and the lettuce ripped into hamburger-size pieces, I take the initiative and pull out the cheddar cheese for Brendan.

"Did you want something to drink?" I ask.

"Just water's fine for me. I'm around booze all the time, so I don't drink very often."

"Good man." I fill two glasses and add ice. "I can't believe your place got done so quickly."

"Money talks," he says. "I got an amazing payoff from the insurance company."

I cock my head to the side. "Really? You must have a great policy."

"Apparently so," he says. "They even waived my deductible, which I wasn't expecting."

"Why would they do that?"

"I didn't ask questions," he says. "Since I'm kind of broke right now, I decided it wasn't in my best interest to make it an issue."

I nod. Even though I don't use my family's money, I'm always aware that I have a safety net. It's easy to take that for granted. Brendan doesn't have that lifeboat.

Still though, I can't help wondering why his insurance company would waive his deductible.

Not that I have a lot of experience with insurance, but I do own a policy on my bakery that I pay for myself. And because I pay it myself, I have a deductible. A rather high one.

I've never had to make a claim, thank goodness, but if I ever do, I certainly won't expect the insurer to waive a deductible that I agreed to. Something smells a little strange here.

But I don't want to spoil my evening with Brendan. He's happy to have this place back, and I'm happy for him.

"How'd you get out of working tonight?" I ask.

"I already had the day off planned, since my place was going to be ready. I wanted to get everything moved back in. Plus, I just hired a new bartender."

"Ah..."

"You know," he says, turning away from the grill, "that was a better christening to that new shower than I ever could've hoped for."

I can't help a smile. "I enjoyed it too."

"I've missed you, Ava."

It's not the first time he's said this, and his words make me warm. "I've missed you too."

"So no more," he says. "No more shutting me out, okay?"

I nod. I really wasn't fair to him over the last week. I just couldn't get that reading out of my mind. The one about my family.

Secret knowledge.

Hypocrisy.

I don't understand any of it.

My family has always been my rock. The people I could depend on and count on. I don't want to think badly of them.

It's just a tarot reading, I remind myself. *They're not always accurate.*

But for me, with my own intuition, they are accurate more often than not, which is why this is bothering me so.

"Earth to Ava."

I jerk upward. "Yeah?"

"You were miles away for a minute." He gives me a chaste kiss on my warm cheek. "What are you thinking about?"

"Something I'd rather not be thinking about, not while I'm with you."

"I'll decide whether that's good or bad later," he says. "In the meantime, burgers are served."

I inhale. You can't be a member of the Steel family and not enjoy the smell of freshly cooked beef. I eat less meat than most of my family, but tonight, I'm looking forward to a good old-fashioned burger.

"Smells great," I say.

"Good." He sets the burgers on his small table and then holds out a chair for me.

"Thank you." I take a seat.

"Not a problem." He pushes the platter of burgers toward me and sits across from me. "Please, help yourself."

I build myself an awesome-looking burger—tomato, lettuce, very little onion, and a touch of mayo—and slide the platter toward Brendan. I take a bite and then squeal as the juices run down my chin. I hastily wipe the drips with my napkin.

"Do I make the juiciest burgers on the planet or what?" Brendan smiles.

"I've got to say, these are fantastic. And that's coming from a woman who was raised on beef."

"This is Steel beef," Brendan says, "but do I take it that no one in your family makes burgers quite this juicy?"

"Aunt Marj comes close," I say, "but she's a professional chef."

"So I beat a professional chef, huh?" Brendan grins. "That's high praise."

"Honestly, Brendan, I have nothing but high praise for you right now."

My cheeks warm at the sentiment I just allowed to come out of my mouth.

I've tried.

I've tried to listen to the cards. To not get swept away with the clear chemistry that Brendan and I share.

In fact, that's a big part of the reason why I steered clear of him for about a week. Even after those amazing two nights together.

The cards have been so strange lately. Never have they given me reason to doubt my family.

But I don't want to think about the cards tonight. I want to enjoy this meal with Brendan and hope he'll forgive me for dripping burger juice down the front of his T-shirt.

"I've been thinking about my tattoo," I say.

"Have you found an image that you like?" He takes a bite of burger.

"Not yet. But it's going to have something to do with the tarot I think."

He swallows, wipes his chin with his napkin. "An image from one of your cards maybe?"

"Yes, but I haven't decided which one."

"Which one speaks to you the most?"

"That's kind of a loaded question because they all speak to me, depending on when I draw them and what question I'm asking."

"Okay, that makes sense."

"But the one that seems to be gravitating toward me right now—and I don't think I want it as a tattoo—is the hierophant."

"What's a hierophant?"

"To the ancient Greeks, a hierophant was a person who brought people to religion. Brought them to the presence of a deity or something else holy. He or she was considered an interpreter of mysteries, of secret knowledge or sacred truth."

"Interesting."

"But in the tarot, it has another interpretation as well. It represents conformity to social standards."

Brendan laughs out loud, nearly choking on his bite of burger. He wipes his mouth. "Sorry about that. But conformity to social standards? That's not you, Ava. That's the opposite of Ava."

"Right? This is a card that I've never drawn for myself, until the night I got that text."

"I suppose that makes sense. You're faced with a mystery regarding the text."

"Right. And I drew it again last Sunday, only in reverse."

"What does it mean in reverse?" Brendan asks.

"Well, the meaning of the cards have to be interpreted based on the question that you're asking at the time."

"All right. What were you asking?"

"I was asking about my family. About the mysteries. And that's when I drew the hierophant card in reverse. And the word that came to my mind? It was *hypocrisy.*"

Brendan's eyes go wide. "With regard to your family?"

"Yes, and I can see you're as surprised as I am."

"I've known the Steels my whole life," he says. "I've always known all of you to be good people. Certainly not hypocrites."

"I know."

"So that's what it means? That card in reverse means hypocrisy?"

I clear my throat. "It's not that simple. The tarot isn't

an either-or kind of thing. The card is still the card, even in reverse. You have to take its original meaning into account as well."

"All right."

"Plus, cards can be interpreted differently depending on the question that is asked and depending on the person who's reading them. It's not an exact science. It's not science at all."

"I'd love to learn more about it. I know nothing about tarot cards."

"Why would you want to learn more about it?"

"Because it's important to you, Ava. And that makes it interesting to me."

I stop my jaw from dropping.

I like Brendan, and boy, the sex is amazing. But with this one statement, I've lost a little piece of my heart to him.

Most guys in my life—and there haven't been that many—have rolled their eyes at the tarot. In fact, one of them thought I was a witch. Which isn't an insult, but in his ignorance, he thought it was.

But not Brendan Murphy.

He accepts me for who I am.

Except that the tarot can't be explained with any simplicity. I've studied it for years, and I'm still a novice in many ways.

"There's no simple way to explain the tarot," I say.

"Give me the condensed version, then."

I laugh. "There is no condensed version, Brendan."

"Okay, I give." He grabs the bottle of ketchup and squirts a small portion onto his plate. "But I do find it interesting. Especially when you did that reading for me. It made me think differently about a lot of things."

"That's really what the tarot is for," I say. "At least the way I use it. Sometimes it spurs something regarding a question I'm seeking answers to. Or regarding something I'm seeking guidance on, even when I don't have a specific question."

"I think it's amazing," he says. "In fact, Ava Steel, I think *you're* amazing."

There go the cheeks again. They're on fire, and I'm pretty sure I'm three shades of red.

But I smile. And I take another bite of my juicy burger.

And I feel . . .

I feel *good*. Even with this mystery surrounding us, even with the budding doubts I'm having about my family, even with the feeling that my mother has been avoiding my questions—I feel *good* in Brendan's presence.

I feel good about taking this chance.

I'm about to say so when his phone buzzes.

"It's my dad. Do you mind?"

"Of course not. Go ahead."

CHAPTER TWENTY-EIGHT

Brendan

"Hi, Dad," I say into the phone.

"Brendan, I'm glad I caught you. Are you working tonight?"

"No. I took the evening off, got someone to fill in. I wanted to enjoy my first night back in my place."

"Oh, I'm sorry. Do you have company?"

"I do, as a matter of fact. Is this important?"

"It is, actually. We got another message."

My pulse quickens slightly. "Through Hardy's office again?"

"Yeah. I'm over there now."

"Why do these things always happen in the middle of my dates?"

"Are you with Ava again?"

"I am."

"Well, since she got the same message the first time, I suppose it's okay if you bring her along."

I glance at Ava, who's still eating her burger. She's wearing nothing but one of my T-shirts. We'll have to stop at her place so she can put on some clean clothes.

"I would tell you it could wait," I say to my father, "but I've got to say I'm curious, and Ava will be too."

Ava's eyebrows rise at her name.

"We'll be there as soon as we can." I end the call.

"What was that all about?" Ava asks.

"My father and I got another message through Hardy's office."

Ava drops her jaw. "I left my phone in the bakery. I wonder if I got another message as well."

"I figured we'd have to stop at the bakery anyway so you can put some clean clothes on."

"Yeah, I can put my dirty jeans on and walk home in the T-shirt, I guess. How cold is it out?"

"I don't know, but it's only three buildings down. We'll take the alley and we'll be fine. You can wear one of my jackets."

"Did your dad say what the message was?"

"He did not. But I'm assuming it's something cryptic again."

"I'll check my phone when we get to my place. I hope it's not dead."

★ ★ ★

Ava's phone *was* dead, so she plugged it in and will check later to see if she got any messages. We walk into the sheriff's office.

"Hey," I say.

"Brendan." Dad looks up from a piece of paper he's holding and hands it to me. "What do you make of this?"

I read the words on the page.

They make absolutely no sense at all.

I hand them to Ava.

She reads out loud.

"When echoes navigate down yonder, many anchors destroy ideas generated about neglect." She looks up at me.

"That's clear as mud." She glances at the paper again. "Wait a minute. The last one said *Ask the Murphys*. This one says *Ask the Murphys and the Steels.*"

I grab the page from her. "I didn't even look that far."

"It says it, clear as day." She turns her gaze to the sheriff. "Hardy, why didn't you call my dad or my uncles?"

"The Murphys were mentioned first," Hardy says.

"And you're here," I say. "You're a Steel."

Ava nods. "True, but everyone knows the patriarch of the family is Uncle Joe. You should probably call him."

"I will," Hardy says, "but before I do, is there anything either of you can tell me that could make any sense out of this? Including why these emails are coming to my office? Especially since you got the same message last time to your phone, Ava."

"Honestly, I don't know," she says, "unless … I'll bet my entire family has some kind of filter on all their email accounts and phone numbers."

"Wouldn't you have that as well, then?" Hardy asks.

"No. I pay my own way, Sheriff. I bought my bakery with money I earned myself, and I pay the mortgage with my profits. I don't use my family's money, and that includes for my phone. I have my own account."

Hardy smiles. "I had heard rumors to that effect. I'm proud of you, Ava."

"Proud of me? Why?"

"Because you're standing on your own two feet."

"And you think my family doesn't stand on their own two feet?"

Hardy's cheeks redden a bit. "I didn't mean anything bad by my statement, Ava."

"I may choose not to use my family's money," Ava says,

"but I assure you, Sheriff, that I love them. And I don't want to hear you say anything bad about them."

"I didn't mean—"

"Sheriff," I interrupt, hoping to bring this conversation to a halt. "Do you have any idea what this message means?"

"Hell no. Neither does your father."

"And neither do I. It doesn't even make sense. Echoes don't navigate. And *down yonder*? When was the last time anyone used the word yonder? And *many anchors destroy ideas generated about neglect*? How can an anchor destroy an idea?"

"I'm not sure it's supposed to make sense," Dad says. "The other one didn't make sense either. There's obviously some kind of code here that we need to break."

"I talked to my mom," Ava says. "I thought she might have some ideas from her years of investigation."

"And did she?" Hardy asks.

"She thinks it's a puzzle of some sort. But we're not sure why it's coming to me and to Brendan. She said she would check some things with her software at home, but she hasn't gotten back to me."

"Hasn't she?" Hardy asks.

Ava shakes her head. "No, and to be frank, it's upsetting. It's almost like she doesn't want to—"

"Doesn't want to what?" my father asks.

Ava looks at her feet. "I can't. I love my family. I love my mom. I'm just making things up at this point. There's no reason why my mom wouldn't be investigating this."

"Wait," Hardy says. "Are you saying that you think your mom is *deliberately* not looking into this?"

"Have *you* looked into it?" Ava asks.

"No. It's not an issue for my office."

"How can it not be an issue for your office?" Ava asks. "The message for the Murphys—and this time for us as well— came *through* your office."

"It did, but no crime has been committed here."

Ava says nothing then.

Hardy's right. It's not a crime to send an email to the sheriff's office.

"We haven't looked any further into it other than letting you guys know it's here."

"Fair enough," I say.

"What's interesting, though," Dad says, "is that these two messages are seemingly unrelated. Which means there *is* some kind of code at work. I can look into that."

"That'd be great, Dad. Now that you're retired, you have more time than Ava and I do."

"Absolutely. I'm glad to do it." He turns to Hardy. "If there's nothing else, I'll get out of your hair, and I'm sure my son would like to get back to his date."

Ava's cheeks turn pink.

My God, she's so beautiful.

"I'll walk you home," I say to Ava.

I plan to walk her to my home, but I don't want to embarrass her in front of all these other people.

She nods. "Thank you."

We walk, hand in hand, through the back alleyway, passing her bakery along the way.

But when we reach the bakery—

I stop, staring at two figures. "What are they doing here?"

Ava's cousins, Donny and Brock, are waiting at the back of the bakery.

"Guys?" Ava says.

"We need to talk to you, cuz."

"All right." She unlocks the door. "You coming up, Brendan?"

Donny and Brock look at each other.

"We need to talk to you alone," Brock says.

"It's okay," I say. "If you need me, I'm only three buildings away."

I brush my lips over Ava's.

Then I head for home.

CHAPTER TWENTY-NINE

Ava

"Thanks for interrupting my date," I say snidely, as they follow me up the stairs to my apartment.

"Got anything to drink up here?" Donny asks as we enter my place.

I point to the kitchen. "Help yourself to whatever you can find. I'm not a waitress."

"What's with the attitude?" This from Brock.

"Sorry."

I do have an attitude, and I realize it's because of what I read in my cards.

The secrets my family is keeping. The hypocrisy that may lie within them.

But it's only a feeling at this point—an interpretation. I could very well be wrong.

It wouldn't be the first time my interpretation of a reading was off. It happens to everyone who practices the tarot.

"Brendan mentioned that he's only a few buildings away," Donny says. "Does that mean his place is fixed already?"

I nod. "Apparently the insurance payoff was huge, and he was able to get everything expedited, so now he's back home. They even waived his deductible, which is strange."

"It's not that strange," Brock says.

I lift my eyebrows. "What's that supposed to mean?"

"It means," Donny says, "that because of a bad decision I made, Brendan's place was empty and available to be trashed."

"Oh my God." I rub my forehead. "Please don't tell me you subsidized his insurance payoff."

"We *paid* his insurance payoff," Donny says. "You really think any insurance company would get money to a person that quickly?"

"Damn it," I say. "Brendan and his family will hate that."

"Which is why Brendan never has to know," Brock says.

"I'm dating the man. I'm not going to keep secrets from him."

"No one is asking you to," Donny says. "Just don't tell him."

"What if he asks me straight-out?"

Donny laughs. "Is he really going to ever ask you, 'Ava, did your family pay my insurance claim?'"

"Seriously?" I rub my temples against a headache I know is coming. "You guys have put me in a shitty position. I hate this. Sometimes I just hate our family's money."

Brock rolls his eyes. "That's pretty clear, since you've chosen not to use it."

"That's not what I mean, and you both know it. But you know what? Money doesn't solve everything."

"It solves a hell of a lot," Donny says.

"But not everything." I whip my hands to my hips. "Why are you here, anyway?"

"Well, it wasn't to spill the beans about Brendan's payoff." Brock eyes Donny. "Nice going, Don."

"Hey, nobody told *me* they were dating." Donny slaps the back of Brock's head. "You couldn't have let me in on that fact?"

"Did the fact that Brendan walked me home and kissed me good night not clue you in?" I ask.

"Yeah, I just didn't think..."

"You didn't *think*," I say. "I know you guys mean well. Our family always means well. But Brendan will hate this. And if I'm going to have any kind of relationship with him—"

"Relationship?" Donny asks. "The two of you are serious?"

"I don't know yet. But I'd like the option."

"He's quite a bit older than you are," Donny says. "He's Dale's age, for God's sake."

"And Dale's wife is ten years younger than he is," I say. "Look, it took me a while to get over the age thing too, but Brendan is a great guy."

"No one said he isn't," Brock says.

"He's an even greater guy than I thought he was. He listens to me. He's interested in what I have to say. He doesn't care that I refuse my family's money or that I believe in the tarot. He doesn't brush me off as some kind of oddball." I sigh. "You still haven't told me why you're here." I look specifically at Brock. "I went to your parents' the other night to get some questions answered, and no one—including you—was willing to help me."

"That's why we're here," Brock says. "We *do* think you should talk to your mom and dad, but Don and I, with Dale's blessing, came to talk to you about what we found out."

Donny clears his throat. "It's not easy, talking about this."

"What? Talking about *what*?"

"Dale and I ... When we were young... I mean, did you ever wonder why the Steels adopted us?"

"Because your mother died. You needed a home."

"Yes, that's all very true. But it's a little more complicated than that. In fact, it was Uncle Ryan and Aunt Ruby, along with

Uncle Talon, who had the biggest hand in rescuing Dale and me."

"Rescuing?" I shake my head. "What are you talking about?"

"Rescuing," Donny says. "Dale and I were taken from our house while our mother was at work."

My mind is turning rapidly to mush. All I can say is, "What?"

"Yes, we were taken from our home"—his voice cracks—"and sold into a human-trafficking ring."

I can't speak. My skin is cold, so cold it's gone numb.

I have no feeling. In fact...my heart may have stopped beating.

Except I'm still here, still alive, so my heart must be beating.

"We were groomed," Donny continues. "Women and children were taken and groomed to...to become *slaves*. Human slaves."

"You okay?" Brock asks.

For a moment, I think Brock is talking to me, but he's not. His gaze is on our blond cousin, who seems more comfortable speaking of this atrocity than he should be.

Donny nods. "Sold to the highest bidder, to anyone who had money enough to pay."

I gulp, audibly, desperately trying to push down the hamburger that is trying to come back up.

"But Dale and I didn't meet that fate, thank God. Because your father and mine rescued us."

Secrets. Family secrets.

The cards sure as hell weren't lying to me.

"My God," I say, fighting tears but wanting to be as strong

as Donny. "I'm so sorry. I'm so, so sorry."

"We're not telling you this so you would feel sorry for Dale and me," Donny says. "It was a long time ago, and Dale and I have done a lot of healing since then. We're telling you because what happened to Dale and me all those years ago seems to be relevant to what's happening with our family now."

"Oh my God." My heart seems to collide with my sternum. "What the hell are you saying?"

"No one's going to be taken," Brock says. "That's not the concern. But all those years ago, our parents thought that trafficking ring had been broken up. Apparently it wasn't."

"Oh my God... Are there children missing from town? How have I not heard about this?"

"No. No one is missing from around here. But the trafficking ring is still operating, and we recently found out that they're operating on our land. They *were*, anyway."

I crumple to the floor then. My legs just stop working. Donny and Brock both help me get back on my feet.

Donny pats my cheek. "Are you okay?"

"Yes. I didn't faint. I just... My legs sort of just...gave out."

They walk me into my living area and help me sit down on the couch. They each take a seat next to me so that I'm in the middle.

"I don't know what to say," I tell Donny. "I feel like an absolute bitch for yelling at you about Brendan and his insurance."

"That's a different story," Donny says. "I made a bad decision. A decision I rectified, but it unfortunately resulted in Brendan's place being trashed."

"What bad decision?"

Donny sighs. "I can't give you any more details at this time, but the result was someone breaking into Brendan's place above the bar."

Normally I'd demand to know everything, but after the bomb Donny just dropped, I don't want to ever yell at him again. I want to hold him to me and protect him.

"And no one knows who did that?" I ask.

Donny shakes his head. "Believe me, I personally went through all the evidence with a fine-tooth comb, and so did Hardy Solomon at the sheriff's office. Whoever trashed it left absolutely no evidence behind. If there was anything hidden somewhere in Brendan's place, it's gone now."

"So you think whoever trashed his place was looking for something?"

"We can't prove it," Donny says, "but that's our working theory."

"Why? Why is this all happening?"

"If we knew," Brock says, "we would tell you. The good news is, we shut down the trafficking ring again. At least as far as our property goes. We've combed every inch of our own property to make sure they're gone."

"Why would they be using our property?" I ask.

"To implicate us, most likely," Donny says. "But we're good. All evidence has been destroyed."

"Why? Why would they want to implicate—" I breathe out. "Right. Because our dads shut them down."

"Right. The stragglers stayed under the radar and began again from scratch with the sole purpose of implicating us in the future. That's our theory."

"But again," Brock says, "we shut it down. My dad and I made sure of it."

"How did you find out all of this?" I ask.

"It's a long story, but people left us evidence. For example, someone left me a safe-deposit key that led us to the first clues," Donny says.

"Who, what, when?"

"Like we said, cuz," Brock says. "It's a long story. So I hope you've got time."

★ ★ ★

My eyes are swollen from crying, my nose clogged. "I don't know what to say."

"The first thing you can say is that you'll keep this to yourself for now," Donny says. "We don't have our fathers' go-ahead to tell you this."

"But there is more," Brock says.

"God, I'm not sure I can take any more." I grab a tissue from the box on my end table.

"Well, we're not going to tell you any more," Donny says. "But you do need to ask your parents."

"Ask them what?"

"First you'll need to tell them that you know about Dale and me," Donny says.

"And then what?"

"Just tell them you want the truth. The truth about your family," Donny says.

"This is all so scary to me."

"We know," Brock says. "It's scary to us too."

"No, you don't understand. Don't laugh at me, but the cards—"

"We won't laugh at you, Ava," Donny says. "We know you take your cards seriously."

"Thank you. I do, and I've been getting some very troubling readings lately. And most of them have to do with our family."

"Anything you want to talk to us about?" Brock says.

"The underlying theme seems to be secrets. Secrets regarding the family dynamic."

Neither Donny nor Brock says a word, but they do steal a glance at each other.

They're hoping I won't notice, but I notice everything. I've been observant since I was a child. Observant and intuitive.

"What aren't you telling me?"

"We've told you all we can," Donny says. "If you want to know more, you need to ask your mom and dad."

A chill breaks over my body, and I visibly shudder.

"It's normal to be apprehensive," Brock says. "God knows I was."

"When?"

"When I confronted my father, demanded the truth from him."

"What truth is there? How is there any more truth than what you've already told me?"

Another stolen glance between them.

"You're really freaking me out here, guys."

"We know, cuz," Donny says. "And we wish we could say more, but we absolutely can't."

I stand then and turn to face them, fire flowing through me. "Brock, I've always thought of you not as a cousin but as a brother. I'm closer to you than I am to my own sister. You, Dave, and me. Huey, Dewey, and Louie, remember?"

Brock smiles, and a nostalgic look passes over his face. "I haven't thought about that since we were kids."

"I'll take this," Donny says. "You and Brock are close, I

know that. And I know it's killing him not to be able to tell you everything. It's killing me too, Ava. I love you and Gina as much as I love Diana and Brianna. So as far as I'm concerned, we *are* all siblings, not cousins. We all grew up together, and we see each other most days. We're as close as any family could be, but families aren't perfect, even as much as ours seems to be on the outside. Every family has skeletons in its closet."

"What kind of skeletons am I going to find in my mom and dad's closet?" I ask, more to myself than to my cousins.

"You'll have to ask them," Brock says.

"My God, you sound like a fucking broken record."

"We need to go," Donny says.

He and Brock rise, now standing next to me.

"No. You absolutely cannot drop a big bomb on me like this and then just leave." I haven't even told them about the new message yet.

"All right," Brock says. "I totally understand. Let me stay here with you tonight. I'll sleep on the couch. I just need to text Rory so she's not waiting up."

"No, that's not what I mean. I'm perfectly safe here."

Though a shiver racks through me as I say the words.

Is anyone *really* safe? Ever? My new security hasn't been installed yet...

Little Donny and Dale probably thought they were safe in their house. I've heard the stories of latchkey kids. My God, I never thought...

"How do these things happen?" I ask. "How do things like this happen in Snow Creek?"

"They happen everywhere, cuz," Donny says. "Unfortunately, Snow Creek isn't immune. The trafficking ring that took Dale and me took some kids from Snow Creek a few decades before."

I go numb again, and shivers pass through me. "Please. No."

"My father was a victim," Donny says. "Dale and I didn't know this until a short time ago."

"Uncle Talon?" I plunk back down on the couch, my head in my hands.

I'm angry. So angry and sad and full of questions. How could any of this happen? My cousins? My uncle? Big strong Dale. Big strong Donny. Big strong Uncle Talon.

But they weren't big and strong when they were children.

So many secrets.

What do my mother and father have to do with all of this? What do they know that Donny and Brock can't tell me?

I need Brendan.

Brock is sweet to offer to stay here, but he's not who I need right now.

I need Brendan Murphy.

Secrets.

So many secrets.

The hierophant.

It's the hierophant.

A chill ripples through me, and I know . . .

I know something dark and ominous is coming.

CHAPTER THIRTY

Brendan

I've just turned out my light when my phone rings. My heart skips when I see the name across my screen.

"Ava?" I say into the phone.

"I'm downstairs in the bar, Brendan. I need to see you. Please."

"Sure, of course. Go up the steps. I'll let you in."

I stumble out of bed and scramble into a pair of jeans.

Ava's face is red and swollen when I answer the door. "My God, have you been crying?"

"No." She falls into my arms. "Yes, I have. But don't hold it against me, okay?"

I kiss the top of her pink head. "I would never. What's wrong, baby? What can I do for you?"

"Right now?" she says. "Take me to bed. Fuck me. Fuck me hard and fast, Brendan. I need an escape."

I'm not one to offer sex as a means of escape, but something in Ava's voice propels me to do as she requests. I like this woman. I think I'm falling in love with her. The last thing I want her to think of when it comes to sex with me is that it's an escape, but right now? I just want to make her feel better.

I want to comfort her.

If a hard fuck is what she needs, I will do it.

After all, I'll enjoy the hell out of it.

"Are you sure you don't want to talk first?"

She shakes her head. "No. I've had enough talking tonight, trust me. No more talking. No more thinking. Please."

I scoop her into my arms, kick the door shut and lock it, and then take her to my bed.

I'm only wearing jeans and nothing else, so I undress her quickly, throwing her clothes in a heap next to the bed.

When she's naked, her blue eyes on fire, her pink hair settled around her shoulders, I peel off my own jeans.

She holds her arms out to me, spreads her legs. In the dim light of my bedroom, her pussy glistens.

She's been thinking about this.

She's wet.

My cock is ready—thick and hard and ready—so I climb on top of her and plunge into her without so much as a kiss to her lips first.

This is what she wants, and this is what I'll give her.

But afterward?

We *will* have a long talk.

Damn, though … Talking is overrated when she's clasping me so completely.

Again I feel like I want to stay inside her forever, but soon the urge overwhelms me, and I pull out and thrust back in.

It doesn't take long for either of us. Surprisingly, she climaxes at the same time I do, and we join together, both shattering, both feeling the sweet edge of release.

I turn to my side then so that I lie facing her. I stroke her silky hair and smooth it off her forehead. She turns toward me, and I take a long look at her beautiful blue eyes, swollen and bloodshot.

"Thank you," she says. "That was just what I needed."

"Sweetheart, what's wrong?"

"It's just too much to process, Brendan. I do want to tell you everything. But I really need to go home. I have to be up early to open the bakery."

"Can Luke or Maya open for you? Just once?"

"No, the place is my responsibility. I need to start the day's bake early. So I should go home."

"You don't have to," I say. "Just set an alarm on your phone."

"I can't sleep here. The sounds from the bar downstairs will keep me awake."

I chuckle. "I guess I've gotten used to it over the years. I don't even hear it. Does it really bother you?"

"Not overly, but I do need to get some sleep, Brendan. And I'm so afraid I won't find any peace tonight. On a normal night, I might be able to tune out the noise from downstairs, but this isn't a normal night. So much is going on in my head."

"All right. I'll walk you back to the bakery."

"No, you don't have to."

"Ava, it's after dark, and I know it's only three buildings down, but—"

"All right," she relents.

Interesting. I expected her to fight me on that, but I'm glad she didn't. No way will I let her leave here alone.

I shove on some clothes quickly as she dresses.

"You ready?" I ask.

She nods, and without speaking to each other again, I take her out the back of the bar so we don't have to walk through everyone.

The bar's hopping tonight, which is unusual on a

weeknight, so I figure I'll check it out when I get back.

I walk Ava to the back of the bakery, where she lets us in, and I walk her to the door that leads to her upstairs apartment.

"You want me to come up?" I ask.

"God, I do, but if you come up, Brendan, neither one of us will get any sleep tonight, and I need to try."

"We don't have to have sex," I say. "I'm happy to hold you. Do whatever it takes to help you sleep."

"You're funny. I wouldn't be able to stay away from your hot body."

I can't help the smile that splits my face. "You said the right thing. I've never been turned down quite so nicely."

"Oh, you're not being turned down." She runs her fingers over my chest. "I mean, this is just for tonight anyway."

I give her a quick kiss on the lips, and when she unlocks the door, I kiss her again. I hear the door to the bakery lock as I leave, and I walk back to the bar.

I walk in, and the first thing I notice is Donny and Brock Steel sitting at the bar.

"Hey, Brendan." Donny motions me over.

"Yeah?"

"How's Ava?"

"She's . . . Why do you ask?"

"We gave her some news tonight. Some news that upset her."

I take the empty stool next to Brock. "So that's what's going on. What kind of news?"

"It's nothing we can tell you," Brock says. "But if she chooses to tell you, we won't stop her."

"Then why don't you two tell me?"

"We can't," Brock says. "It has to do with our family.

We've cleaned up the mess. Part of it, anyway. Let's just say someone—most likely more than one someone—was trying to implicate us in some bad stuff."

I raise my eyebrows. "And it's all cool now?"

"For now, anyway."

"Then why is Ava so upset?"

"Just some family drama she didn't know about," Donny says.

Brock narrows his eyes at Donny.

"Family drama?" I say.

"Yeah," Donny says.

"I get the feeling that you, Brock, consider this more than simple family drama."

"Why do you say that?"

"Because of the stink eye you just gave your cousin there." Donny glares at Brock.

Yep. Something is going on here—something more than mere family drama.

I know better than to press the issue. When the Steels want to remain tight-lipped, they remain tight-lipped. My father said he learned that lesson long ago when he was investigating his uncle's death.

"Can I ask you guys something?"

"Sure," Donny says. "But I can't promise we'll answer."

"Fair enough. Have you gotten any news on that cryptic message that Ava received?"

"The one about Darth Morgen?" Brock says. "No, and it's troubling Ava as well. She thinks her mother has been blowing her off about it."

"Does that seem strange to you?"

"Yeah," Brock says. "It does seem pretty weird to us."

Yet there's a peculiar edge to Brock's voice.

"I suppose it's a little weird," Donny says.

No peculiar edge to his voice at all.

But he's an attorney. He's been trained to stay calm in any situation. Hell, he's probably been trained to present lies as truth. Donny Steel's a good guy, but all lawyers must defend their clients zealously, whether they like them or not.

"So I get the feeling it doesn't seem weird to you at all," I say.

"I think we just said it *does* seem weird," Donny says.

And if I had to bet my last penny on whether Donny was telling me the truth, based solely on his voice and facial expression and body language, I'd say he was.

He's not the problem. Brock is.

Brock has dropped his gaze to the counter.

"Brock?" I say. "You agree?"

"I'll echo what Donny just said." Brock meets my gaze. "We did just say it seems a little strange."

"Okay." I could push the issue, but it won't do me any good. They're staying quiet.

But I'm betting that both Brock and Donny don't think it's strange at all that Ruby would be giving Ava the runaround.

And for the life of me, I can't figure out why.

Ruby seemed genuinely interested in helping us when we met a week ago at the bakery. She said she had apps that could help her decode the message.

I suppose it's possible that her apps didn't help.

But this woman is a detective, the best of the best. The Snow Creek sheriff's office consults with her all the time.

So why would she be putting Ava off?

"Did Ava tell you about the new message that I got?"

Donny keeps his gaze neutral, but Brock's eyebrows rise.

"No," Brock says.

"It was another email that got sent to Hardy's office," I say. "And at the bottom, instead of just saying *Ask the Murphys*, it said *Ask the Murphys and the Steels*."

"Oh?" Donny says. "Well, we're Steels. What is the message?"

I pull out the piece of paper containing the hard copy of the email and hand it to Donny.

He scans it, wrinkles his brow, and hands it to Brock.

Brock scans it. "This doesn't make any sense."

"Well, you're both Steels, and so is Ava. So that makes three of you who have no clue what this is about."

"Not on its face," Donny says. "But clearly, it's some kind of code."

"Right, but a different kind of code from the first message about Darth Morgen," Brock says.

"Not necessarily," Donny says. "I mean, if we could crack the Darth Morgen code, assign each letter a different letter, maybe we would find these codes are the same."

"Right," I say, "and Ava's mom, your aunt, said she had decryption programs that could help with that."

Neither of them says a word.

"You guys have to level with me. I care about your cousin Ava. I care about her a lot."

"Oh?" Donny's eyebrows rise.

"Yes."

"Then what are your intentions?" Donny asks.

It doesn't take a genius to realize that he's more interested in throwing me off track than finding out my true intentions regarding Ava.

But I'll bite. I want to make them comfortable so they might spill some information.

"We're dating. We like each other. My intentions are good, but I'm not ready to propose to her or anything."

"Why not?" Brock asks.

"Did you seriously just ask me that?"

"Well, Donny proposed to Callie after only a few weeks. Same with me and Rory."

I shake my head. "Man, you guys really don't want to discuss these messages with me, do you?"

"What do you mean by that?" Donny's voice reeks of feigned innocence.

The guy is good. I'll give him that.

Brock isn't nearly as good.

"Ava and I have been on two dates," I say. "And you know your cousin better than I do. What do you think she would do if I proposed to her?"

That gets them. They both erupt into laughter.

"See what I mean?" I say.

"But your intentions are good," Brock says.

"Of course they are. I like her. She likes me. She was a little freaked out at the age difference at first, but we've gotten past that."

Neither of them says another word.

"So . . . what about this new message?" I ask.

"I don't fucking know." Brock sighs.

"What does Hardy think?" Donny asks.

"Hardy's not really involved, other than the fact that the messages are coming through his office. But no threat has been made, so there's nothing for the police to investigate."

"True enough," Donny says. "And if there's nothing for the police to investigate, there's definitely nothing for my office to investigate."

"Look," I say. "I care about Ava, and she's a mess right

now. Whatever you guys told her messed her up good."

Brock looks down at the bar again, his lips twisting in a strange way.

Donny, of course, looks completely normal.

"You're good," I say to him.

"What do you mean, *good*?"

"You're good at keeping your face neutral. Your body language neutral." I turn to Brock, stifle a chuckle. "Brock, you're not quite as good."

"What makes you think you can read people?" Donny asks.

"Are you kidding me? I've been a bartender for fifteen years. We're right up there next to psychiatrists with the ability to read people."

Brock scoffs. "I'd put my mother's abilities above yours any day of the week."

I give him a scoff back. "So would I, Steel. But that's not my point. I've been reading people for fifteen years tending bar, and I've gotten pretty damned good at it over the years."

With that, I rise from my stool and leave the bar.

These two people are keeping something from Ava.

I don't know what it is, and it's not my business.

But I will protect Ava. From anyone.

Even from her own family.

CHAPTER THIRTY-ONE

Ava

I spend the next free day I have with Aunt Marjorie, putting the finishing touches on the anniversary party for my parents the Saturday after Thanksgiving.

It's now only a week away, and invitations have gone out. I'll be closing the bakery for Thanksgiving on Thursday and then also Saturday and Sunday, with only limited hours on Friday.

Which means I'm going to be busy, busy, busy tomorrow through Wednesday. People will be coming in to buy their baked goods for Thanksgiving, and on top of all those orders, I have to make pita, olive bread, and baklava for my parents' party.

I normally keep my business just to bread and rolls and some pastries, but for Thanksgiving, I also make pumpkin pies. I have to hire extra help to get everything done. Even in a small town, many people like to purchase professionally made pies rather than make them from scratch. Every year, I sell more pumpkin pies than I did the last.

I have orders for over five hundred this year, including those for the big Steel Thanksgiving spectacular. This time it's going to be held at Uncle Joe and Aunt Melanie's house because we're busy planning for the big party for my parents at

Uncle Talon and Aunt Jade's house two days later.

"Are you going to answer?" Aunt Marjorie's voice invades my thoughts.

"I'm sorry. What?"

"I was asking about you and Brendan," she says.

"Really? I'm sorry. I've got a lot on my mind."

"Clearly," Aunt Marj says. "Everything all right, honey?"

Where to start? I'm not sure how much Aunt Marj knows. I haven't told her about the cryptic messages I've been getting. But Dave knows, and he's Aunt Marj's son.

"Brendan and I are good," I say. "I mean, we've only been out a few times."

"He's a nice young man. Plus, very good-looking."

"He is," I say. "Actually, I should probably talk to you about this, Aunt Marj. I was a little freaked out at first by our age difference, but you and Uncle Bryce have a larger age difference than Brendan and I do."

"That's true. But the age difference never bothered me. I had been crushing on Uncle Bryce since I was a little girl. It bothered him more because he kept thinking of me as that little girl."

"I don't think Brendan sees me that way," I say. "The age difference doesn't seem to bother him."

"That's because he didn't really know you when you were a child. Uncle Bryce and Uncle Joe were best friends from the time they were in kindergarten, so Uncle Bryce remembers when I was born. He was thirteen at the time. Though Brendan and Dale are the same age, they were never close like Uncle Bryce and Uncle Joe are, so Brendan was never around, and he didn't watch you grow up."

"Yeah. True," I say. "He says he started to notice me when I opened the bakery in town."

"See? And that's been what, two years now?" She smiles. "You've had one of the town's most eligible bachelors checking you out. That's something, Ava."

"Then why did he wait so long to do anything about it?"

"He probably was thinking about the age difference as well. And he finally got to the point where it didn't bother him."

"You think?"

"It's just a theory. But he's also very busy, and he knew how busy you were, opening a new business. It probably just wasn't the right time for him."

"Yeah, and honestly? The beginning of my business wasn't the right time for me either."

"So you see? These things work themselves out in time."

"How long did it take for Uncle Bryce to stop thinking of you as a little girl?" I ask.

"Well"—she smiles again as she ties ribbons around one of our wine-themed centerpieces for the party—"I kind of forced him to stop thinking of me in that way. I was determined to have him. I remember when we were first going out, every time he walked into my bedroom, he said all he could remember were the pink and yellow unicorns I used to have all over the walls. Of course, I had redecorated my room since then, but that's what he always saw."

I can't help laughing at the image. "That's so funny. You totally don't seem the unicorn type."

"I know. Growing up with three brothers, I was a regular little tomboy. But my room was the one place where I allowed myself to be a girl."

"So you always knew that Uncle Bryce was the one for you?"

"I did. It just took him a long time to figure it out."

"How long exactly?"

"A while. He already had Henry at that point, and he didn't think I was old enough to be a mother. I was only twenty-five, mind you. But I had to remind him that Jade, my best friend, was also only twenty-five, and at that point, she and Uncle Talon had just adopted Dale and Donny. Plus, she was pregnant with Diana."

"You know," I say, "I never thought about it in that way, but you're right. She was only twenty-five. And Dale was ten."

My lips tremble a bit. Because now I know. I know why Dale and Donny needed a home so badly, and I know why Uncle Talon really wanted to give that to them.

Aunt Marj doesn't know that I know, but then—

"You have a strange look on your face, Ava. Is there something you want to talk about?"

"I—"

"Oh my goodness." The rosiness drains from Aunt Marj's cheeks. "You know, don't you?"

"I don't know what you're talking about."

"Oh, Ava. Please don't lie to me. There's no mistaking the look on your face. I saw it in the mirror when I found out. It must've been Dale or Donny. None of the other kids know."

I swallow. She doesn't know that Brock knows. Of course Dale and Donny know. It happened to them.

"Aunt Marj . . ."

"But why? We all made a decision a long time ago not to poison you kids with the horror our family had been through."

I drop my jaw. "So there *are* secrets. Secrets about our family. Why? Why wouldn't you trust us with these secrets?"

"It's not a matter of trust, Ava. We didn't want to burden any of you with the horrors of the past."

"But now we're being burdened anyway. I don't understand. Why wouldn't my parents tell me everything?"

"That's a difficult question to answer. One I think you should probably talk to them about."

"My parents won't talk to me, Aunt Marjorie. I asked my mother for some information over a week ago, and she hasn't gotten back to me. And it's ridiculous that she hasn't because I know she's a competent detective. More than competent, and I asked for her expertise."

"Ava—"

"Secrets. So many secrets. The cards were right."

"The cards? You mean your tarot?"

"Yes, everything's been pointing me to secrets lately. Something to do with my family. Secret knowledge. And I want to know, Aunt Marj. I want to know exactly what all of you have been keeping from me."

"Ava, you already know more than my children do if you know about Dale and Donny."

I swallow harshly, trying to make the lump in my throat go away. "I've cried so hard about this. I can't even imagine what they went through."

"I can't either. And my own brother went through the same thing. But they all lived through it, and they're stronger for it. All of them found love. And Talon was the perfect father for Dale and Donny because he understood them."

I nod, choking back a sob.

"Also, you need to understand that they have healed. This is decades in the past for them. It seems so new to you because you just found out. But they've moved past it. They're good, strong men. All of them."

I nod.

"Ava, it's so very important that you *not* tell my children about this. I know you and David are close."

"I won't, and I haven't," I say. "But Brock knows, Aunt Marj. And he and Dave are closer than Dave and I are."

"I think you're all pretty close. You're our own Huey, Dewey, and Louie."

I attempt a smile. "I was just thinking about that. It's so funny that I haven't thought about it in years."

"Well, you grew up. All of you became your own people. I suppose David and Brock stayed closer since they went to college together. You went to a different school."

"That was me being a rebel," I say. "And honestly? I missed Dave and Brock so badly those four years. But it was good that I went on my own. It's where I learned to stand on my own two feet and where I found my determination to build my business without the help of my family's name and money."

"I'm not sure you know how proud your parents and your aunts and uncles are of you for that, Ava. But we are. We truly are." She sniffles a bit.

"That means a lot to me. Thank you." I swallow. "But I have to ask, Aunt Marjorie, why did you choose to keep us all in the dark about Dale and Donny? About Uncle Talon?"

And about so many other things?

"It wasn't an easy decision, but at the time, Dale and Donny had just come into the family, and they were healing. Brad and Diana had just been born, and your mother had just found out she was pregnant with you. We were facing a new generation of Steels, and we desperately wanted to leave all the dreadfulness in the past."

"But it's a part of who we are," I say. "There's nothing shameful about it."

"No one was ashamed," Marj says. "But it's a horrific story, as you know. We didn't want to taint the innocent souls coming into our family with what we had been through."

"So it's better that we find out now? It's better to find out that our parents have kept us in the dark our whole lives?"

"Try not to judge us too harshly, Ava. We did what we thought was best at the time."

"I can't believe Aunt Melanie would've gone for this. She's a psychiatrist. She knows secrets are never the answer."

"Aunt Melanie didn't. I didn't say the vote was unanimous."

"Oh my God. You actually had a *vote*?"

"We did. All your aunts and uncles and I voted."

"Was Aunt Melanie the only one who dissented?"

Aunt Marjorie doesn't reply.

"Don't tell me you dissented as well."

She shakes her head. "No, I did not. I wanted to tamp down all of this crap that happened, never have to deal with it again. This all affected me in a horrible way."

"How so?"

Aunt Marj puts down the roll of ribbon. "It's not something I can talk to you about."

I want to fight her, hound her, but what would that accomplish? So instead, I ask, "Who was the other dissenter then? Or was there more than one?"

"No, there was only one."

And I know. I don't even have to think.

"It was my mother, wasn't it?"

Again Aunt Marjorie doesn't reply.

"My mother and Aunt Melanie are best friends. If there was anyone who would be on Aunt Melanie's side in this, it must have been my mother."

"I think that's something you have to ask her about."

Seriously? My mother? My *honesty is always the best policy* mother?

Hypocrisy. Oh my God...

"Yeah, and I would, except that my mother has been ignoring me lately."

Aunt Marj sighs.

"For God's sake, what aren't you telling me?"

"I've told you all I can." She resumes working on the centerpieces. "Probably more than I should have. It's something to approach your own parents about. But can I ask a favor?"

I pause a moment. I love my aunt, but I'm so sick of people keeping information from me. Finally, "Only because you taught me how to cook. How to bake. And I will always owe you for that. And you're my aunt and I love you."

"Thank you, Ava. The favor is this. Please don't ask your parents about this until after their twenty-fifth anniversary celebration."

I drop my mouth open.

"This is a huge anniversary for them," Aunt Marjorie continues. "We've all worked so hard on it already."

I sigh. "Fine," I relent. "But after this party? It's fucking open season."

CHAPTER THIRTY-TWO

Brendan

Thanksgiving Day.

One of only three days—the other two being Christmas Day and New Year's Day—that I close the bar. I'll open back up tomorrow and stay open the rest of the long weekend. Although I won't be working Saturday night, as I'll be attending the twenty-fifth anniversary party for Ava's parents with her.

I was invited anyway, but she specifically asked me to come as her date.

I was flattered beyond belief.

I'm nearly in love with the woman already, but I had no idea she was feeling close enough to ask me to be her date at a Steel family party.

We chatted about Thanksgiving briefly as well and decided to attend our own families' respective celebrations solo.

We'll make our debut to both our families as a couple on Saturday instead.

Besides, the thought of a Steel Thanksgiving kind of freaks me out. Four families and all their offspring and spouses gathering together in Jonah Steel's house this year. How easy to be lost in a sea of Steels.

I'd rather be with my own family. Just the five of us— Mom, Dad, Aunt Ciara, my cousin Carmen, and me. Carmen

232

just got out of a long-term relationship, so she will also be solo.

For some reason, my mom likes to eat at around one p.m. on Thanksgiving rather than at dinnertime. I stopped asking questions long ago. So I'm on my way, walking the few blocks to get to my parents' house.

Carmen opens the door for me before I have a chance to ring the bell. Not that I would ring the bell anyway.

"What's the good word, Carmen?" I ask.

"Men are pigs," she says.

I laugh out loud. "Yeah, most of us are."

"So you admit it."

"Well, personally, I'm not a pig. But anyone who doesn't treat my beautiful cousin right is certainly one."

"True. I'm swearing off men."

"For about five minutes?" I give her a jab as I walk into the house.

"At least fifteen," she says. "So tell me about you and Ava Steel."

"We've been casually dating for a couple of weeks now," I say.

Casual of course meaning we've been sleeping together, but I don't want to tell my cousin that. It's none of her business, and I know Ava doesn't sleep around.

"She's certainly not the type I ever thought you'd go for," Carmen says.

"Why?"

"Don't get me wrong. She's gorgeous and all. All the Steels are. But I could never quite get behind the pink hair."

"I think it works for her," I say.

"She does look good," Carmen admits. "Maybe I'm just a bit envious. I'd love to change my hair color, but I don't think anything would work with my fair skin and freckles."

"What's wrong with your hair? It's the same as mine."

She scoffs. "Not really. Yours is more of a darker auburn. Mine's the color of an orange."

In reality, my cousin is actually very beautiful. I recall her being the junior homecoming attendant the year Rory Pike was queen. I think she was on the court her senior year. Plus she's got an outgoing personality, so she's always been popular. Always had a lot of friends and a lot of boyfriends.

"I'm taking Ava to her parents' anniversary party on Saturday," I continue, "so you can see us as a couple then."

"You mean you're going *with* her? As her date?"

"Yes, ma'am."

"Wow, that's big."

"Why is that big?"

"You know about the Steels, don't you?"

"Probably about as much as you do," I say.

"What I mean is that they have a habit of falling hard and falling fast. Look at how quickly Donny and Brock fell for the Pike sisters."

"Yeah? Well, I'm not a Steel."

"You're not," Carmen says. "But Ava is."

I shake my head. There's no telling my cousin that *I'm* the one who's falling hard. Ava, while she's clearly not indifferent to me, has made it quite clear that she's not ready to get serious with anyone. I'm definitely not getting forever vibes from her.

In fact, she almost seems like she's trying *not* to get serious.

Makes me wonder if her tarot cards told her not to.

I respect her belief in the guidance of the cards, but I hope that's not the case, because I'd really like to have something long-term with Ava Steel. But this is where the age thing could get tricky. I'm thirty-five. I'm ready to settle down. I love the idea of having my own family, of being a father.

Ava probably isn't thinking in those terms yet.

Walking farther into the house, I inhale. I love the smell of turkey and all the fixings—onion, garlic, thyme, sage. Snow Creek is such a beef town, and while Steel Acres and other ranches produce quality beef, it's nice to have a little change of pace.

We only eat turkey once a year. We go back to beef on Christmas and ham on Easter.

But I do love turkey, and I love the turkey pot pie and the wild rice soup that Mom makes with the leftovers during this whole weekend.

I usually eat with my parents all four days.

Except we won't be eating here Saturday night.

We will all be eating at the huge buffet put on by the Steel family to celebrate the twenty-fifth anniversary of Ryan and Ruby Steel.

And I will be there as their daughter's date.

I'm dating a member of the Steel family.

But not just any member.

The most beautiful and unique Steel of all.

Dad hands me a beer, and I grab it and join him in the family room to watch whatever game he has on TV.

Mom is very traditional. She doesn't allow Dad and me anywhere near the kitchen during big meals like this. And that's okay with me. The hamburgers I made for Ava the other night pretty much exhausted my entire culinary repertoire.

I usually live on sandwiches. Two nice slices of Ava's bread slapped together with whatever cold cuts I have in my fridge.

"Who's playing today, Dad?"

"Broncos versus the Packers."

"Who's winning?"

"Broncos are looking good this year, son."

"Great."

My dad is a football fanatic. I remember when I was little, if the Broncos weren't winning, he'd be in a bad mood. He's mellowed a lot since then. Now he only says a few choice curse words when they're not winning, and then he's back to his jovial self.

I take a seat next to him and pretend to enjoy the game.

Until someone rings the doorbell.

That's strange. Everyone's here.

"Brendan," Carmen calls down. "Someone's here to see you."

Me? Who the hell could that be?

"Excuse me, Dad." I rise.

Unless it's Ava Steel, I'm not interested.

And I know it's not Ava Steel.

CHAPTER THIRTY-THREE

Ava

Uncle Joe and Aunt Melanie have put on quite a spread for Thanksgiving. Normally we have holiday dinners at Uncle Talon and Aunt Jade's, since they live in the biggest house, but Joe and Melanie's place is still huge.

My sister, Gina, and my cousins Brianna, Angie, and Sage—the awesome foursome—are all home from college. Gina looks gorgeous as usual, her long dark hair pulled into a side braid. Of course she's dressed for the occasion. Gina always dresses up. Today she's wearing Louboutin leather boots with spiky heels, designer jeans, and a cashmere V-neck sweater.

Yeah, we couldn't be more different.

She hugs me when I arrive. "Ava!"

I hug her back. She's my sister and I love her, although we have absolutely nothing in common. I'm kind of an odd duck as far as she's concerned, and I've grown to be okay with that.

It wasn't easy growing up in my little sister's shadow. Gina is good at so much, and of course she totally outdoes me in the area of raw beauty. The only area I can beat her in is cooking and baking. She's a menace in the kitchen. But damn, the girl has a genius IQ, and she's a gifted artist.

The only thing we do have in common is our bodies. We

both inherited our mother's hourglass figure—boobs, hips, and nice legs. She got our dad's height, though.

The only way to compete with someone like Gina is to *not* compete, which has served me well.

It's why I refused to use the Steel money for my business. Because this way, I'm doing something Gina could never do. I can't afford designer clothes, so I don't wear them. Not that I would wear them anyway, but Gina can't live without them, so she will never forsake her family's money.

"Hey, Ava!" Brianna grabs me for a hug next.

She's the youngest Steel, sibling to Dale, Donny, and Diana. Tall, dark, and gorgeous, of course, and named after Jade's father, Brian Roberts. She's studying agriculture at Mesa and plans to work with her dad in the orchards after she's done with her studies—the only one of Uncle Talon's kids to share his interest. Dale, of course, works at the winery, Donny's an attorney like his mother, and Diana is an architect.

Aunt Marj and Aunt Melanie are in the kitchen, working with the cooks and housekeepers to get everything served.

I love that about the Steels. We may have money coming out of our butts, but not one of us is above doing manual labor. We were all taught that from the time we could walk and talk.

I look around.

Angie and Sage—Aunt Marjorie and Uncle Bryce's twins—are talking to Dave.

Brock and Donny will show up later. The scuttlebutt is that they're eating at the Pike celebration and will show up here—with Rory and Callie—for dessert.

Dale is here with his wife, Ashley, and his mother-in-law, Willow.

I head toward her. She and I will always have something to talk about. My hair.

"Oh, hey, Ava." She smiles and hugs me.

It's funny, actually. Ashley, Willow's daughter and Dale's wife, is not a hugger, but Willow seems to be. All the Steels are huggers. You can't grow up in this family and be uncomfortable around hugging, though I'm probably the least comfortable of everyone.

"I didn't know you were going to be here," I say. "It's great to see you. I love my hair."

"I have to say, kudos to me," Willow says. "I was afraid the color would fade, but it still looks pretty good."

"Yeah, pink always seems to fade. But whatever you mixed in works really well."

"I just used Raine's formula, but I doctored it a little to add some shine."

Dale grabs me into a hug. "Hey, cuz."

Scratch that. Dale is probably the Steel who is the least comfortable hugging. But since he got married to Ashley, he's become a lot more comfortable with it and has dragged his wife along with him.

"It's great to see you guys," I say.

"So what's this we hear about you and Brendan Murphy?" Ashley asks.

"Not much, really. We're dating, I guess."

"That's fantastic," Willow says.

"Yeah, he's great. I was a little freaked out about the age difference at first."

"I hear you." Ashley squeezes Dale's arm. "But when it's right, it's right."

I clear my throat. "It's a little too soon to think about whether it's right or not."

"Really?" Ashley says. "It seems Dale and I were confessing our love within a week or so."

CHANCE

This time Dale clears his throat. "Seems to be the Steel way."

"It's not my way," I say.

Although the words kind of stick in my throat. I *am* feeling some amazing things for Brendan, but I can't help thinking about that first tarot reading. *Don't get swept away.* And then what did I do? I hopped right into bed with him and got swept away.

"Brendan and I are taking it slow."

What a load of crap I just spewed. We've already slept together, and we've gone out quite a bit. But he's certainly not in love with me, and I . . .

Damn.

No, I can't be. Not yet.

"You want something to drink?" Dale asks. "I've got some of your dad's finest here. He was over there tasting this morning."

"I figured he hadn't left the winery yet." I can't help laughing. "He keeps saying he's retiring and you're the new winemaker."

"I don't think he'll ever stay completely out of the winery," Dale says. "But he does let me run things now. Not that we ever disagree. But on the off chance that we do, it's going to be my call from here on out."

"You've got to be kidding me," I say dryly.

Dale wrinkles his forehead. No doubt at the tone of my voice.

I love my mom and dad. Seriously, I would take a bullet for either one of them. I didn't mean to have a snide tone. But after my conversation with Aunt Marj, I can't help but think that they've been hiding something from me my whole life. Something so important that Aunt Marj wants me to wait until after their anniversary party to even bring it up with them.

I glance at my sister. She's knee-deep in conversation with Angie and Sage. The three of them are in their last year of college, and of course they're having the time of their lives.

Gina won't want to be dragged into any family drama. She wants to finish her degree in art. She's been painting since she was a little girl, and she's got so much natural talent, which is odd, because none of the Steels paint.

She does both perceptual and conceptual art, mostly oils on canvas but sometimes watercolor. In fact, every Steel home has one of her creations in it. Mom and Dad's house has one on every freaking wall.

Will she make it as an artist?

I have no doubt. With the Steel money backing her, every gallery in the United States will want to showcase her work.

That's fine.

I'm happy simply showcasing my bread here in Snow Creek.

I'm a small-town girl at heart. But Gina? She'll end up in New York or LA, I'm sure of it.

"Ava?" Dale's voice.

I shake myself out of my thoughts. "Yeah?"

"Are you mad at your parents or something?"

So much for trying to keep my thoughts secret.

"No, of course not."

How can I be mad at them when I don't know what they're keeping from me, if anything?

"Oh, okay. I must've imagined the look."

I should know better. Dale is extremely close to my father, obviously. My father taught him everything he knows about winemaking.

"I'm good." I force a smile.

"Good. Where are your parents, anyway?"

This time I wrinkle my forehead. "They're not here yet?"

"No, they're not. When I saw Ryan earlier at the winery, he said they were going to be a little late."

"They didn't say anything to me. Maybe Gina knows something."

"Nope, we already asked her," Dale says. "She just says they had a quick meeting they had to attend."

"Both of them? On Thanksgiving?"

"Yeah, both of them. Weird, right?"

"I'll say."

What the hell is going on? I hate thinking badly about my parents, but this is all too ominous. First, Mom blows off my calls about the text message. And then Aunt Marj tells me not to approach them until after their anniversary party.

"You know what, Dale? I think I'll have that drink now."

CHAPTER THIRTY-FOUR

Brendan

"Oh." I keep my jaw from dropping on the floor.

Ryan and Ruby Steel are standing in the doorway.

"Hello, Brendan," Ryan says, his lips drawn into a slight frown.

"Mr. Steel."

"Ryan, please."

"Sure, of course. What are you doing here? Shouldn't you be at the Steel family Thanksgiving?"

"Yes, we're heading there, but Ruby and I need to talk to you. It's important."

"Uh...sure. You want to come in?"

"Actually, no," Ruby says. "Can you come with us for a minute?"

"I can come outside and talk to you. But I'm not sure my parents would appreciate me leaving. Dinner will be ready soon."

"Please," Ryan says. "It's important."

"Is Ava okay?"

"Of course. She's fine," Ruby says. "But this *does* concern her. And you."

"You mean the fact that we're seeing each other?"

Ryan shakes his head. "No. I mean, we're happy for you. Really. We've always liked you, Brendan."

"Okay."

I don't really feel that I have to justify who I date, but this *is* Ava's father.

"Let me go tell my mom. You know how long we'll be?"

"No more than half an hour." From Ruby, whose blue eyes look fatigued. She has dark circles that weren't there when Ava and I met her for lunch to talk about the message we both got.

"All right. We probably have a half hour before dinner. But let me just tell her."

I shuffle into the kitchen, my mind racing. What the hell is this all about?

"Hey, Mom," I say. "You have an ETA on dinner?"

"I'd say about half an hour to forty-five minutes."

"Okay. Great. Ryan and Ruby Steel want to talk to me about something, and they want me to go somewhere with them."

"Where do they want you to go?"

"I don't have a clue, but they said it would only take half an hour. Do you mind?"

Mom furrows her brow and then touches her oven-mitted hand to her forehead. "Does this have something to do with Ava? Is she okay?"

"Yes, they've assured me she's okay. I'll be back in half an hour."

She takes off the oven mitt, narrows her gaze. "All right, honey."

I make my escape quickly, just dodging Carmen, who I know is going to want to know why Ryan and Ruby Steel are here.

Once I'm out of the house, Ryan is opening the passenger side door of his Mercedes. "Get in."

The Steels are good people. I trust them implicitly.

So why do I have a feeling I'm heading to my demise?

Get over yourself, I say silently.

Ruby climbs into the back seat. "You have such long legs, Brendan," she says. "I didn't want you to have to sit back here."

Ryan's Mercedes sedan has more than enough room in the back seat for my long legs, but it's a nice gesture.

Or is it?

Ruby's a trained cop. An excellent shot. She could easily stick a gun to the back of my head from where she's sitting.

My God, why is my mind doing this?

Why do I have such a bad feeling?

"Exactly where are you taking me?" I ask.

"Your place," Ryan says.

"We could've walked," I say.

"I know, but we're in a hurry."

Within less than a minute, Ryan's pulling in front of the bar, and we walk in the back way.

"Wow," Ruby says. "It looks great. Your contractor did an excellent job."

"They did. My insurance company was very generous."

Ryan nods. "My brothers have given me some information," he says, "about what you found here. I've seen the copies of the documents they have. I'd like to see the originals, please."

"The originals are in a safe-deposit box," I say.

It's a lie. The originals are in a safe in my closet at my parents' home, but something keeps me from saying those words.

"Where's the safe-deposit box?" Ryan asks.

"In Grand Junction." God, I hate lying. "But if you've seen copies, you've basically seen them."

"All right." Ryan pulls his phone out of his pocket and glances at it. "Let's go tomorrow. You and I."

"Wait. You think I'm going to just *give* you these documents?"

"No, of course not," Ruby says. "But I need to take a look at them. See if we can find any fingerprints on them."

"Well, Dale, Donny, and I have all touched them."

"What about your father?"

"I actually . . . I haven't told him about them."

"You haven't?"

"No. I went straight to Dale and Donny. I mean, Dale and I aren't exactly close, but we are the same age and did go to school together. He was the obvious choice."

Ryan clears his throat. "I understand that your father bought this place from a man named Jeremy Madigan."

"That's what the documents say."

"How did your father know Jeremy Madigan?"

"I'm afraid you'd have to ask him that."

"I see. But you haven't told him about the documents."

"No."

"I have to say, Brendan, that seems a little puzzling to me," Ryan says.

"Why?"

"Because he's the owner of this building, isn't he?"

"He is, but I am as well. When he retired, he added me to the deed via quitclaim. That way we can avoid probate when he passes." Another lie. What the hell is wrong with me? Though my father has drawn up the documents. They just haven't been recorded yet.

"Your father did a lot of investigating when he first came to town," Ruby says.

"That's true."

"Do you know if he investigated the Madigan family?"

"I was a kid. I wasn't even born yet when my father came here. He met my mom here and decided to stay. I came along a year later."

"I understand that," Ryan says. "I'm just wondering, how long did your father investigate his uncle's death?"

"For a while," I say. "But I'm not sure what this has to do with anything right now. Maybe you should be talking to him."

"Yeah," Ryan says. "Maybe we should. But we're concerned because of the messages that you and Ava got."

"My dad knows all about them," I say. "They came to Hardy's office and said to ask the Murphys. He's a Murphy."

"Right," Ryan says. "Has he mentioned the Madigans to you at all?"

"No. Why do you keep asking me that?"

"What about Ava?" Ruby says. "Has she mentioned the Madigans?"

"No. Why would she? None of us even know them. My dad bought this bar from Jeremy Madigan. I don't even know anyone by that name. Do *you* know the Madigans?"

Ryan and Ruby are both silent.

"Should I take that as a yes?"

"Ava has told you," Ruby says, "that I've been giving her the runaround on those messages, hasn't she?"

"She may have mentioned that."

"There are some things Ava doesn't know about our family," Ryan says. "Things that could hurt her. And I'm sure you don't want to see her hurt."

"Of course I don't. I care very much for Ava."

"That's nice to hear," Ruby says. "You're a good man, Brendan."

"Yeah, I am." I stand tall. Ryan Steel is still a little taller, about half an inch. Of course, he's wearing cowboy boots, and I'm not.

I honestly don't have any fear of Ryan Steel.

But I don't want anything to harm Ava.

"Has Ava mentioned anything about her family keeping secrets?"

"No, she hasn't."

That's not exactly the truth, of course. Ava's been very freaked out about the readings she's been getting lately. Something about secret knowledge. Hypocrisy. But I don't feel comfortable telling her parents this without her knowing that I'm talking to them.

This seems thirty shades of wrong.

All of it.

"I have to be honest," I say. "I think the person you should be talking to is Ava."

"She mentioned that you got another message," Ruby says.

"Yeah. I can't make heads or tails out of it. Can you?"

"I don't know," Ruby says. "She hasn't shown it to me."

"She hasn't?"

"No."

"Maybe it's because you haven't given her any information on the first one," I say.

"I need to see that message," Ruby says.

"Look," I say, "if Ava isn't comfortable showing you, I don't feel that I should."

Ryan steps toward me. Is he trying to intimidate me?

I'm not intimidated that easily.

"Please," he says. "We need to see the message."

I sigh. "All right. I'll show it to you, but I'm going to tell Ava."

"Brendan," Ruby says, "I admire your devotion to our daughter. We both do. But we are asking you, as her parents—and this is for her own good—not to tell her that you showed us this message."

"Then I'm sorry. I can't show it to you."

Ryan shovels his fingers through his thick, dark hair. "Damn it, you're going to show it to me—"

"Ryan," Ruby admonishes. "This is not the way. You're not your brother."

Not his brother? He must be talking about Jonah. Everyone in town knows that Jonah can go a little off the deep end sometimes.

"For Ava," Ryan says. "Please. Ruby and I need to see the message."

"Are you saying that harm could come to Ava if I don't show it to you?"

"That's exactly what we're saying," Ruby says. "Please, Brendan."

Nothing like being stuck between a rock and a hard place. How can I keep a secret like this from Ava? But on the other hand? If she could be harmed if I don't do this, how can I *not* do it?

"If you can decipher the message, will you tell me?"

"Yes," Ruby says. "But I may have to ask you not to tell Ava."

"For Christ's sake." I walk to my shelf, pull out a book, and grab a folded-over copy of the email. "This is it." I hand it to Ruby. "It makes absolutely no fucking sense, and Ava and my father had no idea what it could mean either."

CHANCE

I know the message by heart, of course.

I can see that they're as confused as I am, until—

Ruby's eyes widen.

She knows something.

"What is it?"

"Nothing."

Right. She's lying.

"You promised you'd tell me if you could decipher it."

"And I can't," Ruby says. "At least not yet."

Another lie. Whatever it is, Ryan hasn't figured it out yet, but it won't take long for Ruby to tell him.

"We should get you back," Ryan says.

"Please, don't bother. I'll walk."

"Fine." Ruby hands the message back to me.

"Don't you want a copy of it?" I ask.

"That's not necessary," she says. "Happy Thanksgiving, Brendan."

"Sure. Happy Thanksgiving to you too. Please tell Ava I hope I'll see her later."

"We will, son." From Ryan.

Son?

The Steels tend to call everyone younger than they are son.

It doesn't mean anything.

Right now? Ryan and Ruby aren't thinking about me. They're not even thinking about Ava.

They're thinking about that message, and Ruby knows what it means.

And already, I know they won't say anything.

Not to me. Not to their daughter.

Perhaps not even to their own family.

Which means Ava and I have to figure it out on our own.

Ava's smart. She's her mother's daughter. Between the two of us, we *will* figure out what's going on.

And if Ava's in harm's way?

Whoever wants her will have to get through me first.

CHAPTER THIRTY-FIVE

Ava

"Mom, where have you been?" I close in on my mother as soon as she enters Uncle Joe's house.

"Ava, how are you?" She grabs me for a hug.

"Nice try, Mom. What were you and Dad up to today?"

"We just had some things to take care of. Nothing for you to worry about."

"My message, Mom. Why haven't you talked to me about it?"

"I'm still working on it, sweetie. But let's not ruin the holiday with stuff like that."

I'm still working on it.

Right.

My mom will never convince me that she's *that* incompetent. She had it figured out the same day I gave it to her, but for some reason, she's keeping the results from me.

Does it have anything to do with the stuff that I'm not supposed to ask them about until after their anniversary?

It must.

And there must be a reason why Aunt Marj wanted me to wait until after the big party.

I'm so damned curious.

The cards I've been drawing lately . . .

They've got me more freaked than ever.

Family secrets.

Hypocrisy.

Secret knowledge.

What does it all mean?

Darth Morgen. And then that completely incomprehensible message that came in later.

The message I haven't shown my mother yet.

I wish Brendan were here.

The only other person who seems to know anything about this is Brock, and he's over at the Pikes'.

Maybe Aunt Marj has a point.

Maybe I should try to enjoy the holiday and my parents' anniversary. Twenty-five years. Pretty darned amazing.

I'm happy for them.

I sigh.

Then I head into the kitchen to help get everything together.

I'm good in the kitchen, and I may as well go where I'm needed.

★ ★ ★

After dinner, but before dessert, I grab Brock.

"I need to talk to you. Please."

"Okay." He glances over his shoulder. "Rory and Callie are busy talking to Diana. Are you doing okay?"

"How the hell can I be doing okay? Finding out about Dale and Donny. About Uncle Talon. About all the stuff going down on our property."

"And the messages. Have you talked to your mom about them?"

"She won't talk to me. Says we should enjoy the holidays. Which of course makes me think that whatever she's deciphered would make me *not* enjoy the holidays."

Brock says nothing.

"For God's sake, do you know how annoying it is for you to know shit that I don't?"

He opens his mouth, but I hold my hand up to stop him.

"I know, I know. I have to ask my parents. Well, they're not talking. So what the hell else can I do?"

He sighs. "You can try to enjoy the holidays, Ava. That's my best recommendation at this point."

"You're a fucking lot of help."

"Let me get you some dessert."

"You know what? I'm not really in a dessert mood. I think I need to go home."

"Ava . . ."

"No. I'm serious. I need to get the hell out of here." I storm through Uncle Joe's house and out the door, not saying goodbye to my parents, my sister, or anyone else.

It's childish, for sure, but I was suffocating.

It's a half-hour drive back to town to my place, and I speed the whole damned way.

One card.

I'm going to draw one freaking card.

I grab my deck, pull it out of the scarf, shuffle it once, twice, three times.

I don't even bother holding it to my heart and trying to infuse my energy into it.

Right now, I need an answer.

This card. Just one card.

I know it will give me the answers I seek.

I feel it inside my whole being.

I draw the card, set it in front of me on the table, on top of my grandmother's scarf.

And I freeze.

CHAPTER THIRTY-SIX

Brendan

After dinner and dessert, I grab my father. "We need to talk," I say.

"Sure. What's on your mind, son?"

"What can you tell me about the Madigan family?"

He lifts his eyebrows. "Where is *this* coming from?"

"Well, you bought the bar from a guy named Jeremy Madigan."

"I did. It was a long time ago, Brendan."

"Who exactly was Jeremy Madigan?"

"He was a bar owner. I don't really know much else. I believe he had a brother who lived in town too."

"Do you remember his name?"

"Not off the top of my head, but these are facts we can easily find out. Why do you need to know?"

"Ryan and Ruby Steel were asking me about Jeremy Madigan," I say.

"Why?"

"I have no idea. I thought you might have some insight."

He shakes his head. "I think the name came up when I was doing my initial research into my uncle's death," he says. "It was a dead end."

This gets my attention. "How exactly did the name come up?"

"There was some gossip at the time that Jeremy's niece had been involved with Brad Steel."

"Brad Steel meaning Ava's grandfather, right?"

"Right. Apparently they were involved in high school and early on in college as well, until Brad met Daphne Steel."

"Ava's grandmother."

"Right. So of course, that came up as I was doing my research into the Steel family and how my uncle may have died at their wedding. But like I said, it was a dead end."

"Okay. Do you remember the woman's name? Or her father's name?"

"Just her last name. Madigan."

"Yeah, it probably means nothing." I sigh. "Why in the world would Ryan and Ruby be asking me about Jeremy Madigan?"

"Hell if I know. By the time I decided to stay in town and had purchased the bar, I had pretty much forgotten all about the Madigans. Like I said, Jeremy's niece had something to do with Brad Steel at one time, but that was over by the time I got to town. After all, my uncle died at Brad and Daphne's wedding."

"Did any other names come up during your investigation?"

"A few. But they're all dead now."

"Any relation to anyone we know?"

"No. Everything turned out to be a dead end. But I know there's something I'm missing."

"And you think these new messages may have something to do with it?"

"It's just a gut feeling. You know, bartender's gut."

I nod. "I was just saying the same thing to someone. We bartenders learn more about people than their therapists do sometimes."

"We'll figure it out, Brendan. I've had this gut feeling my whole life that the Steels were somehow involved in your uncle's death."

"But the Steels are good people."

"They are. Remember that when your uncle died, none of them were born yet. I'm talking about the Steel patriarch. Bradford Steel."

"But your uncle was supposedly Brad's best friend."

"I know. But he was drugged, son. Drugged at Brad Steel's wedding."

"All the more reason to say that Brad Steel wasn't involved. Why would he drug his best friend at his own wedding?"

"He may not have been involved. At least not directly. But remember, it happened on his land, and not too much later, another young woman disappeared."

"Yes. I've heard the stories."

"This one was Daphne Steel's best friend from college. Her name was Patty Watson."

"So that's why you think it's strange. Both of their best friends were killed."

"Yes, it's always stuck in my gut, kind of like some bad meat. I haven't been able to prove anything, and I did give it up, once your mother and I got married and she announced she was expecting you. We have a good life here in Snow Creek. I love this place. But now? With these new messages coming to light? I know there's something that isn't settled, Brendan. Like I said, I feel it in my gut."

"I hate to say it, Dad, but I feel it too." Like a couple of concrete blocks.

"We're going to figure it out this time, Brendan. Because I just won't rest until I do."

"What about Mom?"

"She'll understand. She always does."

I'm not so sure I agree with my father. He probably knows my mother better than I do, but I can't forget my conversation with her in the garden. About how this consumed my father when they first met. I don't want to see my father get obsessed.

But I want to know the truth.

I want to know what Ruby and Ryan are keeping from Ava.

Except…

If it will harm Ava…

Perhaps I shouldn't know. If I do, I won't be able to keep it from her.

My phone buzzes with a text.

Funny. I was just thinking about Ava.

Can you come over? I need you.

I text her back.

On my way.

CHAPTER THIRTY-SEVEN

Ava

The image on the card is foreboding.

A solid brick tower being struck by lightning. Flames engulfing it, innocent souls jumping from the windows to their deaths to escape.

The tower.

But not *just* the tower.

The tower in reverse.

The common interpretation of this card is danger or crisis. Destruction, but also liberation. Sudden and unforeseen change.

But in reverse? It can mean illness or loss.

Obstacles. Something volatile.

Either way, my intuition is telling me this is not a good sign.

Funny thing about the tarot. Each card has both positive and negative connotations. It's the reader's intuition, and the questions posed, that decide which it will be.

As a tarot reader, I tend to focus on the positive.

I've drawn the tower before, and I read its meaning as liberating, and while there may be obstacles, overcoming them will be part of that liberation.

Right now, though?

I feel as though I've been punched in the gut.

I'm getting no positive feelings at all from this card.

In fact?

I feel like it's inevitable.

Something is changing. Something that's going to affect my life. Something that could destroy my family.

Is it illness? Some kind of loss?

My mother had breast cancer about three years ago. It was only a small lump with no lymph node involvement, and her doctor detected it early. After a lumpectomy and radiation, she's cancer-free. Gina and I have yearly mammograms because Mom was so young when she was diagnosed, and so far all has been good.

But this card is scaring me.

Illness? Is my mother sick again? Is that why she's acting so strange?

Nausea claws at me. No. I can't lose my mother. But if she's sick, that doesn't really explain why she would be keeping information from me about the message Brendan and I received. To the contrary, if she's sick, she'd be telling me things—things I need to know if she—

God, I can't even think the thought.

I sigh. It's probably time to do an entire reading. Pull out the Celtic cross, which I only use on rare occasions.

But something inside me can't bring myself to replace the tower into the deck.

It's staring at me, almost pulsing at me.

And I don't even want to touch it.

I don't consider the tarot to be the be-all and end-all of my life. I use it solely for guidance, and sometimes I choose not to follow what the card seems to be saying to me—a prime example being how I've let myself get swept away with Brendan.

I *can* choose to ignore this card and the feeling it's evoking in me.

Objectively, I know I can pick it up right now, stick it back in the middle of the deck, and shuffle. Do a new reading. A full Celtic cross. Perhaps a cleansing reading.

My phone dings.

I'm here. Down in the alley.

I rush down the stairs and through the bakery to let Brendan in. Then I launch myself into his arms.

"What is it? How can I help?" he asks.

"I'm not sure you can, but I'm really glad you're here." I take his hand and lead him up the stairs to my apartment.

"How was your Thanksgiving?" he asks.

"Odd, honestly. My parents showed up late, which is strange in itself. And of course my mom wouldn't talk to me about the messages. So I came home, Brendan. I felt like I needed to be here, and I needed to draw a card to get some guidance on what's going on."

"So did you?" Then his glance falls on the table.

I nod.

He glances at the tower card sitting on my table. "Is that the card you drew?"

"It is."

"Okay. Let's sit down. Tell me about it."

"I think my mother may be ill."

His eyes widen into circles. "Oh my God. What's wrong?"

"She hasn't told me, specifically, but you do know she had breast cancer in the past, don't you?"

"Yeah. I'm so sorry you had to go through that."

"I don't know if that's what's wrong. But this card... It's the tower, and it usually indicates something bad. Like illness."

"Have you drawn the card before?"

"Yes. Not for a while, but I have."

"And then did something bad happen? Or were you expecting something bad?"

I shake my head. "I've always been able to put a positive spin on the card. It's how I approach the tarot. Like when you draw the card of death. It doesn't usually mean actual death. It usually means change of some sort. Like death of one thing in favor of another."

"And the tower? What's the positive spin on it?"

"Freedom. Liberation. Deliverance from the burning tower. But I'm not getting that feeling at all. I depend on my intuition to interpret the cards, and I'm a positive person, Brendan. I'm always able to see things as if the glass is half full, not empty. But this time..."

"This time you're seeing it half empty."

"Yes." I choke back a sob. "And I've sat here for a while. I've tried to find the positive spin. I've looked inside myself, tried to listen to my intuition. But I'm not getting anything positive about this. And it scares me, Brendan. Not so much that I drew the card, but this card in relation to all the others I've drawn since getting that message."

Brendan doesn't reply. He has a pensive look on his face, and he rubs absently at the auburn stubble on his jawline.

Something is coming down for my family. I want to help them, but I don't know how. My mother won't speak to me, and—

Still, Brendan says nothing.

"You think I've gone off the deep end, don't you?"

He takes my hand, squeezes it. "No, I don't. Not at all."

"Then why aren't you saying anything?"

"I don't know what to say, baby. I don't know how to help you. I wish there were something I could say to ease your mind, but..." He shakes his head. "I've been having the same feelings."

"Oh no. Is one of your parents sick?"

"No," he says. "At least not that I know of. But it's my father. My mother's worried about him, and I wasn't, but now, with you being so concerned about your own family, it makes me think. He went down a spiral years ago, before I was ever born. And now, he thinks he may be able to find new information about what happened to his uncle all those years ago."

"The uncle that died at my grandparents' wedding," I say.

"Yes. He thinks perhaps these messages are related to that, since they're coming to us *and* to your family."

"It's not nonsense. I mean, what other connection do the Murphys have to the Steels?"

"Just the lien on our property."

"Right. But the property was conveyed with the lien, like you said. So this can't be about that."

"No," he admits. "So it must have something to do with my uncle. What else is there?"

"Oh, Brendan." I wipe away a tear. "Today is Thanksgiving. And I try every day to be so grateful for my wonderful life. And part of that wonderful life is my family. My mother and father. I can't lose them."

"There's no need to worry until you know the facts," he says.

"I know that. I'm not a worrier. Like I said, I always put a positive spin on things. But this..." I point to the card. "All I see when I look at this card is something... foreboding. Some kind of impending doom. And Brendan... I'm frightened."

Brendan releases my hand and cups both of my cheeks. "What can I do for you?"

"Make me forget. If only for the next fifteen minutes."

He grins, and my God, he's so handsome. He strokes my cheek with his thumb.

"I assure you, Ava, I can last a lot longer than fifteen minutes."

CHAPTER THIRTY-EIGHT

Brendan

I'm taking Ava to bed.

And keeping a secret from her.

I don't feel good about it.

She's right. Her intuition is on point. Her parents *are* keeping something from her, but of course I don't know what it is. All I know is that it has something to do with Jeremy Madigan and the messages we've been receiving. I don't think Ruby is sick again—I didn't get that feeling at all earlier today—but I can't ease Ava's mind without telling her that her parents came to see me, which they asked me to keep to myself.

A secret.

I hate this.

In this moment, I need Ava as much as she needs me.

Plus . . .

There's the fact that I've fallen in love with this woman.

I haven't wanted to admit it to myself, and I don't expect her to feel the same way. She's so young, and she probably isn't looking for anything permanent.

I will have to live with that.

But I *will* tell her how I feel. When the time is right. And that won't be until I can be honest with her. Until I can look her in the eye and know that we have no secrets from each other.

Which means I'll have to go against her parents' wishes and tell her that they came to visit me.

That can't happen tonight. Her parents are celebrating a milestone anniversary in two days, and I won't ruin that for Ava.

And now I'm done thinking.

I pull Ava to her feet, bring her to me, and kiss her.

Her lips are already parted, and our tongues meet, twirling in beautiful synchrony.

Tonight I'm going to show her there's more to sex with Brendan Murphy than *wham, bam, thank you, ma'am.*

Tonight, I'm going to make love to this woman. With my tongue, with my fingers. I'm going to touch every part of her with my lips.

And if I'm lucky?

She'll do the same for me.

Still clenched together in a kiss, she leads me to her bedroom.

We fall onto the bed together, our lips still joined.

And then hands...

Hands everywhere, pulling at each other's clothes, until we're naked—naked and writhing together.

I break the kiss then, and I trail my lips over her cheek to her earlobe, where I nibble. Then I whisper in her ear. "I'm going to kiss every part of you, Ava. My lips are going to be everywhere tonight. Everywhere."

She sighs against me. "I want you."

"I want you too, baby. And I will have you, but not until I've kissed every part of you."

I begin then, sucking her earlobe into my mouth, tugging on her earring. Then I move toward her jawline, rain tiny kisses across its sculpted beauty.

Then her shoulders, the tops of her chest, and the tops of her gorgeous tits.

Her nipples are pink and hard, and I take one between my lips and suck gently.

She arches her back and moans softly.

With my other hand, I take the other nipple between my thumb and forefinger and gently twist it. Again she writhes, arching her back, sighing, moaning, such honeyed tones.

The texture of her nipple is like velvet, and I twirl my tongue over it, kiss it, and then suck it again. I work the other with my fingers, tugging and pulling, and then squeezing her whole breast.

When I can stand it no longer, I nip the nipple with my teeth while simultaneously pulling on the other with my fingers.

"Oh!" she gasps.

"You like that?" I murmur against her areola.

"God, yes. I love to have my nipples sucked, Brendan. And I swear to God, no one has ever sucked them the way you do."

Oh boy, those are fighting words. Nothing like competing against oneself.

I'll just have to do better.

I switch tactics. I move my mouth to the other nipple and suck it hard. I gently play with the one I just dropped, using my thumb and forefinger to give it a hard twist.

She gasps and undulates her hips.

"Oh God, yes!"

She likes it hard.

Good news for her. So do I.

I clamp over the nipple, suck it hard between my lips, and then I add my teeth and give it a quick nip.

I bite it, just a little bit harder, but not enough to cause her pain.

Until she says, "Harder, Brendan. Please."

Fuck.

My dick is so hard right now, and I know she's already wet for me. I could so easily slide inside her heat, fuck her hard, fuck her fast.

What she wants is for me to bite her nipples harder. This is about her, not me. At least not about me yet.

I'll get mine later.

And if I don't?

Worshiping Ava's body is absolutely worth it, even with no payoff.

I take her at her word, and I bite her hard nipple.

"Yes!" she cries out, reaching above her head and grabbing the rungs of her headboard.

Again. I bite into her flesh. Again. And then once more.

Her fists are clenched around the rungs, her knuckles white. For a moment I imagine her bound with cuffs, unable to move her arms.

The thought of binding a woman has never done much for me . . .

Until this moment.

How beautiful Ava would look tied to the bed, her legs spread, her pussy glistening.

I nibble on her nipple again, suck it, lick it, and then . . .

I close my teeth over it and bite. She thrashes wildly, still holding onto her headboard, begging me to go harder, harder, harder.

"My God, you're making me insane," I whisper against her flesh.

Can she hear me?

I don't know. Doesn't matter. Already I know she feels what I feel. She wants what I want.

But I'm not done.

I have a lot more flesh to taste.

I move my mouth away from the nipple, replacing it with my hand. Both my hands are now working her nipples, twisting, pulling, tugging, as I ease my head downward, kissing the soft flesh of her abdomen.

Her pussy is shaved clean.

And God, it's hot. For a moment I wonder what she would look like if her pubic hair were the same shade as the hair on her head. A luscious pink entrance to the heaven between her legs.

I kiss over her mound, so tempted to slide my tongue just slightly lower to her clit. But I hold myself in check. Time for that later.

I spread her legs, though, because I want to kiss her fleshy inner thighs. Ava has amazing legs. Her inner thighs are moist with her juices, and I lap it up, savoring the tart and tangy taste of her. I move downward to her knees, her calves, her feet. Unpolished toenails that are perfectly square and beautiful.

I kiss each one and then suck slightly on her big toe.

She undulates.

Some women like that and some don't.

Ava clearly does.

So I move to her other foot and massage her instep and take care of her toes.

And now . . . it's time to turn her over.

I ease her onto her belly and continue the foot massage. I don't want to get her too relaxed, because I have plans for the rest of her body. So I move upward, sliding my tongue over her calves and then the inside of her knees.

She wiggles slightly. I found a ticklish spot. I'll remember that for later.

I kiss up her slender thighs to her gorgeous ass, and I spread her cheeks. Her pink asshole puckers at me, and I slide my tongue over it.

She gasps for a moment, but then she relaxes, sighing softly.

Anal sex is something I've never done. I would love for Ava to be my first. Has she done it? I'll ask her some other time.

I squeeze the cheeks of her ass, massaging them softly, and then I move over her, letting my cock dangle between her butt cheeks as I kiss her back, her shoulders, the sides of her beautiful neck.

"Ava," I whisper in her ear, "are you ready for me to slide my cock into you?"

"God, yes, Brendan. Please."

Her legs aren't spread apart very far, which will make for a nice tight entrance.

I reach downward, grab my cock, and slide it between her pussy lips, lubricating it with her juices. Then I nudge the head inside and enter her slowly.

She sighs beneath me, and I take a moment to appreciate every inch of her pussy as she sucks me inside her.

And I stay there.

For a timeless moment, I stay embedded inside her, her pussy tight from the angle and the fact that her legs aren't spread far. She's tighter than she's ever been, and I think I could stay here forever.

But a moment later, my balls begin itching, and I need the

friction. I pull out and thrust back in, this time hard and fast. Then I stay inside again, appreciating how she gloves me.

"Feel good, baby?" I ask.

"God, you have no idea."

"Oh, I think I do."

CHAPTER THIRTY-NINE

Ava

But he doesn't.

He can't possibly feel as good as I feel right now, having his cock burning through me like a torch of fire. When Brendan is inside me, nothing else matters. Nothing else exists.

Just him.

Just me.

Just us.

Except instead of Brendan and Ava, we're some kind of Brendan-Ava hybrid. Our bodies joined, along with our . . .

Dare I think it?

Our souls.

Not our hearts but our souls.

It's a scary thought, and one I haven't had before with any other man.

But somehow, I feel Brendan and I are connected by our souls. And not just when we are connected by our bodies.

He slides out again and thrusts back into me.

And with every plunge of his cock, I feel more like myself.

The problems of my family fade away. The cards fade away.

And all I need is on this bed right now.

Brendan. Brendan in my body, Brendan in my soul.

CHANCE

He slides in and out of me, and every time he pokes against my cervix, I come closer to an orgasm.

"Yes," I sigh into my pillow. "Feels so good. Fuck me, Brendan. Fuck me harder. I'm going to come soon."

I don't have to ask him twice.

He thrusts harder and faster, in and out of me like a jackhammer, and with each thrust, my clit rubs against the bedding, pushing me further ... further ... further ...

Until I leap.

I take the leap of faith, and I soar into the stars, my entire body vibrating as if I'm a stringed instrument and Brendan is playing me expertly with his bow.

"That's it, baby." His voice floats around me. "Come. Come for me. Come for me all night long."

He fucks me, fucks me, fucks me, until—

"God," he groans.

He embeds himself inside me, and I feel each contraction of his cock as he fills me.

He groans again, and I feel it through my whole body. Every part of me is on fire, with the true inferno between my legs, not in my pussy so much as in my very core.

My freaking soul.

Brendan stays on top of me, his entire body touching mine, for a few moments.

A few moments that I relish. As if he's covering me, sheltering me from some storm that is brewing.

And the storm *is* brewing.

Already I know.

In this moment, I let the thoughts flow to the side, drift off the cliff I'm standing on.

Only Brendan and I are on this cliff.

Together, we'll never fall.

★ ★ ★

I'm not sure how long we sleep, but it's still dark when I wake up, entwined with Brendan. I move away from him, check my phone on the nightstand.

One a.m.

I should go back to sleep. Five a.m. will come soon, and I'll have to head downstairs and get the dough rising.

But damn...

Brendan's cock is hard.

I reach between his legs and grasp it.

A groan leaves his throat, but he doesn't wake up.

But I want him. I want him so badly. And even though I really ought to go back to sleep, I can't resist. I crawl back onto the bed, nestle myself on top of him, and lick the head of his dick.

This time he sucks in a breath, and his eyes open.

"Quiet," I say. "Just close your eyes. Enjoy this. I know I will."

"Oh my God, baby."

I suck him between my lips, which is no small feat given his size. He tastes salty and masculine, and already a drop of liquid emerges from the tip. I lick it up, swallow the savory flavor of him. Then I twirl my tongue around the head, suck it gently, and then bring my mouth down upon his length.

He groans—a firm vibration straight from his chest.

My God, he's huge, but I'm determined to give him head. The blow job of a lifetime. By the time he hits the back of my throat, there are still two inches of him left.

Now that he's good and lubed up with my saliva, I add my hand to the mix, twisting it as I slide up and down his cock, applying suction each time I get to the head.

Will he come in my mouth?

No man has ever come in my mouth. I never liked the notion. But the idea of Brendan Murphy shooting down my throat? It's a pretty big turn-on.

"Damn, baby. That lip ring. What you do to me."

His words spur me on. I've never thought of myself as any kind of sexual siren, but Brendan makes me feel desirable. Beautiful even.

I continue working his cock with my lips and my hand, until—

"Stop, baby. You have to stop."

But I don't want to stop, so I don't. I deliberately disobey him, and I feel pretty naughty. I like it.

I continue to work his cock, and then I notice his balls are tightening, his cock is swelling even harder, and—

"I'm going to come, baby. I'm going to come."

I clamp my mouth on him as his dick pulses underneath my tongue. His come squirts into me, warm against my tongue and the back of my throat.

Four and then five squirts.

When he's finally done, I remove my mouth from his cock and swallow.

I swallow his very essence, and I feel even closer to him.

"Fuck," he growls. "That was so hot."

"It was perfect," I say.

"Get your ass over here. Come sit on my face, and I'll return the favor."

I scramble over him, turn around, and lower my pussy onto his lips. He sucks at me right away. No soft swipes to get me moving. There's no need. I'm wet and ready, my clit swollen.

He laps at me, groaning beneath me, and then he slides

HELEN HARDT

his tongue over my clit in such a way that makes me want to shoot to the moon.

"Yes, Brendan," I sigh. "Feels so good."

He doesn't reply, as his mouth is full of my pussy. Instead he shoves his tongue inside me, removes it, slides it over my clit, and then sucks while he simultaneously shoves his finger into my channel.

And that's all it takes.

I'm leaping off the precipice once more, tingles rolling through me like waves crashing on the shore.

I say something, but I don't know what. Words float around me, but they have no meaning. Only my voice and Brendan's groans.

It's a distorted sound, harmony and discord all at once.

I float. I float and I float as I come down from my high.

He's still working my pussy, and my clit is now so sensitive I have to move off him.

"God, you taste like heaven," he says.

"You feel like heaven," I reply. "Ugh. I wish I didn't have to get up in the morning."

"Me too."

"You don't. The bar doesn't open until… When does it open?"

"I usually open it around two."

"Then you've got all kinds of time."

"You didn't let me finish. I'm opening at noon for the weekend. Families and friends are home for Thanksgiving and often want to come into town for a drink. I do great business this weekend. But I'm off Saturday night for your parents' party. In fact, I'm taking the whole day off so we can spend Saturday together," he says.

"We can, but I'll be baking pita and preparing baklava."

"Sounds good to me. It's a date."

"Okay." I smile.

Funny, he didn't ask. He just told me, and I'm okay with that.

I'm okay with all of this. Something about Brendan Murphy grounds me. Makes me feel bigger than myself.

I've never been a woman who thinks a good man can solve every problem. And I'm not saying Brendan has solved mine. My problems still exist, but with him at my side, I feel so much stronger—as well as beautiful and desirable.

As much as I hate to admit it, that feels good.

Women who don't like to feel beautiful and desirable? They're just plain lying.

I used to think I was one of them.

Nope.

I may have made peace with the fact that Gina is the beauty of my family years ago, but that doesn't stop me from enjoying being beautiful myself.

I'll never look like Gina, but it's okay to look like Ava. And if Brendan thinks I'm beautiful? I can't help but enjoy that.

★ ★ ★

My phone alarm rings at five on the button. I'm exhausted, and I'm lying with my head toward the foot of the bed. I simply rolled off Brendan and fell asleep.

His head is on the pillow, and he's snoring softly. Not a loud snore at all, and certainly not enough to have woken me up without my alarm. But it's cute, really. This tiny little snore from such a big man.

I get out of bed carefully so as not to disturb him and tiptoe to the bathroom. I take a quick shower and then dress in sweats, a clean apron, and my hair net.

I go downstairs and gather ingredients to begin the day's bake. My Hobart mixer with the dough hook stands ready. I wish I could hand knead every single loaf, but with the amount of business I do, that's not possible. The Hobart does it for me.

For some of my more specialized loaves, like challah, for example, I still knead by hand. I also hand knead my sourdough, which I mix from my starter each day.

It's just a basic white sourdough loaf. But sometimes, when I'm feeling creative, I add a few things. After last night with Brendan, I want to do something special, so I throw some dried cranberries and walnuts into the sourdough. It will make a nice post-Thanksgiving loaf for people to enjoy with their leftover turkey and stuffing.

An hour later, Maya and Luke arrive. They both help me in the kitchen until we open at eight.

We started serving breakfast sandwiches a few months ago, and they've been a hit. I'm expecting a huge crowd of people who, after preparing a huge meal yesterday, don't want to make breakfast.

And as soon as the clock hits eight, the takeout orders start flying in.

Eggs and bacon on sourdough is my bestseller, followed by a Steel beef burger and a poached egg on an English muffin. I always thought that was a weird combo, but it was my father's idea, and people seem to love it.

My father...

I don't have time to think about what he and my mom might be keeping from me. Maya, Luke, and I are swamped.

"Hey, do you guys need any help down here?"

I jerk toward the sound of Brendan's voice.

"You can't be serious," I say.

"Of course I am. Looks like you could use an extra set of hands."

"You'll need an apron and a hairnet." I point to the closet on the far side of the wall. "Everything's in there."

A few moments later, Brendan returns with his gorgeous red hair tied up in a hairnet.

"Now that is a good look on you," I say, laughing.

I put him to work assembling sandwiches, while I take another batch of loaves out of the oven.

"Have you ever thought of selling pizza crusts?" Brendan asks.

"Yeah. I've had some requests for them. But I can barely keep up with what I do now."

"That's because you're the best damned baker this town has ever seen." Brendan smiles.

"You're sweet."

"I'm only being truthful. You have a gift, Ava. You should think about expanding."

I sigh. Brendan isn't the first person to say this to me. I could easily expand if I poked into my trust fund.

I've just never wanted to do that.

I know it's silly. No one would think twice if I did. But I always wanted to be my own person. Make my own way in this vast world.

Maya is working the cash register, and she's also out front with the few customers who want to eat their breakfast inside the small café.

I don't normally do a lot of eat-in business at breakfast, as

I don't serve coffee. I made that decision when I first opened the bakery because I didn't want to compete with Rita's coffee shop. She brews a fine cup, and I didn't want to take away her business, so my breakfast-sandwich business is mostly takeout.

Brendan is helping Maya up front, so I take time to knead a few more loaves of my special post-Thanksgiving sourdough blend. There's something about having my hands in a ball of dough. Something oddly comforting and meditative. When I'm kneading bread, I tend to get my best ideas, and my intuition seems to flow.

And today … I'm hoping something positive will come to me about the card I drew last night. The tower.

Kneading has never failed me.

But it fails me today.

And the thought is frightening.

The tower. That imposing tower.

Something to do with my parents' secrets.

Illness?

Destruction?

I continue to knead the dough.

But the thoughts … Negative thoughts …

They don't stop.

My mother won't talk to me.

Brendan and I will have to decipher those messages ourselves.

As soon as I close up after lunch?

I'll get to work on it.

CHAPTER FORTY

Brendan

Ava is in better spirits after a few hours of baking. She's helping us in the front now, taking orders, making sandwiches. It's nearly eleven, so I need to get home, clean up, and get ready to open the bar around noon.

I tap her on the shoulder.

"Yeah?"

"I have to go."

"Yeah, I'm surprised you stayed this long." She grabs my hand. "But thanks so much, Brendan. It was great having you here, and we needed the help today."

"I'm happy to do it."

"If you need help at the bar tonight, I'm your girl."

"I might take you up on that. That way we can spend the evening together, even if we're both working again."

"I'd love it, to tell you the truth. You can teach me how to mix drinks."

"Absolutely. Just show up whenever you feel like it."

"I will."

I give her a quick kiss on her lips and then I leave the bakery, but first I make sure to remove the apron and hairnet. Enough people saw me looking like that today. I'm not taking that look into public.

I walk a few buildings to my own place, and someone's waiting for me at the back door.

He looks vaguely familiar, but I can't place him. He's average height, nondescript brown hair, dark-blue eyes. Nice enough looking.

"Can I help you?" I ask.

"Yeah. My name's Pat. Pat Lamone."

I've heard about Pat Lamone. Some of the Steels have mentioned him in passing. Apparently he has a history with the Pike sisters, and it's not good.

"We're not opened yet, Pat."

"I'm not here to have a drink. I need to speak with you."

"What about?"

"About my grandmother. Her name is Sabrina Smith. That's the name she goes by, anyway."

"I'm afraid I don't know what you're talking about," I say.

"Her real name is Dyane Wingdam."

"Again, doesn't ring a bell."

Another figure approaches us.

"You have got to be kidding me," I mutter.

It's Ryan Steel. Ava's father.

Here, at the bar, with me.

"Ryan," I say, "what can I do for you?"

"You can let me in."

"I'm kind of in the middle of something here."

Ryan glances over at Pat. "I know who you are," he says.

"Yeah, I know who you are as well, Mr. Steel."

"So you think you're a Steel relative?" Ryan says.

"Yeah. That's what I hear, anyway."

"Okay," I say. "Clearly this has nothing to do with me, so if you'll both excuse me—"

"Actually, this *does* have something to do with you," Ryan says. "Could we go inside, please?"

"For God's sake." I unlock the door and hold it open. "After you."

Ryan Steel and Pat Lamone traipse into my bar via the back door.

What the hell could this be about? Pat Lamone, who thinks he is related to the Steels, and Ava's father. Both here, at my bar, wanting to talk to me.

Pat about his grandmother, who I don't know from Adam. And Ryan about… Well, I can only guess it has something more to do with those messages Ava and I received.

"All right. I've been helping Ava all morning at the bakery, and as you can see, I'm filthy. I need to take a shower so I can open this place by noon." I glance at the clock on the wall of the bar. "That gives the two of you about three minutes. What the hell do you want?"

CHAPTER FORTY-ONE

Ava

By two o'clock, it's time to close the bakery. I leave Maya and Luke to clean up. I want to go upstairs, get a shower, and go over to the bar to help Brendan. As soon as I get back to my apartment, though, my gaze falls on the card still sitting on the table.

The tower.

Why haven't I put it back into the deck?

But I know why.

I've been waiting. I've been waiting, hoping I could get some kind of positive thought from it.

But nothing has worked.

Not kneading bread this morning.

Hell, not even sex with Brendan last night.

I'm still getting nothing but negative feelings from the damned card.

Mother.

My mother.

I haven't drawn *that* card—the empress—but why is my mom at the forefront of my thoughts?

Because the card sometimes can mean illness, and I'm so very afraid she'll get sick again.

Ill, and about to celebrate her twenty-fifth anniversary.

Plus, she hasn't gotten back to me with her interpretation of the message. She said she had apps that could help decode it. I certainly don't have access to the kind of software my private investigator mother has, but I can easily find apps that may help.

I head to the sink, wash the flour off my hands. Then I fire up my laptop and type *Darth Morgen*.

Nothing I haven't already seen.

My mother was thinking it might have a code embedded in the letters, with each of the letters standing for a different letter. I could start with R. It appears twice so it would be the same letter.

But what if it's not?

What if the code isn't letter per letter but based on something else?

Like perhaps, the letter that precedes it?

God, where to start?

I rise, grab a pad of paper and a pen from a drawer in the kitchen, and come back. I write the letters on the piece of paper.

Darth Morgen.

Then I start playing with them.

What if these letters were rearranged? What if it's one big word? Or several small words? An anagram?

I play with it for a little while, finding several three-letter words and writing them down, but then I laugh.

"What the hell are you doing?" I say out loud. "If you're looking for anagrams, find an anagram maker online."

I don't know why I didn't think of this before. I was so overwhelmed with my developing feelings for Brendan and with the cards that were telling me all kinds of horrible things.

Plus, I was depending on my mother. My ex-cop private-investigator mother who said she could decipher it.

But she kept putting me off.

I do a quick search, and I come up with something called "Dante's Anagram Maker."

Good enough. I type in all the letters of "Darth Morgen."

I close my eyes.

I'm not sure why, except something tells me that if I look, I'll be faced with even more of a mystery.

So I sit for a moment, eyes closed, and I inhale. Exhale. Inhale. Exhale.

I'm still waiting for some kind of positive feeling about the tower card still sitting on the table.

If I can get something—anything—that isn't a negative feeling...

Then I can open my eyes.

And I can begin to solve the mystery of Darth Morgen.

So I wait.

I continue breathing.

But it doesn't work.

Nothing works.

I open my eyes, and I glance at the screen.

And the word I see fills me with hope.

It's not my mother.

My mother's not ill. I feel that, and I know it in my heart, and I breathe a sigh of relief.

Because the first word on the list of anagrams for Darth Morgen is...

Grandmother.

CONTINUE THE STEEL BROTHERS SAGA

WITH BOOK TWENTY-SIX

MESSAGE FROM HELEN HARDT

Dear Reader,

Thank you for reading *Chance*. If you want to find out about my current backlist and future releases, please like my Facebook page and join my mailing list. I often do giveaways. If you're a fan and would like to join my street team to help spread the word about my books, please see the web addresses below. I regularly do awesome giveaways for my street team members.

If you enjoyed the story, please take the time to leave a review on a site like Amazon or Goodreads. I welcome all feedback. I wish you all the best!

Helen

Facebook
Facebook.com/HelenHardt

Newsletter
HelenHardt.com/SignUp

Street Team
Facebook.com/Groups/HardtAndSoul

ALSO BY HELEN HARDT

The Steel Brothers Saga:
Craving
Obsession
Possession
Melt
Burn
Surrender
Shattered
Twisted
Unraveled
Breathless
Ravenous
Insatiable
Fate
Legacy
Descent
Awakened
Cherished
Freed
Spark
Flame
Blaze
Smolder
Flare
Scorch
Chance
Fortune
Destiny

Blood Bond Saga:
Unchained
Unhinged
Undaunted
Unmasked
Undefeated

Misadventures Series:
Misadventures with a Rock Star
Misadventures of a Good Wife (with Meredith Wild)

The Temptation Saga:
Tempting Dusty
Teasing Annie
Taking Catie
Taming Angelina
Treasuring Amber
Trusting Sydney
Tantalizing Maria

The Sex and the Season Series:
Lily and the Duke
Rose in Bloom
Lady Alexandra's Lover
Sophie's Voice

Daughters of the Prairie:
The Outlaw's Angel
Lessons of the Heart
Song of the Raven

Cougar Chronicles:
The Cowboy and the Cougar
Calendar Boy

Anthologies Collection:
Destination Desire
Her Two Lovers

ACKNOWLEDGMENTS

What do you think of Ava and Brendan? They are a fun couple to write, and they're both a breath of fresh air. We're diving deep into Steel history with this couple, and you're in for some surprises. Stay tuned!

Huge thanks to the always brilliant team at Waterhouse Press: Audrey Bobak, Haley Boudreaux, Jesse Kench, Jon Mac, Amber Maxwell, Dave McInerney, Michele Hamner Moore, Chrissie Saunders, Scott Saunders, Kurt Vachon, and Meredith Wild.

Thanks also to the women and men of Hardt and Soul. Your endless and unwavering support keeps me going.

To my family and friends, thank you for your encouragement. Special shout out to Dean—aka Mr. Hardt—and to our amazing sons, Eric and Grant. Special thanks to Eric for giving *Chance* a much-needed edit before I handed it in to Scott at Waterhouse.

Thank you most of all to my readers. Without you, none of this would be possible. I am grateful every day that I'm able to do what I love—write stories for you!

Ava and Brendan will return soon in *Fortune*!

ABOUT THE AUTHOR

#1 *New York Times,* #1 *USA Today,* and #1 *Wall Street Journal* bestselling author Helen Hardt's passion for the written word began with the books her mother read to her at bedtime. She wrote her first story at age six and hasn't stopped since. In addition to being an award-winning author of romantic fiction, she's a mother, an attorney, a black belt in Taekwondo, a grammar geek, an appreciator of fine red wine, and a lover of Ben & Jerry's ice cream. She writes from her home in Colorado, where she lives with her family. Helen loves to hear from readers.

Visit her at HelenHardt.com